WOMEN
WERE HIS LADDER
TO SUCCESS...

*With dashing ease and with a scoundrel's
heartlessness, George Duroy
swept women off their feet and into his power.*

GUY DE MAUPASSANT, master builder of
world literature, is justly renowned for his
short stories. He has never been adequately
recognized for his achievement in the novel; in
Bel Ami he reaches his fullest flowering as a
novelist.

Henri René Albert Guy de Maupassant

In a brief ten-year span of writing, during a life that ended tragically, Guy de Maupassant produced some thirty volumes of material. A master of the short story form, he earned an immediate reputation upon publication of *Boule de suif* in 1880, thus creating his first masterpiece.

The son of a Paris stockbroker, Maupassant began to write at an early age. The French novelist Flaubert, to whom the young Maupassant showed samples, was unimpressed with them, though he encouraged the novice to persevere.

From such an inauspicious beginning have come such great works as: *Une Vie, Clair de lune, Miss Harriet,* and the fully developed genius of *Bel Ami.*

A victim of general paralysis, hallucinations and the imprudent use of drugs, Maupassant died in Paris in 1893. He is buried in the cemetery of Montparnasse.

BEL AMI

By Guy de Maupassant

THE POPULAR LIVING CLASSICS LIBRARY · NEW YORK

All POPULAR LIBRARY LIVING CLASSICS are carefully
selected by the POPULAR LIBRARY Editorial Board and represent titles by the world's greatest authors.

POPULAR LIBRARY LIVING CLASSICS EDITION
Published in September, 1963

I. A Lean Pocket

When the cashier had given him the change out of his five-franc piece, George Duroy left the restaurant.

As he had a good carriage, by nature as well as from his military training, he drew himself up, twirled his mustache, and threw upon the lingering customers a rapid and sweeping glance—one of those glances which take in everything within their range like a cast net.

The women looked up at him in turn—three little work-girls, a middle-aged music mistress, disheveled, untidy, and wearing a bonnet always dusty and a dress always awry, and two shopkeepers' wives dining with their husbands—all regular customers at this popular-price establishment.

When he was on the sidewalk, he stood still a moment, asking himself what he should do. It was the 28th of June, and he had just three francs forty centimes in his pocket to carry him to the end of the month. This meant the option of two dinners without luncheon or two luncheons without dinner. He reflected that as the earlier repasts cost twenty sous apiece, and the latter thirty, he would, if he were content with the luncheons, be one franc twenty centimes to the good, which would further represent two repasts of bread and sausage and two "bocks" on the boulevard. This latter item was his greatest extravagance and his chief pleasure of a night; and he began to descend the Rue Notre Dame de Lorette.

He walked as in the days when he had worn a hussar uniform, his chest thrown out and his legs slightly apart, as if he had just left the saddle, pushing his way through the crowded street, and shouldering people to avoid having to step aside. He wore his somewhat shabby hat slightly on one side, and brought his heels smartly down on the pavement. He seemed ever ready to defy somebody or something, the passers-by, the houses, the whole city, retaining all the swagger of a dashing soldier reduced to the rank of a civilian.

Although wearing a sixty-franc suit, he was not devoid of a certain somewhat loud though real air of fashion. Tall, well built, fair, with a curly mustache twisted up at the ends, bright blue eyes with small pupils, and reddish-brown hair curling naturally and parted in the middle, he bore a strong resemblance to the dare-devil of popular romances.

When George Duroy reached the boulevard he paused again, undecided as to what he should do. He now thought of going on to the Champs Elysées and the Avenue du Bois Boulogne to seek a little fresh air under the trees, but another wish tormented him, the desire for a love affair.

What shape would it take? He did not know, but he had been waiting it for three months, night and day. Occasionally, thanks to his good looks and gallant bearing, he gleaned a few crumbs of love here and there, but he was always hoping for something further and better.

He liked, however, the localities frequented by the lower class of women; he liked their balls, their cafés, and their amusements. He liked to rub shoulders with them, speak to them, chaff them, feel himself near them. He did not despise them with the innate contempt of a well-born man. He turned toward the Madeleine, following the stream of people which moved along, overcome by the heat. The larger cafés, filled with customers, were overflowing on to the pavement, and displayed their drinking public under the dazzling glare of their street lamps. Duroy had slackened his pace; an intense thirst parched his throat.

A hot thirst, a summer evening's thirst, had taken possession of him, and he imagined the delightful sensation of cool drinks flowing into his mouth. But if he drank only two bocks in the evening, farewell to the slender supper of the morrow, and he was only too well acquainted with periods of short commons at the end of the month.

He said to himself: "I must hold out till ten o'clock, and then I'll have my bock at the American café. Confound it, how thirsty I am, though." And he glanced at the men seated at the tables drinking, all the people who could quench their thirst as they pleased. He went on, passing in front of the cafés with a sprightly, swaggering air, guessing at a glance from their dress and bearing how much money each customer ought to have about him. The sight of these men quietly sitting there filled him with wrath. If their pockets were searched, gold, silver, and coppers would be found in them. On an average, each one must have at least two louis. There were certainly a hundred in the café; a hundred times two louis is four thousand francs. He murmured, "The swine," as he walked, swaggering, past them. If he could have got hold of one of them at a nice dark street corner he would have twisted his neck without scruple, as he did the country folk's fowls on field-days.

And he recalled his two years in Africa and the way in which he robbed the Arabs when stationed at little outposts in the South. A bright and cruel smile flitted across his lips at the recollection of an escapade which had cost the lives of three men of the Ouled-Alane tribe, and had furnished him and his comrades with a score of fowls, a couple of sheep, some gold, and food for laughter for six months.

The culprits had never been found, and, what is more, they had hardly been looked for, the Arab being looked upon somewhat as the natural prey of the soldier.

In Paris it was another thing. One could not plunder gracefully, sword by side and revolver in hand, far from civil authority and with impunity. He felt in his heart all the instincts of a non-commissioned officer let loose in a conquered country. He certainly regretted his two years in the desert. What a pity he had not stayed there! But, then, he had hoped for something better in returning home. And now—ah! yes, now he was getting it, was he not?

He clicked his tongue as if to verify the parched state of his palate.

The crowd swept past him slowly, and he kept thinking: "Set of hogs! All these idiots have money in their waistcoat pockets." He pushed against people and softly whistled a lively tune. Gentlemen whom he thus elbowed turned round grumbling; women murmured: "What a brute!"

He passed the Vaudeville Théâtre and stopped before the American café, asking himself whether he should not drink a bock, so greatly did this thirst torture him. Before making up his mind, he glanced at the illuminated clock. It was a quarter past nine. He knew himself; as soon as the glassful of beer was before him, he would gulp it down. What would he do then up to eleven o'clock?

He passed on. "I will go as far as the Madeleine," he said, "and walk back slowly."

As he reached the corner of the Place de l'Opéra, he passed a stout young fellow, whose face he vaguely recollected having seen somewhere. He began to follow him, turning over his recollections and repeating to himself half aloud: "Where the deuce did I know that fellow?"

He searched without being able to recollect, and then all at once, by a strange trick of memory, the same man appeared to him thinner, younger, and clad in a hussar uniform. He exclaimed aloud: "Why, Forestier!" and stepping out he tapped the other on the shoulder. The promenader turned round and looked at him and then said: "What is it, sir?"

Duroy broke into a laugh. "Don't you know me?" said he.

"No."

"George Duroy, of the Sixth Hussars."

Forestier held out his hands, exclaiming: "Why, old fellow! How are you?"

"Very well, and you?"

"Oh, not very brilliant. Just imagine, I have a chest made of papier mâché just now. I cough six months out of twelve, in consequence of a cold I caught at Bougival the year of my return to Paris, four years ago."

And Forestier, taking his old comrade's arm, spoke to him of his illness, related the consultations, opinions, and advice of the doctors, and the difficulty of following this advice in his position. He was told to spend the winter in the South, but how could he? He was married, and was a journalist with a good position.

"I am political editor of the *Vie Française*. I write the proceedings in the Senate for the *Salut*, and from time to time literary criticisms for the *Planète*. So I have made my way."

Duroy looked at him with surprise. He was greatly changed, matured. He had now the manner, bearing, and dress of a man in a good position and sure of himself, and the paunch of a man who dines well. Formerly he had been thin, slight, supple, heedless, brawling, noisy, and always ready for a spree. In three years, Paris had turned him into someone quite different, stout and serious, with some white hairs about his temples, though he was not more than twenty-seven.

Forestier asked: "Where are you going?"

Duroy answered: "Nowhere; I am just taking a stroll before turning in."

"Well, will you come with me to the *Vie Française*, where I have some proofs to correct, and then we will take a bock together?"

"All right."

They began to walk on, arm-in-arm, with that easy familiarity that exists between schoolmates and between men in the same regiment.

"What are you doing in Paris?" asked Forestier.

Duroy shrugged his shoulders. "Simply starving. As soon as I finished my term of service I came here—to make a fortune, or rather for the sake of living in Paris; and, for six months, I have been a clerk in the offices of the Northern Railway at fifteen hundred francs a year, no more."

Forestier murmured: "Hang it, that's not much!"

"I should think not. But how can I get out of it? I am alone; I don't know any one; I can get no introductions. It is not good will that is lacking, but means."

His comrade looked him over from head to foot, like a practical man examining a subject, and then said, in a tone of conviction: "You see, my boy, everything depends upon assurance here. A clever fellow can more easily become a minister than an under-secretary. One must obtrude one's self on people; not ask things of them. But how the deuce is it that you could not get hold of anything better than a clerkship on the Northern Railway?"

Duroy replied: "I looked about everywhere, but could not find anything. But I have something in view just now: I have been offered a position as riding master at Pellerin's. There I shall get three thousand francs at the lowest."

Forestier stopped short. "Don't do that; it is stupid, when you ought to be earning ten thousand francs. You would nip your future in the bud. In your office, at any rate, you are hidden; no one knows you; you can get out of it, if you are strong enough, and make your own way. But once a riding master, and it is all over. It is as if you were head waiter at a place where all Paris goes to dine. When once you have given riding lessons to people in society or to their children, they will never be able to look upon you as an equal."

He remained silent for a few moments evidently reflecting, and then asked:

"Have you a bachelor's degree?"

"No; I failed twice."

"That is no matter as long as you studied for it. If any one mentions Cicero or Tiberius, you know pretty well what they are talking about?"

"Yes; pretty well."

"Good; no one knows any more, with the exception of a score of idiots who have taken the trouble. It is not difficult to pass as being well informed; the great thing is not to be caught in some blunder. You can manœuvre, avoid the difficulty, turn the tables, and floor others by means of a dictionary. Men are all as stupid as geese and ignorant as donkeys."

He spoke with the quiet self-possession of one who knows life, and smiled as he watched the crowd go by. But all at once he began to cough, and stood still till the paroxysm was over, adding, in a tone of discouragement: "Isn't it terrible not to be able to get rid of this cough? And we are in the middle of summer. Oh, this winter I shall go and get cured at Mentone. Health before everything."

They halted on the Boulevard Poissonnière before a large glass door, on the inner side of which an open newspaper was pasted. Three passers-by had stopped and were reading it.

Above the door, in large letters of flame, outlined by gas jets, were the words *La Vie Française*.

Forestier pushed the door open, saying, "Come in." Duroy entered, ascended a handsome but dirty staircase visible from the street, passed through an anteroom where two messengers bowed to his companion, and reached a kind of waiting room, shabby and dusty, upholstered in dirty green Utrecht velvet, covered with spots and stains, and worn in places as if mice had gnawed it.

"Sit down," said Forestier, "I will be back in five minutes."

And he disappeared through one of the three doors opening into the room.

A strange, special, indescribable odor, the odor of a newspaper office, floated in the air of the room. Duroy remained motionless, slightly intimidated, above all, surprised. From time to time men passed hurriedly before him, coming in at one door and going out at another before he had time to look at them.

Others, too, arrived, serious, important-looking men, wearing tall hats with flat brims, as if this shape distinguished them from the rest of mankind.

Forestier reappeared holding the arm of a tall thin fellow, between thirty and forty years of age, in evening dress, very dark, with his mustache ends twirled into sharp points, and with an insolent, self-satisfied bearing.

Forestier said to him: "Good night, dear master!"

The other shook hands with him, saying: "Good night,

my dear fellow," and went downstairs whistling, with his cane under his arm.

Duroy asked: "Who is that?"

"Jacques Rival, you know; the celebrated news editor, the duelist. He has just been correcting his proofs. Garin, Montel, and he are the three best news editors as regards intelligent setting forth of facts that we have in Paris. He gets thirty thousand francs a year here for two articles a week."

As they were leaving they met a short, stout man, with long hair and untidy appearance, who was puffing as he came up the stairs.

Forestier bowed low to him. "Norbert de Varenne," said he, "the poet; the author of *'Soleils Morts';* another who gets big pay. Every story he writes for us costs three hundred francs, and the longest do not run two hundred lines. But let us turn into the Neapolitan café; I am beginning to choke with thirst."

As soon as they were seated at a table in the café, Forestier called for two bocks, and drank off his own at a single draught, while Duroy sipped his beer in slow mouthfuls, tasting and relishing it as if it were something rare and precious.

His companion was silent, and seemed to be reflecting. Suddenly he exclaimed: "Why don't you try journalism?"

The other looked at him with surprise, and then said: "But, you know, I have never written anything."

"Bah; every one must begin. I could give you a job to hunt up information for me—to make calls and inquiries. You would have two hundred and fifty francs a month to start with, and your cab hire. Shall I speak to the manager about it?"

"Certainly!"

"Very well, then; come and dine with me tomorrow. I shall only have five or six people—the proprietor,

Monsieur Walter and his wife; Jacques Rival, and Norbert de Varenne, whom you have just seen; and a lady, a friend of my wife. Is it settled?"

Duroy hesitated, blushing and perplexed. At length he murmured: "You see, I have no clothes."

Forestier was astounded. "You have no dress clothes? Hang it all, they are indispensable, though. In Paris one would be better off without a bed than without a dress suit."

Then, suddenly, feeling in his waistcoat pocket, he drew out some gold, took two louis, placed them in front of his old comrade, and said, in a cordial and familiar tone: "You will pay me back when you can. Hire the clothes you want or arrange to pay by installments, whichever you like, but come and dine with me to-morrow, half-past seven, number seventeen, Rue Fontaine."

Duroy, confused, picked up the money, stammering: "You are too good; I am very much obliged to you; you may be sure I shall not forget."

The other interrupted him. "All right. Another bock, eh? Waiter, two bocks."

Then, when they had drunk them, the journalist said: "Shall we stroll about a bit for an hour?"

"Certainly."

And they set out again in the direction of the Madeleine.

Duroy, rather perplexed, did not know what to say; at length he made up his mind. "I have never been in the Folies Bergère. I should not mind taking a look in there," he said.

"The Folies Bergère," exclaimed his companion; "the deuce, we shall roast there as in an oven. Well, all right, it is always amusing there."

And they turned their steps toward the Rue du Faubourg Montmartre.

The illuminated front of the establishment threw a bright light down the four streets which meet in front of it. A string of cabs were waiting for the close of the performance.

Forestier was walking in when Duroy stopped him. "You are passing the box office," said he.

"I never pay," was the reply, in a tone of importance.

When he approached the doormen they bowed, and one of them held out his hand. The journalist asked: "Have you a good box?"

"Certainly, Monsieur Forestier."

He took the seat check held out to him, pushed the padded door with its leather borders, and they found themselves in the auditorium.

A cloud of tobacco smoke veiled like a faint mist the stage and the further side of the theatre.

The tall mirrors behind them reflected their backs and the faces of passers-by.

Forestier pushed his way through the groups, advancing quickly with the air of a man entitled to consideration.

He went up to an usher: "Box seventeen," said he. "This way, sir."

And they were shut up in a little open box draped with red, and holding four chairs of the same color, so near to one another that one could scarcely slip in between them. The two friends sat down. To the right as to the left, following a long curved line the two ends of which joined the proscenium, a row of similar cribs held people seated in like fashion, with only their heads and chests visible.

On the stage, three young fellows in fleshings were executing feats in turn upon a trapeze.

Duroy scarcely noticed the performance, and with head averted, kept his eyes on the promenade behind him, full of men.

Said Forestier to him: "Look at the stalls; nothing but middle-class folks with their wives and children, good know-nothings who come here to see the show. In the boxes, men about town, some artists, some second-rate girls; and, behind us, the strangest mixture in Paris. Who are these men? Watch them. There are some of every kind, of every profession, and every caste; but black-guardism predominates. There are clerks of all kinds— bankers' clerks, government clerks, shopmen, reporters, pimps, officers in civilians' clothes, swells in evening dress, who have dined out, and who have dropped in here on their way from the Opéra to the Théâtre des Italiens; and then again, too, quite a crowd of suspicious folk who defy analysis. As to the women, only one type. We have known them for the last ten years; we see them every evening all the year round in the same places, except when they are making a sojourn at St. Lazare or at Lourcine."

Duroy no longer heard him. One of these women was leaning against their box and looking at him. She was a stout brunette, her skin whitened with paint, her black eyes lengthened at the corners with pencil and shaded by enormous and artificial eyebrows; and her painted lips, red as a fresh wound, gave her a bestial, ardent, unnatural appearance.

She motioned with her head to one of her friends who was passing, a blonde with red hair, and stout, like herself, and said to her, in a voice loud enough to be heard: "There is a pretty fellow!"

Forestier turned and tapped Duroy on the knee with a smile. "That is meant for you; you are a success, my dear fellow. I congratulate you."

The ex-officer blushed, and mechanically fingered the two pieces of gold in his waistcoat pockets.

The curtain had dropped, and the orchestra was now playing a waltz.

Duroy said: "Supposing we take a turn round the promenade."

"Just as you like."

They left their box, and were at once swept away by the stream of promenaders. Pushed, pressed, squeezed, jostled, they went on, having before their eyes a crowd of hats. The girls, in pairs, passed amidst this throng with facility, gliding between elbows and backs as if quite at home, perfectly at their ease, like fish in water, amidst this masculine flood.

Duroy, charmed, let himself be swept along, drinking in with intoxication the air vitiated by tobacco and the odor of humanity. But Forestier sweated, puffed, and coughed.

"Let us go into the garden," said he.

And, turning to the left, they entered a kind of covered garden, cooled by two large, ugly fountains. Men and women were drinking at zinc tables placed beneath evergreen trees growing in boxes.

"Another bock, eh?" said Forestier.

"Willingly."

They sat down and watched the passing throng.

But the stout brunette who just before had been leaning against the box occupied by the two comrades reappeared, walking proudly arm-in-arm with the stout blonde.

She smiled on perceiving Duroy, as though their eyes had already exchanged secrets, and, taking a chair, sat down quietly opposite him, and, making her friend sit down too, gave the order in a clear voice: "Waiter, two grenadines!"

Forestier, rather surprised, said: "You make yourself quite at home."

She replied: "It is your friend that captivates me. I believe that I could make a fool of myself for his sake."

Duroy, intimidated, could find nothing to say. He twisted his curly mustache, smiling in a silly fashion. The waiter brought the drinks, which the women drank off at a draught, they then arose, and the brunette, with a friendly nod of the head and a tap on the arm with her fan, said to Duroy: "You are not very talkative."

And they went off, swinging their trains.

Forestier laughed. "I say, old fellow, you are very successful with the women. You must see to it. It may be a help to you." He was silent for a moment, and then continued in the dreamy tone of men who think aloud: "It is through them, too, that one gets on quickest."

And as Duroy still smiled without replying, he asked: "Are you going to stop any longer? I have had enough of it; I am going home."

The other murmured: "Yes, I shall stay a little longer. It is not too late."

Forestier rose. "Well, good night, then. Till to-morrow. Don't forget. Seventeen, Rue Fontaine, at half past seven."

"That is settled! Till to-morrow. Thanks."

They shook hands, and Forestier walked away.

As soon as he had disappeared Duroy felt himself free.

He soon caught sight of the two women, the blonde and the brunette, who were still making their way through the throng of men.

He went straight up to them, and when he was quite close his courage failed him.

The brunette said: "Have you found your tongue again?"

He stammered, "By Jove!" without being able to say anything else.

The three stood together, checking the stream of promenaders, the current of which swept around them.

She asked: "Will you walk with me?"

As they went out he thought that he could easily hire a suit of dress clothes for the next evening.

II. An Important Dinner-Party

"Monsieur Forestier?"

"Third floor, the door on the left," the janitress had replied, in an amiable tone which betokened consideration for her tenant, and George Duroy ascended the stairs.

He felt somewhat abashed, awkward and ill at ease. He was wearing a dress suit for the first time in his life, and was uneasy about the general effect of his toilet. He felt it was altogether defective, from his boots, which were not of patent leather, though neat, for he was naturally smart about his footgear, to his shirt, which he had bought that very morning for four francs fifty centimes at the Magasin du Louvre, and the limp front of which was already rumpled.

His trousers, rather too loose, set off his legs badly, seeming to flap about the calf with that creased appearance which second-hand clothes present. The coat alone did not look bad, being, by chance, almost a perfect fit.

He was slowly ascending the stairs with beating heart and anxious mind, tortured above all by the fear of appearing ridiculous, when suddenly he saw in front of him a gentleman in full dress looking at him. They were

so close to one another that Duroy took a step back
and then remained standing in amazement; it was himself, reflected in a tall mirror on the first floor landing.
A thrill of pleasure shot through him to find himself
so much more presentable than he had imagined.

Only having a small shaving-glass in his room, he
had not been able to see his whole figure at once, and
as he only had imperfect glimpses of the various items of
his improvised toilet, he had mentally exaggerated his
imperfections, and harped to himself on the idea of
appearing grotesque.

But on suddenly coming upon his reflection in the
mirror, he had not even recognized himself; he had
taken himself for some one else, for a gentleman whom
at the first glance he had thought very well dressed and
fashionable-looking. And now, looking at himself carefully, he recognized that really the general effect was
satisfactory.

He studied himself as actors do when learning their
parts. He smiled, held out his hand, made gestures, expressed sentiments of astonishment, pleasure, and approbation, and essayed smiles and glances, with a view
to displaying his gallantry toward the ladies, to let them
see that he admired them and desired their acquaintance.

On reaching the second story he noticed another
mirror, and slackened his pace to view himself in it as
he went by. His bearing seemed to him really graceful.
He walked well. And now he was filled with unbounded
confidence in himself. Certainly he must be successful
with such an appearance, the wish to succeed, and his
native resolution and independence of mind. He wanted
to run, to jump, as he ascended the last flight of stairs.
He stopped in front of the third mirror, twirled his
mustache as he had a trick of doing, took off his hat to
run his fingers through his hair, and muttered half

aloud, as he often did: "What a capital notion!" Then
raising his hand to the bell-handle, he rang.

The door opened almost at once, and he found himself face to face with a man-servant in plain clothes,
serious, clean shaven, and so perfect in his get-up that
Duroy became uneasy again without understanding the
reason of his vague emotion, due, perhaps, to an un-
witting comparison of the cut of their respective garments. The man-servant, who had patent leather shoes,
asked, as he took the overcoat which Duroy had carried
on his arm, to avoid exposing the stains on it: "Whom
shall I announce?"

And he announced the name through a draped back
portière leading into a drawing-room.

But Duroy, suddenly losing his assurance, felt himself breathless and paralyzed by fear. He was about to
take his first step in the world he had looked forward to
and longed for. He advanced nevertheless. A fair young
woman, quite alone, was standing awaiting him in a
large brilliantly lighted room full of plants, like a greenhouse.

He stopped short, quite disconcerted. Who was this
lady who was smiling at him? Then he remembered
that Forestier was married, and the thought that this
pretty and elegent blonde must be his friend's wife put
the finishing touch to his alarm.

He stammered: "Madame, I am——"

She held out her hand, saying: "I know, monsieur;
Charles has told me of your meeting last evening, and
I am very pleased that he had the happy thought of
asking you to dine with us today."

He blushed up to his ears, not knowing what to say,
and felt himself being inspected from head to foot,
weighed and criticised.

He longed to excuse himself, to invent some pretext

for explaining the deficiencies of his toilet, but he could not think of one, and did not dare touch on this difficult subject.

He sat down on an armchair she pointed out to him, and as he felt the soft, springy, velvet-covered seat yield beneath his weight, as he felt himself, as it were, supported and clasped by the padded back and arms, it seemed to him that he was entering upon a new and enchanting life, that he was taking possession of something delightful, that he was becoming somebody, that he was saved, and he looked at Madame Forestier, who had not taken her eyes off him.

She was dressed in pale blue cashmere, which set off the outline of her slender waist and full bust. Her arms and neck issued from a cloud of white lace, with which the bodice and short sleeves were trimmed, and her fair hair, dressed high, left a little fair fluffy cloud above the nape of her neck.

Duroy recovered his assurance beneath her glance, which reminded him, without his knowing why, of that of the girl he met at the Folies Bergère. She had gray eyes, of a bluish tinge, which imparted to them a strange expression; a thin nose, full lips, a rather full chin, and irregular but attractive features, full of archness and charm. It was one of those faces every trait of which reveals a special grace and seems to have its meaning— every movement to say or to hide something.

After a brief silence she asked: "Have you been long in Paris?"

He replied slowly, recovering his self-possession: "A few months only, madame. I have a berth in one of the railway companies, but Forestier holds out the hope that I may, thanks to him, enter journalism."

She smiled more perceptibly and kindly, and murmured, lowering her voice: "Yes, I know."

The bell had rung again. The servant announced "Madame de Marelle."

This was a little brunette, who entered briskly, and seemed to be outlined—moulded, as it were—from head to foot in a dark dress made quite plainly. A red rose fastened in her black hair caught the eye at once, and seemed to stamp her physiognomy, accentuate her distinctive character, and give the marked tone required.

A little girl in short frocks followed her.

Madame Forestier darted forward, exclaiming: "Good evening, Clotilde."

They kissed one another, and then the child offered her forehead, with the assurance of a grown-up person, saying: "Good evening, cousin."

Madame Forestier kissed her, and then introduced them, saying: "Monsieur George Duroy, an old friend of Charles; Madame de Marelle, my friend, and a kind of relative." She added: "You know we do not put on any airs here. You quite understand, don't you?"

The young man bowed.

The door opened again, and a short, stout gentleman appeared, having on his arm a tall, handsome woman, much younger than himself, and of distinguished appearance and grave bearing. They were Monsieur Walter, a Jew from the South of France, deputy, financier, capitalist, and manager of the *Vie Française*, and his wife, the daughter of Monsieur Basile Ravalau, the banker.

Then came, one following the other, Jacques Rival, very elegant, and Norbert de Varenne, whose coat-collar was rather shiny from the friction of the long locks that fell down on his shoulders, scattering over them a few specks of dandruff. His badly tied cravat looked as if it had already done duty. He advanced with the airs and graces of an old beau, and, taking Madame Forestier's hand, he imprinted a kiss on her wrist. As he bent forward, his long hair spread like water over her bare arm.

Forestier entered in his turn, offering excuses for being late. He had been detained at the office of the paper by the Morel affair. Monsieur Morel, a Radical deputy, had just addressed a question to the Ministry respecting a vote of credit for the colonization of Algeria.

The servant announced: "Dinner is served, Madame," and they passed into the dining room.

Duroy found himself seated between Madame de Marelle and her daughter. He again felt ill at ease, being afraid of making some mistake in the conventional handling of forks, spoons and glasses. There were four glasses, one of a pale bluish tint. What could one drink in that?

Nothing was said while the soup was being consumed, and then Norbert de Varenne asked: "Have you read the Gauthier case? What a funny business it is!"

And a discussion of this blackmailing case followed. They did not speak of it as the events recorded in newspapers are spoken of in private families, but as a disease is discussed among doctors, or vegetables by market gardeners. They were neither shocked nor astonished at the facts, but sought out their hidden and secret motives with professional curiosity, and an utter indifference to the crime itself. The women, too, were interested in this investigation. And other recent events were discussed, commented upon, turned so as to show every side of them, and weighed correctly, with the practical glance and from the especial standpoint of dealers in news and vendors of the drama of life at so much a line, just as articles destined for sale are examined, turned over, and weighed by tradesmen. Then it was a question of a duel, and Jacques Rival spoke. That was his business, no one else could handle it.

Duroy dared not put in a word. He glanced from time

to time at his neighbor, who captivated him. A diamond, suspended by a thread of gold, dangled from her ear like a drop of water that had rolled down it. From time to time she made an observation which always brought a smile to her hearer's lips. She had a quaint, neat, unexpected wit, the wit of an experienced woman of the world who views things with indifference, and judges them with a superficial and benevolent skepticism.

Duroy sought in vain for some compliment to pay her, and, not finding one, occupied himself with her daughter, filling her glass, holding the dishes for her as they were passed, and helping her. The child, more sedate than her mother, thanked him in a serious tone, with a little bow, saying: "You are very good, sir," and listened to her elders with a little thoughtful air.

The dinner was very good, and every one was enraptured. Monsieur Walter ate like an ogre, hardly spoke, and glanced sideways under his glasses at the dishes offered to him. Norbert de Varenne kept him company, and from time to time let drops of gravy fall on his shirt front. Forestier, silent and serious, watched everything, exchanging glances of intelligence with his wife, like confederates engaged together on a difficult task which is going on swimmingly.

Duroy had found the wine to his liking, and let his glass be filled every time. A delicious cheerfulness stole over him, a warm cheerfulness, that mounted from the stomach to the head, flowed through his limbs, and penetrated him throughout. He felt himself permeated by a sense of absolute well-being of life and thought, of body and soul.

He longed to speak to bring himself into notice, to be listened to, appreciated like those men whose slightest words are enjoyed.

But the conversation, which had been going on uninterruptedly, linking ideas one to another, jumping from one topic to another at a chance word, a mere trifle, and skimming over a thousand matters, turned again on the great question put by Monsieur Morel in the Chamber representing the colonization of Algeria.

Monsieur Walter, between two courses, made a few jests, for his wit was skeptical and broad. Forestier told about his editorial for the following day. Jacques Rival demanded a military government with land grants to all officers after thirty years of colonial service.

"By this plan," he said, "you will create an energetic class of colonists, who will have already learned to love and understand the country, and will be acquainted with its language, and with all those grave local questions which are a stumbling block to all newcomers."

Norbert de Varenne interrupted him with "Yes, they will be acquainted with everything except agriculture. They will speak Arabic, but they will not know how to plant out beet-root and how to sow wheat. They will be even skillful at fencing, but very shaky as regards manures. On the contrary, this new land should be thrown absolutely open to every one. Intelligent men will achieve a position there, the others will go under. It is the social law."

A brief silence followed, and the listeners smiled.

George Duroy opened his mouth and said, feeling as much surprised at the sound of his own voice as if he had never heard himself speak: "What is chiefly lacking there is good land. The really fertile estates cost as much as they do in France, and are bought up as investments by rich Parisians. The real colonists, the poor fellows who leave home for lack of bread, are forced into the desert, where nothing will grow for want of water."

Every one looked at him, and he felt himself blushing. Monsieur Walter asked: "Do you know Algeria, sir?" George replied: "Yes, sir; I was there nearly two years and a half, and I was quartered in all three provinces."

Suddenly, unmindful of the Morel question, Norbert de Varenne interrogated him respecting a detail of manners and customs of which he had been informed by an officer. It was with respect to the Mzab, that strange little Arab republic sprung up in the midst of the Sahara, in the driest part of that burning region.

Duroy had twice visited the Mzab, and he narrated some of the customs of this singular country, where drops of water are valued as gold; where every inhabitant is bound to discharge all public duties; and where commercial honesty is carried further than among civilized nations.

He spoke with a certain raciness excited by the wine and by the wish to please, and told regimental anecdotes, incidents of Arab life and military adventure. He even hit on some telling phrases to depict these bare and yellow lands, eternally laid waste by the devouring fire of the sun.

All the women had their eyes turned upon him, and Madame Walter said, in her deliberate tones: "You could make a charming series of articles out of your recollections."

Walter looked at the young fellow over the top of his spectacles, as was his custom when he wanted to see any one's face distinctly. He looked at the dishes from beneath them.

Forestier seized the opportunity: "My dear sir, I had already spoken to you about Monsieur George Duroy, asking you to let me have him for my assistant in gleaning political tips. Since Marambot left us, I have no one to send in quest of urgent and confidential information, and the paper suffers in consequence."

Daddy Walter became serious, and pushed his spectacles up on to his forehead, in order to look Duroy well in the face. Then he said: "It is true that Monsieur Duroy has evidently an original turn of thought. If he will come and have a chat with us to-morrow at three o'clock, we will settle the matter." Then, after a short silence, turning right round toward George, he added: "But write us a little series of entertaining articles on Algeria at once. Relate your experiences, and mix up the colonization question with them as you did just now. They are facts, genuine facts, and I am sure that they will greatly please our readers. But be quick. I must have the first article to-morrow or the day after, while the subject is being discussed in the Chamber, in order to catch the public."

Madame Walter added, with that serious grace which characterized everything she did, and which lent an air of kindness to her words: "And you have a charming title, 'Recollections of a Chasseur d'Afrique?' Is it not, Monsieur Norbert?"

The old poet, who had won renown late in life, feared and hated newcomers. He replied dryly: "Yes, excellent, provided that the keynote be followed, for that is the great difficulty; the exact key, what in music is called the pitch."

Madame Forestier cast on Duroy a smiling and protective glance, the glance of a connoisseur, which seemed to say: "Yes, you will get on." Madame de Marelle had turned toward him several times, and the diamond in her ear quivered incessantly as though the drop of water were about to fall.

The little girl remained quiet and serious, her head bent over her plate.

But the servant passed round the table, filling the blue glasses with Johannisberg, and Forestier proposed a toast, drinking with a bow to Monsieur Walter: "Prosperity to the *Vie Française*."

Every one bowed toward the proprietor, who smiled, and Duroy, intoxicated with success, emptied his glass at a draught. He would have emptied a whole barrel after the same fashion; it seemed to him that he could have eaten a bullock or strangled a lion. He felt a super-human strength in his limbs, unconquerable resolution and unbounded hope in his mind. He was now at home among these people. He had just taken his position, won his place. His glance rested on their faces with a new-born assurance, and he ventured for the first time to address his neighbor.

"You have the prettiest earrings I have ever seen, Madame."

She turned toward him with a smile. "It was an idea of my own to have the diamonds hung like that, just at the end of a thread. They really look like dewdrops, do they not?"

He murmured, ashamed of his own daring, and afraid of making a fool of himself:

"It is charming; but the ear, too, helps to set it off."

She thanked him with a look, one of those woman's looks that go straight to the heart. And as he turned his head he again met Madame Forestier's eye, always kindly, but now, as he thought, sparkling with a livelier mirth, an archness, an encouragement. All the men were now talking at once, with gesticulations and raised voices. They were discussing the great project of the metro-politan railway. The subject was not exhausted till dessert was finished, every one having a deal to say about the slowness of the methods of transit in Paris, the in-convenience of the tramway, the delays of omnibus traveling, and the rudeness of cabmen.

Then they left the dining-room to take coffee. Duroy, in jest, offered his arm to the little girl. She gravely thanked him, and raised herself on tiptoe in order to rest her hand on it.

On returning to the drawing-room he again experi-enced the sensation of entering a greenhouse. In each of

the four corners of the room tall palms unfolded their
shapely leaves, rising to the ceiling and there spreading
downward.

On each side of the fireplace were india rubber plants
like round columns, with the dark-green leaves spreading
out one above the other; and on the piano two unknown
shrubs, one covered with crimson flowers, the other all
white, had the appearance of artificial plants, appearing
too perfect to be real.

The air was cool, and laden with a soft, vague perfume
that could scarcely be defined. The young fellow, now
more himself, considered the room attentively. It was not
large; nothing attracted the eye except the shrubs, no
striking bright color, but one felt at ease in it; one felt
soothed and refreshed, and, as it were, caressed by one's
surroundings.

"Do you take coffee, Monsieur Duroy?" And Madame
Forestier held out a cup toward him with that smile
which never left her lips.

"Thank you, Madame."

He took the cup, and as he bent forward to take a
lump of sugar from the sugar basin carried by the little
girl, Madame Forestier said to him in a low voice: "Be
attentive to Madame Walter."

Then she drew back before he could answer.

He first drank his coffee, which he was afraid of spill-
ing on the carpet; then, his mind more at ease, he
sought for some excuse to approach the wife of his new
chief and begin a conversation. All at once he noticed
that she was holding an empty cup in her hand, and as
she was at some distance from a table, did not know
where to put it. He darted forward with "Allow me,
Madame?"

"Thank you, sir."

He took away the cup, and then returned.

"If you knew, Madame," he began, "the happy hours

the *Vie Française* helped me to pass when I was away in the desert. It is really the only paper that is readable out of France, for it is more literary, wittier, and less monotonous than the others. There is something of everything in it."

She smiled with amiable indifference, and answered, seriously:

"Monsieur Walter took a great deal of trouble to create this type of newspaper which supplies a need of the day."

And they began to chat. He had an easy flow of small talk, a charm in his voice and look, and an irresistible seductiveness about his mustache. It curled coquettishly about his lips, reddish brown, with a paler tint at its curled tips.

They chatted about Paris, its suburbs, the banks of the Seine, watering places, summer amusements, all the current topics on which one can talk for ever without wearying one's self.

Then as Monsieur Norbert de Varenne approached with a liqueur glass in his hand, Duroy discreetly withdrew.

Madame de Marelle, who had been speaking with Madame Forestier, summoned him.

"Well, Monsieur," she said abruptly, "so you want to try your hand at journalism?"

He spoke vaguely of his projects, and then recommenced with her the conversation he had just had with Madame Walter; but as he understood his subject better he did it more justice, repeating as his own the things he had just heard. And he continually looked his companion in the eyes, as though to give a deep meaning to what he was saying.

She, in her turn, related anecdotes with the easy flow of spirits of a woman who knows she is witty and is always seeking to appear so, and becoming familiar she laid her hand from time to time on his arm, and lowered her voice to make trifling remarks which thus assumed a character of intimacy. He would have liked to have shown his devotion for her on the spot, to have defended her, shown her what he was worth, and his delay in his replies to her showed the preoccupation of his mind.

But suddenly, without any reason, Madame de Marelle called "Laurine!" and the little girl came.

"Sit down here, child; you will catch cold near the window."

Duroy was seized with a wild longing to kiss the child. It was as though some part of the kiss would reach the mother.

He asked in a gallant and at the same time fatherly tone: "Will you allow me to kiss you, Mademoiselle?"

The child looked up at him in surprise.

"Answer, my dear," said Madame de Marelle, laughingly.

"Yes, sir, this time; but it will not do always."

Duroy, sitting down, lifted Laurine on to his knees and brushed the fine curly hair above her forehead with his lips.

Her mother was surprised. "What! she has not run away; it is astounding. Usually she will only let ladies kiss her. You are irresistible, Monsieur Duroy."

He blushed without answering, and gently jogged the little girl on his knee.

Madame Forestier drew near, and exclaimed with astonishment: "What! Laurine tamed! what a miracle!"

Jacques Rival also came up, cigar in mouth, and Duroy rose to take leave, afraid of spoiling, by some unlucky remark, the work done, his task of conquest begun.

He bowed, softly pressed the little outstretched hands of the women, and then heartily shook those of the men. He noted that the hand of Jacques Rival, warm and dry, answered cordially to his grip; that of Norbert de

Varenne, damp and cold, slipped through his fingers; that of Daddy Walter, cold and flabby, was without expression or energy; and that of Forestier was plump and moist. His friend said to him in a low tone: "To-morrow at three o'clock; do not forget."

"Oh! no, do not fear."

When he found himself once more on the stairs, he felt a great longing to run down them, so great was his joy, and he darted forward, going down two steps at a time, but suddenly he caught sight of a large mirror on the second floor landing of a gentleman in a hurry, and he stopped short, ashamed, as if he had been caught tripping.

Then he looked at himself in the glass for some time, astonished at being really such a handsome fellow, smiled complacently, and, taking leave of his reflection, bowed low to it as one bows to a personage of importance.

III. The First Step

When George Duroy found himself in the street, he hesitated as to what he should do. He wanted to run, to dream, to walk about thinking of the future as he breathed the soft night air, but the thought of the series of articles asked for by Mr. Walter haunted him, and he decided to go home at once and set to work.

He walked along quickly, reached the outer boulevard, and followed it as far as the Rue Boursault, where he dwelt. The house, six stories high, was inhabited by a score of small households of tradespeople and workmen, and he experienced a sickening sensation of disgust, longing to leave the place and live like well-to-do people in a clean dwelling, as he ascended the stairs, lighting his way with wax matches up the dirty steps, littered with bits of paper, cigarette ends, and scraps of kitchen refuse.

The young fellow's room on the fifth floor looked into a kind of abyss, the huge cut of the Western Railway just above the exit to the tunnel by the Batignolles Station. Duroy opened his window and leaned against the rusty iron cross bar.

Beneath him, at the bottom of the dark hole, three motionless red lights resembled the eyes of huge wild animals, and further on a glimpse could be caught of others and of others again still further. Every moment whistles, prolonged or brief, pierced the silence of the night, some close at hand, others scarcely audible, coming from the direction of Asnières. Their modulations were akin to those of the human voice; one of them was approaching, with its plaintive appeal growing louder and louder every moment, and soon a big yellow light appeared, advancing with a loud noise, and Duroy watched the string of railway carriages swallowed up in the tunnel.

Then he said to himself: "Come, let's get to work."

He placed his light upon the table, but at the moment of commencing he found that he had only a quire of letter paper in the place. More's the pity, but he would make use of it by opening out each sheet to its full extent. He dipped his pen in ink, and wrote at the head of the page, in his best hand, "Souvenirs d'un Chasseur d'Afrique."

Then he tried to frame the opening sentence. He remained with his head on his hands and his eyes fixed on the white sheet spread out before him. What should he say? He could no longer recall anything of what he had been relating a little while back; not an anecdote, not a fact, nothing.

All at once the thought struck him: "I must begin with my departure."

And he wrote: "It was in 1874, about the middle of May, when France, exhausted, was resting after the catastrophes of the terrible year."

He stopped short, not knowing how to lead up to what should follow—his embarkation, his voyage, his first impressions.

After ten minutes' reflection, he resolved to put off the introduction till the morrow, and set to work at once to describe Algiers.

And he traced on his paper the words: "Algiers is a white city," without being able to state anything further. He recalled in his mind the pretty white city, tumbling as it were like a cascade of flat-roofed dwellings from the summit of its hills to the sea, but he could no longer find a word to express what he had seen or what he had felt.

After a violent effort, he added: "It is partly inhabited by Arabs."

Then he threw down his pen and rose from his chair.

On his little iron bedstead, hollowed in the center by the weight of his body, he saw his everyday garments lying, worn and limp, and ugly as the clothing at the Morgue. On a straw-bottomed chair his tall hat, his only one, brim uppermost, seemed to be awaiting an alms.

The wall paper, gray with blue bouquets, showed as many stains as flowers, old, suspicious-looking stains, the origin of which could not be defined; crushed insects or drops of oil, finger tips smeared with pomatum, or soapy water scattered while washing. It smacked of shabby genteel poverty, the poverty of a Paris lodging house. Anger rose within him at the wretchedness of his mode of living. He said to himself that he must get out of it at once; that he must finish with this irksome existence the very next day.

A frantic desire to work suddenly taking possession of him again, he sat down once more at the table, and began anew to seek for phrases to describe the strange and charming physiognomy of Algiers, that anteroom of vast and mysterious Africa; the Africa of wandering Arabs and unknown tribes of negroes; that unexplored Africa whose improbable-looking animals, seemingly made to figure in fairy tales, are sometimes shown us in zoölogical gardens; ostriches, those exaggerated fowls; gazelles, those sacred goats; surprising and grotesque giraffes, grave-looking camels, monstrous hippopotami, shapeless rhinoceroses, and gorillas, those frightful-looking brothers of mankind.

He vaguely felt ideas occurring to him; he might perhaps have uttered them, but he could not put them into writing. And his impotence exasperating him, he got up again, his hands damp with perspiration and his temples throbbing.

His eyes falling on his washing bill, brought up that evening by the concierge, he was suddenly seized with wild despair. All his joy vanished in a twinkling, with his confidence in himself and his faith in the future. It was all up; he could not do anything, he would never be anybody; he felt played out, incapable, good for nothing, damned.

And he went and leaned out of the window again, just as a train issued from the tunnel with a loud and violent noise. It was going away far off, across the fields and plains toward the sea. And the recollection of his parents stirred in Duroy's breast. It would pass near them, that train, within a few leagues of their house. He saw it again, the little house at the entrance to the village of Canteleu, on the summit of the slope overlooking Rouen and the immense valley of the Seine.

His father and mother kept a little inn, a place where the tradesfolk of the suburbs of Rouen came out to lunch on Sunday and called "A la Belle Vue." They had wanted to make a gentleman of their son, and had sent him to college. Having finished his studies, and failing in his examination for the degree of B. A., he had entered the army with the intention of becoming an officer, a colonel, a general. But, disgusted with military life long before the completion of his five years' term of service, he had dreamed of making a fortune in Paris.

He came there at the expiration of his term of service, despite the entreaties of his father and mother, who, their visions having fled, wanted now to have him at home with them. In his turn, he hoped to achieve a future; he foresaw a triumph by means as yet vaguely defined in his mind, but which he felt sure he could scheme out and further.

His comrades used to say of him: "He is a sharp fellow, a schemer, he will look out for himself," and he had promised himself to act up to his character.

His inborn conscience of a Norman, blunted by the daily dealings of garrison life, rendered elastic by pillaging exploits in Africa, illicit commissions, shady tricks in business; spurred on, too, by the notions of honor current in the army, military bravado, patriotic sentiments, the fine-sounding tales current among non-commissioned officers, and the vain glory of the profession of arms, had become a kind of trick box in which something of everything was to be found.

But the wish to succeed reigned sovereign in it.

He had, without noticing it, begun to dream again, as

he did every evening. He pictured to himself some splendid love adventure which should bring about all at once the realization of his hopes. He married the daughter of some banker or nobleman whom he met in the street and captivated at the first glance.

The shrill whistle of a locomotive, issuing from the tunnel like a big rabbit bolting out of its hole and tearing at full speed along the rails toward the round house, where it was to rest, awoke him from his dream.

Then, repossessed by the vague and joyful hope which ever haunted his mind, he wafted a kiss into the night, a kiss of love addressed to the vision of the woman he was awaiting, a kiss of desire addressed to the fortune he coveted. Then he closed his window, and began to undress, murmuring:

"I shall feel in a better mood for it to-morrow. My thoughts are not clear to-night. Perhaps, too, I have had just a little too much to drink. One can't work well under those circumstances."

He got into bed, blew out his light, and went off to sleep almost immediately.

He awoke early, as one wakes on mornings of hope or of anxiety, and, jumping out of bed, opened his window to drink a cup of fresh air, as he phrased it.

The houses of the Rue de Rome opposite, on the other side of the broad railway cut, glittering in the rays of the rising sun, seemed to be painted with white light. Afar off on the right a glimpse was caught of the slopes of Argenteuil, the hills of Sannois, and the windmills of Orgemont, through a light bluish mist, like a floating and transparent veil cast across the horizon.

Duroy remained for some minutes gazing at the distant landscape, and he murmured: "It would be devilish nice out there a day like this." Then he bethought himself that he must set to work, and that at once, and also send his janitor's lad, at a cost of ten sous, to the office to say that he was ill.

He sat down at his table, dipped his pen in the ink, leaned his forehead on his hand, and sought for ideas. All in vain—nothing came.

He was not discouraged, however. He thought: "Bah, I am not accustomed to it. It is a trade to be learned like all other trades. I must have some help the first time. I will go and find Forestier, who will start my article going in ten minutes."

And he dressed himself.

When he got into the street he came to the conclusion that it was still too early to present himself at the residence of his friend, who must be a late sleeper. He therefore walked slowly along beneath the trees of the outer boulevard. It was not yet nine o'clock when he reached the Parc Monceau, fresh from its morning watering. Sitting down on a bench, he began to dream again. A well-dressed young man was walking up and down at a short distance, awaiting a woman, no doubt. Yes; she appeared, closely veiled and walking rapidly, and taking his arm, after a brief clasp of the hand, they walked off together. A riotous need of love broke out in Duroy's heart, a need of amours at once distinguished and delicate. He rose and resumed his journey, thinking of Forestier. What luck the fellow had! He reached the door at the moment his friend was coming out of it.

"You here at this time of day! What do you want of me?"

Duroy, taken aback at meeting him thus, just as he was starting out, stammered: "You see, you see, I can't manage to write my articles; you know the article Monsieur Walter asked me to write on Algeria. It is not very surprising, considering that I have never written anything. Practice is needed for that as for everything else.

I shall get used to it very quickly, I am sure, but I do not know how to set about beginning. I have plenty of ideas, but I cannot manage to express them."

He stopped, hesitatingly, and Forestier smiled somewhat slyly, saying: "I know how it is."

Duroy went on: "Yes, it must happen to every one when they first begin. Well, I came, I came to ask you for some help. In ten minutes you can give me a start, you can show me how to shape it. It will be giving me a good lesson in style, and really without you I do not see how I can manage it."

Forestier still smiled, and, tapping his old comrade on the arm, said: "Go in and see my wife; she will settle your business quite as well as I could. I have trained her to that kind of work. I myself have not time this morning, or I would willingly have done it for you."

Duroy, suddenly abashed, hesitated, feeling afraid.

"But I cannot call on her at this time of the day."

"Oh! yes, she is up. You will find her in my study arranging some notes for me."

Duroy refused to go upstairs, saying: "No. I can't think of such a thing."

Forestier took him by the shoulders, twisted him round on his heels, and, pushing him toward the staircase, said: "Go along, you great donkey, when I tell you to. You are not going to oblige me to go up these flights of stairs again to introduce you and explain the fix you are in."

Then Duroy made up his mind. "Thanks, then, I will go up," he said. "I shall tell her that you forced me, positively forced me to come and see her."

"All right. She won't scratch your eyes out. Above all, don't forget our appointment for three o'clock."

"Oh, never fear!"

Forestier hastened off, and Duroy began to ascend the stairs slowly, step by step, thinking over what he should say, and feeling uneasy as to his probable reception.

The manservant, wearing a blue apron and holding a broom in his hand, opened the door to him.

"Master is not at home," he said, without waiting to be spoken to.

Duroy persisted.

"Ask Madame Forestier," said he, "whether she will receive me, and tell her that I have come from her husband, whom I met in the street."

Then he waited while the man went away, returned and, opening a door on the right, said: "Madame will see you, sir."

She was seated in an office armchair in a small room, the walls of which were wholly hidden by books carefully ranged on shelves of black wood. The bindings, of various tints, red, yellow, green, violet, and blue, gave some color and liveliness to these monotonous lines of volumes.

She turned round, still smiling. She was wrapped in a white dressing-gown, trimmed with lace, and as she held out her hand, displayed her bare arm in its wide sleeve.

"So soon?" she said, and then added: "That is not meant for a reproach, but a simple question."

"Oh, Madame, I did not wish to come up, but your husband, whom I met downstairs, obliged me to do so. I am so confused that I dare not tell you what brings me."

She pointed to a chair, saying: "Sit down and tell me about it."

She was twirling a pen quill between her fingers, and in front of her was a half-written page, interrupted by the young fellow's arrival. She seemed quite at home at this work table, as much at her ease as if in her drawing-room engaged in every-day duties. A faint perfume emanated from her dressing gown, the fresh perfume of a recent toilet. Duroy sought to divine, fancied he could trace, the outline of her plump, youthful figure through the soft material enveloping it.

She went on, as he did not reply: "Well, come, tell me what it is?"

He murmured, hesitatingly: "Well, you see—but I really dare not—I was working last night very late and quite early this morning on the article upon Algeria, upon which Monsieur Walter asked me to write, and I could not get on with it—I tore up all my attempts. I am not accustomed to this kind of work, and I came to ask Forestier to help me this once——"

She interrupted him, laughing heartily. "And he told you to come and see me? That is a nice thing."

"Yes, Madame. He said that you will get me out of my difficulty better than himself, but I did not dare, I did not wish to—you understand."

She rose, saying: "It will be delightful to work in collaboration with you like that. I am charmed at the notion. Come, sit down in my place, for they know my handwriting at the office. And we will soon turn out a good article."

He sat down, took a pen, spread a sheet of paper before him, and waited.

Madame Forestier, standing by, watched him make these preparations, then took a cigarette from the mantel-shelf and lit it.

"I cannot work without smoking," said she. "Come, what are you going to say?"

He lifted his head toward her with astonishment.

"But that is just what I don't know, since that is what I came to see you about."

She replied: "Oh! I will put it in order for you. I will make the sauce, but then I want the joint."

He remained embarrassed before her. At length he

said hesitatingly: "I should like to relate my journey there from the beginning."

Then she sat down before him on the other side of the table, and looking him in the eyes:

"Well, tell it me first; for myself alone, you understand, slowly and without forgetting anything, and I will select what is to be used of it."

But as he did not know where to commence, she began to question him as a priest would have done in the confessional, putting precise questions which recalled to him forgotten details, people encountered and faces merely caught sight of.

When she had made him speak thus for about a quarter of an hour, she suddenly interrupted him with:

"Now we will begin. In the first place, we will imagine that you are narrating your impressions to a friend, which will allow you to write a lot of tomfoolery, to make remarks of all kinds, to be natural and funny if we can. Begin:

"MY DEAR HENRY: You wish to know what Algeria is like, and you shall. I will send you, having nothing else to do in the little cabin of dried mud which serves me as a habitation, a kind of journal of my life, day by day, and hour by hour. It will be a little spicy at times unfortunately, but you are not obliged to show it to your lady friends."

She paused to relight her cigarette, which had gone out, and the faint creaking of the quill on the paper stopped, too.

"Let us continue," said she.

"Algeria is a great French possession on the frontiers of the great unknown countries called the Desert, the Sahara, Central Africa, etc., etc.

"Algiers is the door, the pretty white door of this strange continent.

"But it is first necessary to get to it, which is not a rosy task for every one. I am, you know, an excellent horseman, for I break in the colonel's horses; but a man may be a very good rider and a very bad sailor. That is my case.

"You remember Surgeon-Major Simbretas, whom we used to call Old Ipecacuanha, and how when we thought ourselves ripe for a twenty-four hours' stay in the infirmary, that blessed sojourning place, we would go to see him.

"How he used to sit on his chair, with his fat legs in his red trousers wide apart, his hands on his knees, and his elbows stuck out, rolling his great eyes, and gnawing his white mustache.

"You remember his favorite prescription:

"This man's stomach is out of order. Give him a dose of emetic number three, according to my formula, and then twelve hours off duty, and he will be all right."

"It was a sovereign remedy, that emetic—sovereign and irresistible. One swallowed it because one had to. Then when one had undergone the effects of Old Ipecacuanha's prescription, one enjoyed twelve well-earned hours' rest.

"Well, my dear fellow, to reach Africa it is necessary to undergo for forty hours the effects of another kind of irresistible emetic, according to the prescription of the Compagnie Transatlantique."

She rubbed her hands, delighted with the idea.

She got up and walked about, after lighting another cigarette, and dictated as she puffed out little whiffs of smoke, which, issuing at first through a little orifice in the midst of her compressed lips, slowly spread and gradually disappeared, leaving in the air faint gray lines, a kind of transparent mist, like a spider's web. Sometimes with her open hand she would brush aside these light traces; at others she would cut them asunder with her forefinger, and then watch with serious attention the two halves of the almost impenetrable vapor slowly disappear.

Duroy, with his eyes, followed all her gestures, her attitudes, the movements of her form and features, busied with this vague pastime which did not preoccupy her thoughts.

She now imagined the incidents of the journey, sketched traveling companions invented by herself, and a love affair.

Then, sitting down again, she questioned Duroy on the topography of Algeria, of which she was absolutely ignorant. In ten minutes, she knew as much about it as he did, and she dictated a little chapter of political and colonial geography to coach the reader in such matters and prepare him to understand the serious questions which were to be brought forward in the following articles. She continued by a trip into the provinces of Orana, a fantastic trip, in which it was, above all, a question of women, Moorish, Jewish, and Spanish.

"That is what interests most," she said.

She wound up by a sojourn at Saïda, at the foot of the great tablelands; and by a pretty little intrigue between the non-commissioned George Duroy and a Spanish work-girl employed at the *alfa* factory at Aïn el Hadjar. She described their rendezvous at night amidst the bare, stony hills, with jackals, hyenas, and Arab dogs, yelling, barking, and howling among the rocks.

And she gleefully uttered the words, "To be continued." Then, rising, she added: "That is how one writes an article, my dear sir. Sign it, if you please."

He hesitated.

"But sign it, I tell you."

Then he began to laugh, and wrote at the bottom of the page, "George Duroy."

She went on smoking as she walked up and down;

and he still kept looking at her, unable to find anything to say to thank her, happy to be with her, filled with gratitude, and with the pleasure of this new-born intimacy. It seemed to him that everything around him was part of her, everything, down to the walls covered with books. The chairs, the furniture, the air in which the perfume of tobacco was floating, had about them something good, sweet, and charming, which emanated from her.

Suddenly she asked: "What do you think of my friend, Madame de Marelle?"

He was surprised, and answered: "I think—I think—her very charming."

"Is she not?"

"Yes, indeed."

He longed to add: "But not as charming as yourself," but dared not.

She resumed: "And if you only knew how funny, original, and intelligent she is. She is a Bohemian—a true Bohemian. That is why her husband scarcely cares for her. He only sees her defects, and does not appreciate her good qualities."

Duroy felt stupefied at learning that Madame de Marelle was married, and yet it was only natural she should be.

He said: "Oh! she is married, then. And what is her husband?"

Madame Forestier gently shrugged her shoulders, and raised her eyebrows, with a gesture of incomprehensible meaning.

"Oh! he is an inspector on the Northern Railway. He spends eight days out of the month in Paris. What his wife calls 'obligatory duty,' or 'week of drudgery,' or 'holy week.' When you know her better, you will see how bright and charming she is. Go and call on her one of these days."

Duroy no longer thought of leaving. It seemed to him that he was going to remain here forever; that he was at home.

But the door opened noiselessly, and a tall gentleman entered without being announced. He stopped short on seeing a stranger. Madame Forestier seemed troubled for a moment; then she said in natural tones, though a slight rosy flush had risen to her cheeks:

"Come in, my dear sir. I must introduce one of Charles's old friends, Monsieur George Duroy, a future journalist." Then, in another tone, she added: "Our best and most intimate friend, the Comte de Vaudrec."

The two men bowed, looking each other in the eyes, and Duroy at once took his leave.

There was no attempt to detain him. He stammered a few thanks, grasped the outstretched hand of Madame Forestier, bowed again to the newcomer, who preserved the cold, grave air of a man of position, and went out quite disturbed, as if he had made a fool of himself.

On finding himself once more in the street, he felt sad and uneasy, haunted by the vague idea of some hidden annoyance. He walked on, asking himself whence came this sudden melancholy. He could not tell, but the stern face of the Comte de Vaudrec, already somewhat aged, with gray hair, and the calmly insolent look of a very wealthy man, constantly recurred to his recollection. He noted that the arrival of this unknown, breaking off a charming *tête-à-tête*, had produced in him that chilly, despairing sensation that a word overheard, a trifle noticed, the least thing, suffices sometimes to bring about. It seemed to him, too, that this man, without his being able to guess why, was displeased at finding him there.

He had nothing more to do till three o'clock, and it was not yet noon. He had still six francs fifty centimes in his pocket, and he went and lunched at the Bouillon Duval. Then he prowled about the boulevard, and as

three o'clock struck, ascended the advertisement stair-
way of the *Vie Française*.

The office boys were seated with folded arms on a
bench, while, at an enclosed desk, an employé was sort-
ing the mail that had just arrived. The entire get-up
of the place, intended to impress visitors, was perfect.
Every one had the appearance, bearing, dignity, and
smartness suitable to the anteroom of a large daily newspaper.

"Monsieur Walter, if you please?" inquired Duroy.

"The manager is engaged, sir," replied the doorkeeper.
"Will you take a seat, sir?" and he indicated the waiting room, already full of people.

There were men grave, important-looking and wearing
the ribbon of an order; and men with no linen apparent,
whose frock coats, buttoned up to the chin, bore upon
the breast stains recalling the outlines of continents and
seas on geographical maps. There were three women
among them. One of them was pretty, smiling, and over-
dressed, and had the air of a gay woman; her neighbor, with a wrinkled, tragic countenance, also stylishly
dressed, but in a more severe fashion, had about her that
something worn and artificial that old actresses generally
have; a kind of false youth.

The third woman, in mourning, sat in a corner with
the air of a grieving widow. Duroy thought that she
had come to ask for charity.

However, no one was ushered into the room beyond,
and more than twenty minutes had elapsed.

Duroy was seized with an idea, and, going back to
the doorkeeper, said: "Monsieur Walter made an appointment for me to call on him here at three o'clock.
At all events, see whether my friend Monsieur Forestier
is here."

He was at once ushered along a lengthy passage which

brought him to a large room, where four gentlemen were writing at a large table covered with green leather.

Forestier, standing before the fireplace, was smoking a cigarette. He turned his head as Duroy entered, saying: "Oh! here you are! Have you seen the governor?"

"Come with me, I will take you in to see the governor; otherwise, you might be getting moldy here till seven in the evening."

They recrossed the waiting room, in which the same people were waiting in the same order. As soon as Forestier appeared, the young woman and the old actress, rising quickly, came up to him. He took them aside, one after the other, into the bay window, and, although they took care to talk in low tones, Duroy noticed that they were on familiar terms.

Then, having passed through two padded doors, they entered the manager's room. The business which had detained him for an hour or so was nothing more than a game of ecarté with some of the gentlemen with flat-brimmed hats whom Duroy had noticed the night before.

Monsieur Walter dealt and played with concentrated attention and cautiously, while his adversary threw down, picked up, and handled the light bits of colored pasteboard with the swiftness, skill, and grace of a practiced player. Norbert de Varenne, seated in the managerial armchair, was writing an article; Jacques Rival, stretched at full length on a couch, was smoking a cigar with his eyes closed.

The room smelt close with that blended odor of leather-covered furniture, stale tobacco, and printing ink peculiar to editors' rooms and familiar to all journalists. Upon the black wood table, inlaid with brass, lay an incredible pile of papers, letters, cards, newspapers, magazines, bills, and printed matter of every description.

Forestier shook hands with the watchers standing behind the card players, and without a word watched the progress of the game, then as soon as Daddy Walter had won he said: "Here is my friend Duroy."

The manager glanced sharply at the young fellow over the glasses of his spectacles, and said:

"Have you brought my article? It would fit in very well to-day with the Morel debate."

Duroy took the sheets of paper folded in four from his pocket, saying: "Here it is, sir."

The manager seemed pleased, and remarked with a smile: "Very good, very good. You are a man of your word. You must look through this for me, Forestier."

But Forestier hastened to reply: "It is not worth while, Monsieur Walter. I went over it with him to give him a lesson in the tricks of the trade. It is very well done."

And the manager, who was gathering up the cards dealt by a tall, thin gentleman, a deputy belonging to the Left Centre, remarked with indifference. "All right, then."

Forestier, however, did not let him begin the new game, but, stooping, murmured in his ear: "You know you promised me to take on Duroy to replace Marambot. Shall I engage him on the same terms?"

"Yes, certainly."

Taking his friend's arm, the journalist led him away from the table, while Monsieur Walter resumed the game.

Norbert de Varenne had not lifted his head; he did not appear to have seen or recognized Duroy. Jacques Rival, on the contrary, had shaken his hand with the marked and demonstrative energy of a good fellow who may be reckoned upon in case of any little difficulty.

They passed through the waiting room again, and as every one looked at them, Forestier said to the youngest of the women, in a tone loud enough to be heard by the rest: "The manager will see you directly. He is just now engaged with two members of the Budget Committee."

Then he passed swiftly on, with a hurried, business-like air, as though about to draft at once an article of the utmost importance.

As soon as they were back in the editor's room, Forestier said to Duroy: "Report here every day at three o'clock, and I will tell you the places you are to go to during the day, or evening, or the next morning. One— I will give you, first of all, a letter of introduction to the chief of police, who will put you in touch with one of his subordinates. You will arrange with him to obtain all the important news, official and quasi-official information, you know. In all matters of detail you will apply to Saint-Potin, who is up in the work. You can see him by-and-by, or to-morrow. Above all, cultivate the knack of dragging information out of the men I send you to see and of obtaining an entrance everywhere, in spite of closed doors. You will receive for this a salary of two hundred francs a month, with two sous a line for the paragraphs you glean and two sous a line for all articles written by you, to order, on different subjects."

Duroy drank a glass of beer with his new comrades, and then said to his friend: "What am I to do now?"

"I have nothing for you to-day. You can go if you want to."

"And our—our—article, will it go in to-night?"

"Yes, but do not bother yourself about it; I will correct the proofs. Write the continuation for to-morrow, and come here at three o'clock, the same as to-day."

After shaking hands with every one, Duroy went down the gorgeous staircase with a light heart.

IV. Lessons in Journalism

Duroy slept badly, so excited was he by the wish to see his article in print. He was up as soon as it was daylight, and was prowling about the streets long before the hour at which the porters from the newspaper offices run with their papers from kiosk to kiosk.

He went on to the Saint Lazare terminus, knowing that the *Vie Française* would be delivered there before it reached his own district. As he was still too early, he wandered up and down on the footpath.

He saw the newspaper vendor arrive, open her news-stand, and then saw a man bearing on his head a pile of papers. He rushed forward. There were the *Figaro*, the *Gil Blas*, the *Gaulois*, the *Événement*, and two or three morning journals, but the *Vie Française* was not among them. Fear seized him. Suppose the "Souvenirs d'un Chasseur d'Afrique" had been kept over for the next day, or that by chance, they had not at the last moment seemed suitable to Daddy Walter!

Turning back to the kiosque, he saw that the paper was on sale without his having seen it.

He darted forward, unfolded it after having thrown down three sous, and ran through the headings of the articles on the first page. Nothing. His heart began to beat, and he experienced strong emotion on reading at the foot of a column in large letters, "George Duroy." It was in; what happiness!

He began to walk along unconsciously, the paper in his hand and his hat on one side of his head, with a longing to stop the passers-by in order to say to them: "Buy this, buy this, there is an article by me in it." He would have liked to have bellowed with all the power of his lungs, like some vendor of papers at night on the boulevards, "Read the *Vie Française*; read George Duroy's article, 'Souvenirs d'un Chasseur d'Afrique.'"

And suddenly he felt a wish to read this article himself, to read it in a public place, a café, in sight of all. He looked about for some establishment already filled with customers. He had to walk in search of one for some time. He sat down at last outside a kind of wine shop, where several customers were already installed, and began to read his article, and several times said aloud: "Very good, very well put," to attract the attention of his neighbors, and inspire them with the wish to know what there was in this sheet. Then, on going away, he left it on the table.

He thought: "What shall I do now?" And he decided to go to his office, take his month's salary, and tender his resignation. He felt a thrill of anticipatory pleasure at the thought of the faces that would be pulled by the chief of his room and by his colleagues. The notion of the bewilderment of the chief above all charmed him.

He walked slowly, so as not to get there too early, the cashier's office not opening before ten o'clock.

His office was a large gloomy room in which gas had to be kept burning almost all day long in winter. It looked into a narrow courtyard, with other offices on the farther side of it. There were eight clerks there, besides a sub-chief hidden behind a screen in one corner.

Duroy first went to get the hundred and eighteen francs twenty-five centimes inclosed in a yellow envelope, and placed in the drawer of the pay clerk, and then, with a conquering air, entered the large room in which he had already spent so many days.

As soon as he came in the sub-chief, Monsieur Potel, called out to him: "Ah! it is you, Monsieur Duroy? The chief has already asked for you several times. You know that he will not allow any one to plead illness two days running without a doctor's certificate."

Duroy, who was standing in the middle of the room preparing his sensational effect, replied in a loud voice: "As if I cared whether he does or not!"

There was a movement of amazement among the clerks, and Monsieur Potel's face appeared, filled with astonishment, above the screen which shut him up as in a box. At length the sub-chief said hesitatingly: "What did you say?"

"I said that it makes no difference to me. I have only called to-day to tender my resignation. I am engaged on the staff of the *Vie Française* at five hundred francs a month, and extra pay for all I write. Indeed, I made my *début* this morning."

The effect was overwhelming. No one stirred.

Duroy went on: "I will go and inform Monsieur Perthuis, and then come and wish you good-by."

And he went in search of the chief, who exclaimed on seeing him: "Ah! here you are. You know that I won't have——"

His late employé cut him short: "It's not worth while roaring like that."

Monsieur Perthuis, a stout man, as red as a turkey-cock, was choked with astonishment.

Duroy continued: "I have had enough of this crib. I made my *début* this morning in journalism, where I am assured of a very good position. I have the honor to bid you good-day."

And he went out. He was avenged.

As he promised, he went and shook hands with his old colleagues, who scarcely dared speak to him, for they had overheard his conversation with the chief, the door having remained open.

He found himself in the street again, with his salary in his pocket. He had a substantial breakfast at a good but cheap restaurant he was acquainted with, and having again purchased the *Vie Française,* and left it on the table, went into several shops, where he bought some trifles, solely for the sake of ordering them to be sent home, and giving his name—"George Duroy," with the addition, "I am the editor of the *Vie Française."*

Then he gave the name of the street and the number, taking care to add: "Leave it with the janitor."

As he had still some time to spare, he went into the shop of a lithographer, who wrote visiting cards at a moment's notice, before the eyes of passers-by, and had a hundred, bearing his new occupation under his name, printed off while he waited.

Then he went to the office of the paper.

Forestier received him loftily, as one receives a subordinate. "Ah! here you are. Good. I have several things for you to attend to. Just wait ten minutes. I will finish what I am about."

And he went on with a letter he was writing.

At the other end of the large table a fat, bald, little man, with a very pale puffy face, and a white and shining head, was writing with his nose on the paper owing to extreme short-sightedness. Forestier said to him: "I say, Saint-Potin, when are you going to interview those people?"

"At four o'clock."

"Take young Duroy with you, and show him the tricks of the trade."

Then, turning to his friend, Forestier added: "Have

you brought the continuation of the Algerian article? The opening this morning was very successful."

Duroy, taken aback, stammered: "No. I thought I should have time this afternoon. I had heaps of things to do. I was not able."

The other shrugged his shoulder with a dissatisfied air. "If you are not more exact than that you will spoil your future. Daddy Walter was reckoning on your copy. I will tell him it will be ready to-morrow. If you think you are to be paid for doing nothing, you are mistaken."

Then, after a short silence, he added: "The deuce! One must strike the iron while it is hot."

Saint-Potin rose, saying: "I am ready."

Then Forestier, leaning back in his chair, assumed a serious attitude in order to give his instructions, and turning to Duroy, said: "See here. Within the last two days the Chinese general, Li Theng Fao, has arrived at the Hôtel Continental, and the Rajah Taposahib Ramaderao Pali at the Hôtel Bristol. You will go and interview them." Turning to Saint-Potin, he continued: "Don't forget the main points I told you about. Ask the general and the rajah their opinion upon the action of England in the East, their ideas upon her system of colonization and domination, and their hopes respecting the intervention of Europe, and especially of France." He was silent for a moment, and then added in a theatrical aside: "It will be most interesting to our readers to learn at the same time what is thought in China and in India upon these matters which are of such intense interest at this moment." He continued, for the benefit of Duroy: "Watch how Saint-Potin sets to work; he is a capital reporter, and try to learn the trick of pumping a man dry in five minutes."

As soon as they had crossed the threshold, Saint-Potin began to laugh, and said to Duroy: "There's a bluffer for you. He even tried to bluff us. One would really think he took us for his readers."

They reached the boulevard, and the reporter observed: "Will you have a drink?"

"Certainly. It is awfully hot."

They turned into a café and ordered cooling drinks. Saint-Potin began to talk. He talked about the paper and every one connected with it with an abundance of astonishing details.

"The governor? A regular Jew.

"And yet a good fellow who believes in nothing, and does every one. His paper, which is Governmental, Catholic, Liberal, Republican, Orleanist, pay your money and take your choice, was only started to help him in his speculations on the Bourse, and bolster up his other schemes. At that game he is very clever, and nets millions through companies without four sous of genuine capital.

"And he says things worthy of Balzac, the old shark. The other day I was in his room with that old tub, Norbert, and that Don Quixote, Rival, when Montelin, our business manager, came in with his morocco portfolio, that portfolio that every one in Paris knows, under his arm. Walter raised his head and asked, 'What news?' Montelin answered simply, 'I have just paid the sixteen thousand francs we owed the paper maker.' The governor gave a jump, an astonishing jump. 'What do you mean?' said he. 'I have just paid Monsieur Privas,' replied Montelin. 'But you are mad.' 'Why?' 'Why—why—why——' He took off his spectacles and wiped them. 'Why? Because we could have obtained a reduction of from four to five thousand francs.' Montelin replied, in astonishment: 'But, sir, all the accounts were correct, checked up by me and passed by yourself.' Then the governor, quite serious again, observed: 'What a fool you are! Don't you know, Monsieur Montelin, that one should always let one's debts mount up, in order to offer to compromise?'"

And Saint-Potin added, with a knowing shake of his head: "Eh! isn't that worthy of Balzac?"

Duroy had not read Balzac, but he replied: "By Jove, yes."

Then the reporter spoke of Madame Walter, an old goose; of Norbert de Varenne, an old failure; of Rival, a copy of Fervacques. Next he came to Forestier. "As to him, he has been lucky in marrying his wife, that is all."

Duroy asked: "What is his wife, really?"

Saint-Potin rubbed his hands. "Oh! a deep one, a smart woman. Comte de Vaudrec gave her a dowry and married her off."

Duroy suddenly felt a cold shiver run through him, a tingling of the nerves, a longing to smack this prattler on the face. But he merely interrupted him by asking:

"And your name is Saint-Potin?"

The other replied, simply enough:

"No, my name is Thomas. It is in the office that they have nicknamed me Saint-Potin."

Duroy, as he paid for the drinks, observed: "But it seems to me that time is getting on, and that we have two noble foreigners to call on."

Saint-Potin began to laugh. "You are still green. So you fancy that I am going to ask that Chinaman and that Hindoo what they think of England? As if I did not know better than themselves what they ought to think in order to please the readers of the *Vie Française*. I have already interviewed five hundred of these Chinese, Persians, Hindoos, Chilians, Japanese, and others. They all reply the same, according to me. I have only to take my article on the last comer and copy it word for word. What has to be changed, though, is their appearance, their names, their titles, their age, and their suite. Oh! on that point it does not do to make a mistake, for I should be snapped up sharp by the *Figaro* or the *Gaulois*. But on these matters the hall porters at the Hôtel Bristol and the Hôtel Continental will put me right in five minutes. We will smoke a cigar as we walk there. Five francs cab hire to charge to the paper. That is how one sets about it, my dear fellow, when one is practical."

"It must be worth something to be a reporter under these circumstances," said Duroy.

The journalist replied mysteriously: "Yes, but nothing pays so well as paragraphs, on account of the veiled advertisements."

They had got up and were passing down the boulevard toward the Madeleine. Saint-Potin suddenly observed to his companion: "You know if you have anything else to do, I shall not need you in any way."

Duroy shook hands and left him. The notion of the article to be written that evening worried him, and he began to think.

Having dined at a wine shop near the Arc de Triomphe, he walked slowly home along the outer boulevards and sat down at his table to work. But as soon as he had the sheet of blank paper before his eyes, all the materials that he had accumulated fled from his mind as though his brain had evaporated.

After an hour of effort, and five sheets of paper disfigured by opening phrases that had no continuation, he said to himself: "I am not yet broken in to the business. I must have another lesson." And all at once the prospect of another morning's work with Madame Forestier filled him with anticipation.

It was past ten when he rang his friend's bell.

The manservant replied: "Master is busy at work."

Duroy had not thought that the husband might be

at home. He insisted, however, saying: "Tell him that I have called on a matter requiring immediate attention."

After waiting five minutes, he was shown into the study in which he had passed such a pleasant morning. In the chair he had occupied, Forestier was now seated writing, while his wife in the same white gown leaned against the mantelpiece and dictated, cigarette in mouth.

Duroy, halting on the threshold, murmured: "I really beg your pardon; I am afraid I am disturbing you."

His friend, turning his face toward him—an angry face, too—growled: "What is it you want now? Be quick; we are pressed for time."

The intruder, taken aback, stammered: "It is nothing; I beg your pardon."

But Forestier, growing angry, exclaimed: "Come, hang it all, don't waste time about it; you have not forced your way in just for the sake of wishing us good morning, I suppose?"

Then Duroy, greatly perturbed, made up his mind.

"No—you see—the fact is—I can't quite manage my article—and you were—so—so kind last time—that I hoped—that I ventured to come——"

Forestier cut him short. "You have plenty of assurance. So you think I am to do your work, and that all you have to do is to call on the cashier at the end of the month to draw your screw? No; that is too good."

The young woman went on smoking without saying a word, and with a vague smile, which seemed like an amiable mask, concealing the irony of her thoughts.

Duroy, coloring up, stammered: "Excuse me—I thought——" Then suddenly, and in a clear voice, he went on: "I beg your pardon a thousand times, Madame, while again thanking you most sincerely for the charming article you produced for me yesterday." He bowed, remarked to Charles: "I shall be at the office at three;" and went out.

He walked home rapidly, grumbling: "Well, I will do it all alone, and they shall see——"

Scarcely had he got in than, excited by anger, he began to write. He continued the adventure begun by Madame Forestier, heaping up details of catch-penny romance, surprising incidents and inflated descriptions, with the style of a schoolboy and the phraseology of the barrack-room. Within an hour, he had finished an article which was a chaos of nonsense, and took it with every assurance to the *Vie Française*.

The first person he met was Saint-Potin, who, grasping his hand with the energy of an accomplice, said: "You have read my interview with the Chinese and the Hindoo? Isn't it funny? It has amused every one. And I did not even get a glimpse of them."

Duroy, who had not read anything, at once took up the paper and ran his eye over a long article, headed: "India and China," while the reporter pointed out the most interesting passages.

Forestier came in hurriedly, saying:

"Good; I want both of you." And he mentioned a number of political items that would have to be obtained that very afternoon. Duroy held out his article. "Here is the continuation about Algeria."

"Very good; hand it over and I will give it to the governor."

That was all.

Saint-Potin led away his new colleague, and when they were in the passage, he said to him. "Have you seen the cashier?"

"No; why?"

"Why? To draw your money. You see, you should always draw a month in advance. One never knows what may happen."

"Why—I ask for nothing better."

"I will introduce you to the cashier. He will make no difficulty about it. They pay well here."

Duroy went and drew his two hundred francs, with twenty-eight more for his article of the day before, which, added to what remained of his salary from the railway company, gave him three hundred and forty francs in his pocket. He had never owned such a sum, and thought himself possessed of wealth for an indefinite period.

When evening had come, Duroy, who had nothing more to do, thought of going again to the Folies-Bergère, and putting a bold face on it, went up to the box office.

"I am George Duroy, on the staff of the *Vie Française*. I came here the other day with Monsieur Forestier, who promised to see about my being given a pass. I do not know whether he has thought of it."

The list was referred to. His name was not entered. However, the box-office keeper, a very affable man, at once said: "You can go in all the same, sir, and write to the manager, who, I am sure, will attend to it."

He went in and almost immediately met Rachel, the woman he had met the first evening. She came up to him, saying: "Good evening, ducky. Are you quite well?"

"Very well, thanks; and you?"

"I am all right. Do you know I have dreamed of you twice since last time."

And, lifting her eyes toward the young man's moustache, she took his arm and leaned lovingly upon it.

"Let us go and have a grenadine first of all," she remarked. "And then we will take a stroll together. I should like to go to the Opéra like this, with you, to show you off."

*　　*　　*

It was broad day when he arose the next morning, and the notion occurred to him to buy the *Vie Française*. He opened the paper with feverish hand. His article was not there, and he stood on the footpath, anxiously running his eye down the printed columns with the hope of at length finding what he was in search of. A weight suddenly oppressed his heart.

Entering the office some hours later, he went to see Monsieur Walter.

"I was surprised at not seeing my second article on Algeria in the paper this morning, sir," said he.

The manager raised his head, and replied in a dry tone: "I gave it to your friend Forestier, and asked him to read it through. He did not think it up to the mark; you must rewrite it."

Duroy, in a rage, went out without saying a word, and abruptly entering his old comrade's room, said: "Why didn't you let my article go in this morning?"

"The governor thought it poor, and told me to give it back to you to do over again. There it is." And he pointed to the copy, unfolded, beneath a paper weight.

Duroy, abashed, could find nothing to say in reply, and as he was putting his prose into his pocket, Forestier went on: "To-day you must first of all go to the police department." And he proceeded to give a list of business errands and items of news to be attended to.

Duroy went off without being able to think of the cutting remark he wished to utter. He brought back his article the next day. It was returned to him again.

Having rewritten it a third time and finding it still refused, he understood that he was trying to go ahead too fast, and that Forestier's hand alone could help him on his way. He did not, therefore, say anything more about the "Souvenirs d'un Chasseur d'Afrique," but resolved to be adaptable and crafty, since it was necessary, and, while awaiting something better, to zealously discharge his duties as a reporter.

He became familiar with the secrets of theatrical and political life, with the waiting-rooms of statesmen and the lobby of the Chamber of Deputies; the important countenances of Cabinet officials, and the grim looks of sleepy doorkeepers. He was in continual communication with ministers, janitors, generals, police agents, princes, pimps, courtesans, ambassadors, bishops, priests, adventurers, men of fashion, card-sharpers, cab-drivers, waiters, and many others, having become the interested yet indifferent friend of all these; confounding them together in his estimation, measuring them with the same measure, judging them with the same eye, through having to see them every day at any hour, without any change of ideas, and to converse with them all on the same matter, bearing on his own business. He compared himself to a man who had to drink of samples of every kind of wine one after the other, and who would soon be unable to tell Château Margaux from Argenteuil.

He soon became a remarkable reporter. However, as he only got ten centimes a line in addition to his salary of two hundred francs a month, and as life on the boulevards and in cafés and restaurants is costly, he never had a penny, and was disgusted with his poverty. There must be some trick, he thought, as he saw some of his colleagues with their pockets full of money without ever being able to understand what secret methods they employed to procure this abundance. He enviously suspected unknown and suspicious transactions, services rendered, a whole system of graft carried on and tolerated. He would have to solve the mystery, enter into a tacit partnership, obtrude himself on the comrades who were dividing the spoils without him.

And of an evening, as he watched the trains go by from his window, he would think over the best method to attain this end.

V. The First Affair

Two months had gone by, September was at hand, and the rapid fortune which Duroy had hoped for seemed to him slow in coming. He was, above all, distressed at the social mediocrity of his position, and did not see by what path he could scale the heights on which one finds respect, power, and money. He felt shut up in the middle-class calling of a reporter, so walled in as to be unable to get out of it. He was appreciated, but only in accordance with his position. Even Forestier, to whom he rendered a thousand services, no longer invited him to dinner, and treated him in every way as an inferior, though still accosting him as a friend.

From time to time, it is true, Duroy, seizing an opportunity, got in a short article, and having acquired through his news items a mastery over his pen, and a tact which he lacked when he wrote his second article on Algeria, no longer ran any risk of having his descriptions of facts refused. But between this and drawing on his imagination for a story, or writing authoritatively on political questions, there was as great a difference as between driving in the Bois de Boulogne as the coachman or as the owner of the carriage. That which humiliated him above everything was to see the doors of society closed to him, not to meet people on equal terms, to be unable to have close friendships with those of the opposite sex, although several well-known actresses had occasionally received him with an interested familiarity.

He had often thought of calling on Madame Forestier, but the recollection of their last meeting checked and humiliated him; and, besides, he was awaiting an invitation to do so from her husband. Then the recollection of Madame de Marelle occurred to him, and recalling that she had asked him to come and see her, he called one afternoon when he had nothing to do.

"I am always at home till three o'clock," she had said.

He rang at the bell of her residence, a fourth floor in the Rue de Verneuil, at half-past two.

At the sound of the bell a servant opened the door, an untidy girl, who tied her cap-strings as she replied: "Yes, Madame is at home, but I don't know whether she is up."

And she pushed open the drawing-room door, which was ajar. Duroy went in. The room was fairly large, scantily furnished, and neglected-looking.

Duroy sat down immediately. He waited a long time. Then the door opened and Madame de Marelle came running in, wearing a Japanese morning gown of rose-colored silk, embroidered with golden landscapes, blue flowers, and white birds.

"How good of you to come and see me!" she exclaimed. "I had made up my mind that you had forgotten me."

She held out both her hands with a delighted air, and Duroy, whom the commonplace appearance of the room had put at his ease, kissed one of them, as he had seen Norbert de Varenne do.

She begged him to sit down, and then, looking him

over from head to foot, said: "How you have changed! You have improved in looks. Paris has done you good. Come, tell me the news."

And they began to gossip at once, as if they had been old acquaintances.

Suddenly Madame de Marelle exclaimed in astonishment: "It is strange how I get on with you. It seems to me as though I had known you for ten years. We shall become good friends, no doubt. Are you willing?"

He answered: "Certainly," with a smile which said still more.

She went on talking, each phrase sparkling with that ready wit of which she had acquired the habit, just as a workman acquires the knack needed to accomplish a task that seems difficult to others. He listened, thinking: "All this is worth remembering. A man could write charming articles of Paris gossip by getting her to chat over the events of the day."

Some one tapped softly, very softly, at the door by which she had entered, and she called out: "You can come in, pet."

Her little girl made her appearance, walked straight up to Duroy, and held out her hand to him. The astonished mother murmured: "But this is a complete conquest. I no longer recognize her."

The young fellow, having kissed the child, made her sit down beside him, and with a serious manner asked her pleasant questions as to what she had been doing since they last met. She replied, in her little flutelike voice, with her grave and grownup air.

The clock struck three, and the journalist rose.

"Come often," said Madame de Marelle, "and we will chat as we have done to-day; it will always give me pleasure. But how is it one no longer sees you at the Forestiers'?"

He replied: "Oh! for no special reason. I have been very busy. I hope to meet you there again one of these days."

He went out, his heart full of hope, though without knowing why.

He did not speak to Forestier of this visit. But he retained a recollection of it the following days, and more than the recollection.

He paid a second visit a few days later.

The maid ushered him into the drawing-room, and Laurine at once appeared. She no longer held out her hand, but her forehead, and said: "Mamma told me to request you to wait for her. She will be a quarter of an hour, because she is not dressed yet. I will keep you company."

Duroy, who was amused by the ceremonious manners of the little girl, replied: "Certainly, Mademoiselle. I shall be delighted to pass a quarter of an hour with you, but I warn you that for my part I am not at all serious, and that I play all day long, so I suggest a game of tag."

The girl was astounded; then she smiled as a woman would have done at this idea, which shocked her a little as well as astonished her, and murmured: "Rooms are not meant to play in."

He said: "It is all the same to me. I play everywhere. Come, catch me."

And he began to run round the table, enticing her to come after him, which she did, smiling with a species of polite condescension. Suddenly, just as she thought she had got him, he seized her in his arms, and, lifting her to the ceiling, exclaimed: "Tag."

The delighted child wriggled her legs to escape, and laughed with all her heart.

Madame de Marelle came in at that moment, and was amazed. "What, Laurine, Laurine playing! You are a sorcerer, sir."

He put down the little girl, kissed her mother's hand, and they sat down with the child between them. They began to chat, but Laurine, usually so silent, kept talking all the while, and had to be sent to her room. She obeyed without a word, but with tears in her eyes.

As soon as they were alone Madame de Marelle lowered her voice. "You do not know, but I have a grand scheme, and I have thought of you. This it is. As I dine every week at the Forestiers', I return their hospitality from time to time at some restaurant. I do not like to entertain company at home; my household is not arranged for that, and, besides, I do not understand anything about domestic affairs. I like to live as I please. So I entertain them now and then at a restaurant, but it is not very lively when there are only we three, and my own acquaintances scarcely assimilate with them. I tell you all this in order to explain a somewhat irregular invitation. You understand, do you not, that I want you to make one of us on Saturday at the Café Riche, at half-past seven. You know the place?"

He accepted with pleasure, and she went on: "There will be only four of us."

He left her, retaining, as before, the sense of her continued presence as in a species of hallucination. And he awaited the day of the dinner with growing impatience.

Having hired, the second time, an evening suit—his funds not yet allowing him to buy one—he arrived first at the rendezvous, a few minutes before the time. He was ushered up to the second story, and into a small private dining room hung with red and white, its single window opening on to the boulevard. A square table, laid for four, displayed a white cloth, so shining that it seemed to be varnished, and glasses and silver that glittered brightly in the light of the twelve candles of two tall candelabra. He heard throughout the huge house a confused murmur, the murmur of a large restaurant, the clattering of glass and silver, the hurried steps of the waiters, deadened by the carpets in the passages, and the opening of doors, letting out the sound of voices from the numerous private rooms in which people were dining. Forestier came in and shook hands with him, with a cordial familiarity which he never displayed at the offices of the *Vie Française*.

"The ladies are coming together," said he; "these little dinners are very pleasant."

Then he glanced at the table, turned off a gas jet that was turned low, closed one sash of the window on account of the draught, and chose a sheltered place for himself, with the remark: "I must be careful; I have been better for a month, and now I feel worse again these last few days. I must have caught cold on Tuesday coming out of the theatre."

The door was opened, and, followed by a waiter, the two ladies appeared.

As Duroy bowed to Madame Forestier she scolded him for not having come to see her again; then she added, with a smile in the direction of her friend: "I know what it is; you prefer Madame de Marelle; you can find time to visit her."

They sat down to table, and the waiter having handed the wine card to Forestier, Madame de Marelle exclaimed: "Give these gentlemen whatever they like, but for us iced champagne, the best, sweet champagne."

The Ostend oysters were brought in, tiny and plump, like little ears enclosed in shells, and melting between the tongue and the palate like salted bonbons. Then, after the soup, a trout was served, as rose-tinted as a young girl, and the guests began to talk.

They spoke at first of a current scandal. And then they began to talk of love. Without admitting it to be eternal, Duroy understood it as enduring, creating a bond, a tender friendship, a confidence. The union of the senses was only a seal to the union of hearts. But he was angry at the outrageous jealousies, melodramatic scenes, and unpleasantnesses which almost always accompany ruptures.

When he ceased speaking, Madame de Marelle replied: "Yes, it is the only good thing in life, and we often spoil it by preposterous unreasonableness."

Madame Forestier, who was toying with her knife, added: "Yes—yes—it is pleasant to be loved."

And she seemed to be carrying her dream farther, to be thinking things that she dared not give words to.

As the first entrée was slow in coming, they sipped from time to time a mouthful of champagne, and nibbled bits of crust. And the thought of love slowly intoxicated their souls, as the bright wine, rolling drop by drop down their throats, fired their blood and perturbed their minds.

The waiter brought in some lamb cutlets, delicate and tender, upon a thick layer of asparagus tips.

"Ah! this is good," exclaimed Forestier; and they ate slowly, enjoying the delicate meal and the vegetables as smooth as cream.

Duroy resumed: "For my part, when I love a woman, everything else in the world disappears." He said this in a tone of conviction.

Madame Forestier murmured, in her indifferent tone: "There is no happiness comparable to that of the first hand-clasp, when the one asks: 'Do you love me?' and the other replies, 'Yes.'"

Madame de Marelle, who had just tossed off a fresh glass of champagne, said gayly, as she put down her glass: "For my part, I am not so platonic."

And all began to smile with kindling eyes at these words.

Forestier, stretched out in his seat on the divan, rested his arms on the cushions, and said, in a serious tone:

"This frankness does you honor, and proves that you are a practical woman."

And the conversation, descending from highflown theories concerning love, strayed into the flowery garden of polite smut. The roast, consisting of partridges flanked by quails, had been served; then came green peas, and then a dish of *foies gras,* accompanied by a curly lettuce salad. They had partaken of all these things without distinguishing their taste, without noticing it, solely preoccupied with their subject.

Dessert came, and then coffee; and the liqueurs produced a still greater warmth and agitation in their excited imaginations.

Cigarettes were lighted, and, all at once, Forestier began to cough. It was a terrible fit, that seemed to tear his chest, and with red face and forehead damp with perspiration, he choked behind his napkin. When the fit was over he growled angrily: "These feeds are very bad for me; they are stupid." All his good humor had vanished at the apprehension of illness that haunted his thoughts. "Let us go home," said he.

Madame de Marelle rang for the waiter, and asked for the bill. It was brought almost immediately. She tried to read it, but the figures danced before her eyes, and she passed it to Duroy, saying: "Here, pay for me; I can't see straight."

And at the same time she threw him her purse. The bill amounted to a hundred and thirty francs. Duroy checked it, and then handed over two notes and received back the change, saying in a low tone: "What shall I give the waiter?"

"What you like; I do not know."

He put five francs on the salver, and handed back the purse, saying: "Shall I see you to your door?"

"Certainly. I am incapable of finding my way alone."

They shook hands with the Forestiers, and Duroy

called a cab. He felt through his sleeve the warmth of her shoulder, and he could find nothing to say to her, absolutely nothing, his mind being paralyzed by the imperative desire to seize her in his arms.

She did not speak either, but remained motionless in her corner. He would have thought that she was asleep if he had not seen her eyes gleam every time a ray of light entered the carriage.

"What was she thinking?" He felt that he must not speak, that a word, a single word, breaking this silence would destroy his chances.

But the cab having shortly stopped before the house in which they resided, Duroy had no time to seek passionate phrases to thank her and express his admiration. She did not stir. Duroy got out first to help her to alight.

At length she got out of the cab, and, without saying a word, he rang the bell, and as the door opened, said trembling: "When shall I see you again?"

She murmured so softly that he scarcely heard it: "Come and lunch with me to-morrow." And she disappeared in the entry, pushing to the heavy door, which closed with a noise like a cannon. He gave the driver five francs, and began to walk along with rapid and triumphant steps, and heart overflowing with joy.

He was somewhat agitated the next day as he ascended Madame de Marelle's staircase. How would she receive him? And supposing she should not receive him at all?

The little servant opened the door. She looked the same as usual. He felt reassured, as though he had expected the servant to look disturbed. He asked: "Is your mistress quite well?"

She replied: "Oh, yes, sir; the same as ever," and showed him into the drawing-room.

He went straight to the mirror to ascertain the state of his hair and his toilet, and was arranging his necktie before it, when he saw in it the young woman watching him as she stood at the door leading from her room. He pretended not to have noticed her, and the pair looked at one another for a few moments in the glass, observing and watching before finding themselves face to face. He turned round. She had not moved, and seemed to be waiting. He darted forward, stammering: "My dear! my dear!"

She held out her arms and fell upon his breast; then, having raised her head toward him, their lips met.

"It is easier than I should have imagined," he thought. "It is all going on very well."

He smiled without saying a word, while striving to throw a world of love into his looks. She, too, smiled, with that smile with which women show their consent, and murmured: "We are alone. I have sent Laurine to lunch with one of her young friends."

"Thank you," he said. "I will worship you."

They sat down side by side on the sofa. He wanted to start a clever and attractive chat, but not being able to do so to his liking, stammered: "Then you are not too angry with me?"

She put her hand on his mouth, saying: "Be quiet."

They sat in silence, looking into one another's eyes.

The door opened, and the servant announced that luncheon was ready. Duroy gravely offered his arm.

They sat down opposite one another, continually gazing and smiling at each other, solely taken up with each other. They ate without knowing what they were eating. He felt a foot, a little foot, straying under the table. He took it between his own and kept it there. The servant came and went, bringing and taking away the dishes with a careless air, without seeming to notice anything.

When they had finished they returned to the drawing-room, and resumed their place on the sofa, side by side. Little by little he drew closer to her, striving to take her in his arms. But she calmly repulsed him, saying: "Take care; some one may come in."

He murmured: "When can I see you quite alone, to tell you how I love you?"

She leaned over toward him, and whispered: "I will come and pay you a visit some of these days."

She named a day in the latter half of the week. He begged her to come sooner, playing with and squeezing her hands. She was amazed to see him implore her with such ardor, and took off a day at a time. But he kept repeating: "To-morrow, only say to-morrow."

She consented at length. "Yes, to-morrow. At five o'clock."

The sound of the doorbell made them start, and with a bound they separated to a distance. She murmured: "It must be Laurine."

The child made her appearance, stopped short in amazement, and then ran to Duroy, clapping her hands with pleasure at seeing him, and exclaiming: "Ah! Bel-Ami."

Madame de Marelle began to laugh. "What! Bel-Ami! Laurine has baptized you. It's a nice little nickname for you, and I will call you Bel-Ami, too."

He had taken the little girl on his knee, and he had to play with her all the games he had taught her. He rose to take his leave at twenty minutes to three, to go to the office, and on the staircase, through the half-closed door, he still whispered: "To-morrow at five."

She answered: "Yes," with a smile, and disappeared.

As soon as he had got through his day's work he speculated how he should arrange his room, and hide as far as possible the poverty of the place. The idea struck him of pinning some little Japanese trifles on the walls, and he bought for five francs quite a collection of paper ornaments, little fans and screens, with which he hid

the most glaring of the stains on the wall paper. He
pasted on the window panes transparent pictures representing boats floating down rivers, flocks of birds flying
across rosy skies, multi-colored ladies on balconies, and
processions of little black men on plains covered with
snow. His room soon looked like the inside of a Chinese
lantern. He thought the effect satisfactory, and passed
the evening in pasting on the ceiling birds that he cut
out from the colored sheets remaining over. Then he
went to bed.

He went home early the next day, carrying a paper bag
of cakes and a bottle of Madeira, purchased at the
grocer's.

Then he waited.

She came at about a quarter-past five; and, attracted
by the bright colors of the pictures, exclaimed: "Why,
how pretty your place is! But there are a great number
of people on the stairs."

Her visit was a short one, and half an hour later he
escorted her back to the cabstand in the Rue de Rome.
When she was in the carriage he murmured: "Tuesday,
at the same time."

As the driver whipped up his horse, she exclaimed:
"Good-by, Bel-Ami;" and the old vehicle jagged along
behind its old white horse.

For three weeks Duroy received Madame de Marelle
in this way every two or three days, now in the afternoon
and now in the morning. While he was expecting her
one afternoon, a loud uproar on the stairs drew him to
his door. A child was crying. A man's angry voice
shouted: "What is that little devil howling about now?"
The snapping, exasperated voice of a woman replied:
"It is that woman who comes to see the penny-a-liner
upstairs; she has upset Nicholas on the landing. It is
people like that who pay no attention to children on the
staircase."

Duroy drew back, distracted, for he could hear the quick rustling of skirts and a hurried step ascending the stairs to the floor beneath him. There was presently a knock at the door, which he had closed. He opened it, and Madame de Marelle rushed into the room, terrified and breathless, stammering: "Did you hear?"

He pretended to know nothing. "No; what?"

"How they have insulted me."

"Who? Who?"

"The wretches who live down below."

"Why no; what does it all mean? Tell me."

She began to sob, without being able to utter a word. He had to take off her bonnet and moisten her forehead with a wet towel. She was choking, and when her emotion had somewhat abated, all her wrathful indignation burst forth. She wanted him to go down at once to thrash them, to kill them.

He repeated: "But they are only working people, peasants. Just think, you would have to go to court. One cannot lower one's self to have anything to do with such people."

She passed on to another idea. "What shall we do now? For my part, I cannot come here again."

He replied: "It is very simple; I will move."

She murmured: "Yes, but that will take some time." Then, all at once, she framed a plan, and, reassured, added softly: "No, I know what to do; let me act, do not trouble yourself about anything. I will send you a telegram to-morrow morning."

As he usually rose late, he was still in bed the next day, when about eleven o'clock he received the promised telegram. He opened it and read:

"Meet me at five, 127 Rue de Constantinople. Rooms hired by Madame Duroy.   CLO."

At five o'clock to the minute he entered the janitor's

room in a large furnished-room house, and asked: "Is this where Madame Duroy has taken rooms?"

"Yes, sir."

"You will show me to them, if you please."

The man, doubtless used to delicate situations in which prudence is necessary, looked him straight in the eyes, and then, selecting one of the long range of keys, said: "You are Monsieur Duroy?"

"Yes, certainly."

The man opened the door of a small, two-room apartment on the ground floor, opposite his own. The sitting room had a flowered wall paper, mahogany furniture covered with green rep with a yellow design, and a thin, flowered carpet through which one could feel the wooden flooring.

Duroy, uneasy and displeased, thought: "This place will cost goodness knows how much. I shall have to borrow again. It is idiotic, what she has done."

The door opened, and Clotilde came in like a whirlwind, with outstretched arms and rustling skirts. She was delighted. "Isn't it nice, eh? Isn't it nice? And on the ground floor, too; no stairs to go up."

He kissed her coldly, not daring to put the question that rose to his lips. She had placed a large parcel on the little round table in the middle of the room. And she played at moving in, finding a place for everything, and deriving great amusement from it.

"It will be very convenient. If I get wet, for instance, while I am out, I can run in here to dry myself. We shall have a key, besides the one left with the doorkeeper, in case we forget it. I have taken the place for three months, in your name, of course, since I could not give my own."

Then he said: "You will let me know when the rent is to be paid."

She replied simply: "But it is paid, dear."

"Then I owe it you?"

"No, no, my dear; this is a little fancy of my own."

He seemed annoyed. "Oh, no, indeed; I can't allow that."

She implored him, but he held out, refusing with an irritated air, and then he yielded, thinking that, after all, it was fair. And when she had gone, he murmured, rubbing his hands, and without inquiring in the depths of his heart why he thought so: "She is very interesting."

He received, a few days later, another telegram:

"My husband returns to-night after six weeks' inspection, so we shall have a week off.   CLO."

Duroy felt astounded. He no longer thought of her as being married. But here was a man whose face he would have liked to see just once, in order to know him. He patiently awaited the husband's departure, but he passed two evenings at the Folies-Bergère, which wound up with Rachel.

Then, one morning, came a fresh telegram:

"To-day at five.   CLO."

When they met, she said: "If you like, you may take me to dinner somewhere. I have kept myself disengaged."

It was the beginning of the month, and although he had some time before drawn his salary in advance, and was living from day to day upon money gleaned on every side, Duroy happened to be in funds, and was pleased at the opportunity of spending something upon her.

They started off, therefore, about seven, and gained the outer boulevard. She leaned on his arm, and whispered in his ear: "If you only knew how happy it makes me to walk out on your arm; how I love to feel you beside me."

He said: "Would you like to go to Père Lathuile's?"

"Oh, no; it is too swell. I should like something funny, out of the way; a restaurant that salesmen and working-girls go to. I adore dining at a country inn. Oh, if we had only been able to go into the country."

As he knew no such place in the neighborhood, they wandered along the boulevard, and ended by going into a wine shop where there was a dining-room. She had seen through the windows two bareheaded girls seated at table with two soldiers. Three cab drivers were dining at the farther end of the long and narrow room, and an individual, impossible to classify under any calling, was smoking, stretched on a chair, with his legs stuck out in front of him, his hands in the waistband of his trousers, and his head thrown back over the top bar. His jacket was a museum of stains, and in its swollen pockets could be noted the neck of a bottle, a piece of bread, a parcel wrapped up in a newspaper, and a dangling piece of string. He had thick, tangled, curly hair, covered with dandruff, and his cap was on the floor, under his chair.

The entrance of Clotilde created a sensation, due to the elegance of her toilet. The two couples ceased whispering together, the three cab drivers left off arguing, and the man who was smoking, having taken his pipe from his mouth and expectorated, turned his head slightly to look.

Madame de Marelle murmured: "It is very nice; we shall be very comfortable here. Another time I will dress like a working-girl." And she sat down, without embarrassment or disgust, before the greasy wooden table, shiny from grease, washed by spilt liquors, and streaky from a hurried wipe with the waiter's napkin. Duroy, somewhat ill at ease and slightly ashamed, sought a peg to hang his hat on. Not finding one, he put it on a chair.

They had a ragout, a slice of melon, and a salad. Clotilde repeated: "I delight in this. I have low tastes.

I like this better than the Café Anglais." Then she added: "If you want to complete my enjoyment, you will take me to a dancing place. I know a very funny one close by, called the Reine Blanche."

Duroy, surprised at this, asked: "Whoever could have taken you there?"

He looked at her and saw her blush, somewhat disturbed, as though his sudden question aroused within her some delicate recollections. After one of those feminine hesitations, so short that they can scarcely be guessed, she replied: "A friend of mine," and then, after a brief silence, added, "who is dead." And she cast down her eyes with a very natural sadness.

Duroy, for the first time, thought of all that he did not know as regarded the past life of this woman. A vague jealousy, a species of enmity, awoke within him; an enmity against all that he did not know. He looked at her, irritated at the mystery wrapped up within that pretty, silent head, which was thinking, perhaps, at that very moment, of the other, the others, regretfully. How he would have liked to have looked into her recollections —to have known all.

She repeated: "Will you take me to the Reine Blanche? That will be a perfect treat."

He thought: "What matters the past? I am very foolish to bother about it," and smilingly replied: "Certainly, darling." When they were in the street she resumed, in that low and mysterious tone in which confidences are made: "I dared not ask you this until now, but you cannot imagine how I love these escapades in places ladies do not go to. During the carnival I will dress up as a schoolboy. I make such a capital boy."

When they entered the ballroom she kept close to him, gazing with delighted eyes on the young people, and from time to time, as though to secure herself from any possible danger, saying, as she noticed some serious and motionless police officer: "That is a strong-looking fellow." In a quarter of an hour she had had enough of it, and he escorted her home.

Then began quite a series of expeditions to all the queer places where the populace amuse themselves, and Duroy saw that she had quite a liking for this vagabondage of students bent on a spree. She came to their meeting place in a cotton frock and a servant's cap—a theatrical servant's cap—on her head; and despite the elegant and studied simplicity of her toilet, she retained her rings, her bracelets, and her diamond earrings, saying, when he begged her to remove them: "Bah! They will think they are paste."

She thought she was admirably disguised, and although she was really only concealed after the fashion of an ostrich, she went into drinking-places of the worst repute. She wanted Duroy to dress himself like a workman, but he resisted, and retained his correct attire, not even consenting to exchange his tall hat for one of soft felt. She consoled herself for his obstinacy by the reflection that she would be taken for a chambermaid engaged in a love affair with a gentleman, and thought this delightful. In this guise they went into popular wine shops, and sat down on rickety chairs at old wooden tables in smoke-filled rooms. A cloud of rank tobacco smoke, blended with the odor of fried fish remaining from dinner, filled the room; men in blouses shouted at one another as they tossed off *petits verres;* and the astonished waiter stared at this strange couple as he placed before them two cocktails. Trembling, half-afraid, and yet charmed, she began to sip the red liquid, looking round her with uneasy and kindling eye. Each cherry she swallowed gave her the sensation of a sin committed, each drop of the burning liquor flowing down her throat gave her the enjoyment as of a forbidden pleasure.

Then she would say: "Let us go," and they would leave. She would pass rapidly, with bent head and the short steps of an actress leaving the stage, among the drinkers, who, with their elbows on the tables, watched her go by with suspicious and dissatisfied glances; and when she had crossed the threshold she would give a deep sigh, as if she had just escaped some terrible danger.

Sometimes she asked Duroy, with a shudder: "If I were insulted in these places, what would you do?"

He would answer, with a swaggering air: "Take your part, *parbleu!*"

And she would clasp his arm with happiness, with, perhaps, a vague wish to be insulted and defended, to see men fight on her account, even such men as those, with her admirer.

But these outings, taking place two or three times a week, began to weary Duroy, who had found it difficult to raise the ten francs necessary for the cake and the drinks. He now had great difficulty in making his expenses, more so than when he was a clerk in the Northern Railway; for having spent lavishly during his first months of journalism, in the constant hope of gaining large sums in a day or two, he had exhausted all his resources and all means of procuring money. A very simple method, that of borrowing from the cashier, was very soon exhausted; and he already owed the paper four months' salary, besides six hundred francs advanced for work. He owed, besides, a hundred francs to Forestier, three hundred to Jacques Rival, who was generous with his money; and he was also harassed by a number of small debts of from five francs to twenty. Saint-Potin, consulted as to the means of raising another hundred francs, had discovered no expedient, although a man of inventive mind, and Duroy was exasperated at this poverty, of which he was more sensible now than formerly, since he had more wants. A sullen rage against

every one smouldered within him, and an ever-increasing
irritation, which manifested itself at the most trivial
causes. He sometimes asked himself how he could have
spent an average of a thousand francs a month, without
any extras or any foolish extravagances, and he found
that, with a luncheon at eight francs and a dinner at
twelve, partaken of in some large café on the boulevards,
he soon got rid of a louis, which, added to ten francs
pocket money—that pocket money that melts away, one
does not know how—makes a total of thirty francs. But
thirty francs a day is nine hundred francs at the end of
the month. And he did not reckon in this the cost of
clothes, boots, linen, washing, etc.

So on the 14th December he found himself without a
sou in his pocket, and without the slightest idea how to
get any money. He went without luncheon, and passed
the afternoon working at the newspaper office, cross and
preoccupied. About four o'clock he received a telegram
from Madame de Marelle:

"Shall we dine together and have a lark afterward?"

He at once replied: "Cannot dine." Then he reflected
that he would be very stupid to deprive himself of the
pleasant moments she might afford him, and added:
"But will await you at nine at our place." And, having
sent one of the messengers with this, to save the cost of
a telegram, he began to reflect what he should do to
procure himself a dinner.

At seven o'clock he had not yet hit upon anything,
and felt terribly empty. Then, in despair, he resorted
to strategy. He let all his colleagues depart, one after
the other, and when he was alone, rang sharply. Monsieur
Walter's messenger, left in charge of his office, came in.
Duroy was standing, feeling in his pockets, and said in
an abrupt voice: "Foucart, I have left my purse at home,
and I have to go and dine at the Luxembourg. Lend me
fifty sous for my cab."

The man took three francs from his waistcoat pocket, and said: "Do you want any more, sir?"

"No, no, that will be enough. Thanks."

And, having seized the coins, Duroy ran downstairs and dined at a popular-price restaurant to which he drifted on his days of poverty.

At nine o'clock he was awaiting Madame de Marelle, with his feet on the fender, in the little sitting room. She came in, lively and animated, from the keen air of the street. "If you like," said she, "we will first go for a stroll. The weather is splendid for walking."

He replied, in a grumbling tone: "Why go out? We are very comfortable here."

She said, without taking off her bonnet: "If you knew, the moonlight is beautiful. It is splendid walking about to-night."

"Perhaps so, but I do not care for walking about!"

He had said this in an angry fashion. She was struck and hurt by it, and asked: "What is the matter with you? Why do you act like that? I should like to go for a stroll, and I don't see why that should annoy you."

He got up in a rage. "It does not annoy me. It is a bother, that is all."

She was a woman whom resistance irritated and im- politeness exasperated, and she said disdainfully and with angry calm: "I am not accustomed to be spoken to like that. I will go alone, then. Good-by."

He saw that it was serious, and darting toward her, seized her hands, saying: "Forgive me, forgive me. I am very nervous this evening, very irritable. I have had vexations and annoyances, you know—matters of busi- ness."

She replied, somewhat softened, but not calmed down:

"That does not concern me, and I will not bear the brunt of your ill temper."

"Listen, darling. I did not want to hurt you; I was not thinking of what I was saying."

He had forced her to sit down, and kneeling before her, went on: "Have you forgiven me? Tell me you have forgiven me!"

She murmured coldly: "Very well, but do not do so again;" and rising, she added: "Now let us go for a stroll."

He stammered: "Clo, my little Clo, I have a reason."

She stopped, and, looking him full in the face, said: "You are lying. What is the reason?"

He caught her by the shoulders, and, in despair, ready to acknowledge anything in order to avoid a rupture, he said in a despairing tone: "I have not a sou. That is the reason."

She stopped short, and looking into his eyes to read the truth in them, said: "What do you say?"

He had flushed up to the roots of his hair. "I say that I have not a sou. Do you understand? Not twenty sous, not ten, not enough to pay for a glass of liqueur in any café we may go into. You force me to confess what I am ashamed of. It was, however, impossible for me to go out with you, and when we were seated with refreshments before us to tell you quietly that I could not pay for them."

She was still looking him in the face. "Well—is it all true?"

In a moment he had turned out all his pockets, those of his trousers, coat, and waistcoat, and murmured: "There, are you satisfied now?"

Suddenly opening her arms, in an outburst of passion, she threw them around his neck, crying: "Oh, my poor boy, if I had only known. How did it happen?"

She made him sit down, and obliged him to tell her how this misfortune had come about.

He invented a touching story. He had been obliged to assist his father, who had got into difficulties. He had not only handed over to him all his savings, but had even incurred heavy debts on his behalf. He added: "I shall have to starve for at least six months, for I have exhausted all my resources. It cannot be helped; there are crises in every life. Money, after all, is not worth troubling about."

She whispered: "I will lend you some; will you let me?"

He answered, with dignity: "You are very kind, pet; but do not think of that, I beg of you. You would hurt my feelings."

She was silent for some time, and then she remarked smilingly: "How nice it is when one is in your position to find money you had forgotten in your pocket—a coin that had got in between the cloth and the lining."

He replied in a tone of conviction: "Ah, yes, indeed!"

She insisted on walking home, under the pretence that the moon was beautiful, and went into ecstasies over it. It was a cold, still night at the beginning of winter. Pedestrians and horses went by quickly, spurred by a sharp frost. Heels rang on the pavement.

As she left him she said: "Shall we meet again the day after to-morrow?"

"Certainly."

"At the same time."

"Good-by, dearest."

Then he walked home rapidly, wondering what he could think up on the morrow to help him out of his difficulty. But as he opened the door of his room, and fumbled in his waistcoat pocket for a match, he was stupefied to find a coin under his fingers. As soon as he struck a light he hastened to examine it. It was a louis. He thought he had gone crazy. He turned it over and

over, wondering by what miracle it could have found
its way there. It certainly could not have fallen from
heaven into his pocket.

Then, all at once, he guessed, and he went to bed,
his heart filled with anger and humiliation.

He woke late. He was hungry. He tried to go to sleep
again, in order not to get up till two o'clock, and then
said to himself: "That will not forward matters. I must
end by finding some money." Then he went out, hoping
that an idea might occur to him in the street. It did not,
but at every restaurant he passed a longing to eat made
his mouth water. As by noon he had failed to hit on any
plan, he suddenly made up his mind: "I will pay for
breakfast out of Clotilde's twenty francs. That will not
hinder me from paying her back to-morrow."

He therefore lunched for two francs fifty centimes. On
reaching the office, he also gave three francs to the
messenger, saying: "Here, Foucart, here is the money
you lent me last night for my cab."

He worked till seven o'clock. Then he went and
dined, taking another three francs. The two evening
bocks brought the expenditure of the day up to nine
francs thirty centimes. But as he could not get any more
credit or create fresh resources in twenty-four hours, he
borrowed another six francs fifty centimes the next day
from the twenty he was going to return that very evening,
so that he came to keep his appointment with just four
francs twenty centimes in his pocket.

He was in a deuce of a temper, and promised himself
that he would pretty soon explain things. He would say
to Madame de Marelle: "You know, I found the twenty
francs you slipped into my pocket the other day. I cannot give them back to you now, because my situation is
unaltered, and I have not had time to occupy myself
with money matters. But I will give them you the next
time we meet."

She came in, anxious, full of alarm. How would he receive her?

He said to himself: "It will be time enough to enter into the matter by and by. I will find an opportunity of doing so."

He did not find the opportunity, and said nothing, shrinking from broaching this delicate subject. She did not speak of going out, and was in every way charming. They separated early, after making an appointment for the Wednesday of the following week, for Madame de Marelle was engaged to dine out several days in succession.

The next day, as Duroy, on paying for his breakfast, felt for the four remaining coins, he perceived that there were five, and one of them a gold one. At first he thought that he had received it by mistake in his change the day before; then he understood it, and his heart throbbed with humiliation at this persistent charity. How he regretted not having said anything! If he had spoken energetically, this would not have happened.

For four days he made efforts, as numerous as they were fruitless, to raise five louis, and spent Clotilde's second coin. Although he had said to her savagely: "Don't play that joke of the other evenings again, or I shall get angry," she managed to slip another twenty francs into his pocket the next time they met.

When he found them he swore bitterly, and transferred them to his waistcoat to have them under his hand, for he had not a sou. He appeased his conscience by this argument: "I will give it her all back in a lump. After all, it is only borrowed money and can be repaid."

At length the cashier at the newspaper office agreed, on his urgent appeal, to let him have five francs daily. It was just enough to live upon, but not enough to repay sixty francs with. But as Clotilde was again seized with a passion for nocturnal expeditions to all the

suspicious localities in Paris, he ended by not being un-
bearably annoyed at finding a yellow coin in one of his
pockets, one even in his boot, and another time in his
watch-case, after these escapades.

One evening she said to him: "Would you believe
that I have never been to the Folies-Bergère? Will you
take me there?"

He hesitated a moment, afraid of meeting Rachel.
Then he thought: "Bah! I am not married, after all. If
that girl sees me, she will understand the state of things,
and will not speak to me. Besides, we will have a box."

He had another reason for his decision. He was well
pleased at this opportunity of offering Madame de
Marelle a box at the theater without its costing anything. It was a kind of compensation.

They went in, and were received with bows by the
acting manager. An immense crowd filled the foyer, and
they had great difficulty in making their way through
the swarm of men and women. At length they reached
their box and settled themselves in it, shut in between
the motionless orchestra and the restless gallery.

Suddenly she said: "There is a stout, dark girl who
keeps watching us all the time. I thought just now that
she was going to speak to us. Did you notice her?"

He answered: "No, you must be mistaken." But he
had already noticed her. It was Rachel, who was walking
up and down past their box, with anger in her eyes and
hard words upon her lips.

Duroy had brushed against her in making his way
through the crowd, and she had whispered: "Good
evening," with a wink which signified, "I understand."
But he did not reply to this mark of attention, for fear
of being seen by Madame de Marelle, and he had passed
on coldly, with haughty look and disdainful lips. The
woman, incited by unconscious jealousy, turned back,
brushed against him again, and said in louder tones:

"Good evening, George." He had not answered even then. Then she had made up her mind to be recognized and greeted, and she kept continually passing the box, awaiting a favorable moment.

As soon as she saw that Madame de Marelle was looking at her, she touched Duroy's shoulder, saying: "Good evening; are you quite well?"

He made an angry movement, and exclaimed in exasperated tones: "What do you mean by speaking to me? Be off, or I will have you locked up."

Then, with fiery eye and swelling bosom, she screamed out: "So that's it, is it? Ah, you scamp! It is no reason because you are with some one else that you should cut me to-day. If you had only nodded to me when I passed you just now, I should have left you alone. But you wanted to put on airs. I'll pay you out! Ah! so you won't say good evening when you meet me?"

She would have gone on for a long time, but Madame de Marelle had opened the door of the box and fled through the crowd, blindly seeking the way out. Duroy darted after her, and strove to rejoin her, while Rachel, seeing them flee, yelled triumphantly: "Stop her, stop her; she has stolen my sweetheart!"

Every one began to laugh. Two gentlemen, in joke, seized the fugitive by the shoulders and sought to bring her back. But Duroy, having caught up with her, freed her forcibly and led her away into the street. She jumped into an empty cab standing at the door. He jumped in after her, and when the driver asked, "Where to, sir?" replied, "Wherever you like!"

The cab slowly moved off, jolting over the cobble stones. Clotilde, seized by a kind of hysterical attack, sat choking and gasping, with her hands covering her face, and Duroy neither knew what to do nor what to say. At last, as he heard her sobbing, he stammered out:

"Clo, just listen; let me explain. It it not my fault. I used to know that woman some time ago, you know——"

She suddenly took the hands from her face, and overcome by the wrath of a loving and deceived woman, a furious wrath that enabled her to recover her speech, she stammered out in rapid, broken sentences: "Oh, you wretch—you wretch—what a scoundrel you are! Can it be possible? How shameful! Oh, *mon Dieu!* How shameful!"

Suddenly she leaned out of the window, and, catching the driver by the sleeve, cried: "Stop!" And opening the door, sprang out.

George wanted to follow, but she cried: "I forbid you to get out!" in such loud tones that the passers-by began to gather about her, and Duroy did not move, for fear of a scandal. She then took her purse from her pocket and looked for some change by the light of the cab lantern, and taking out two francs fifty centimes, she put them·in the driver's hand, saying in ringing tones:

"There is your fare. I am paying you, and now take this blackguard to the Rue Boursault, Batignolles."

Those surrounding her began to laugh. A gentleman said: "Well done, little woman," and a young scalawag standing close to the cab thrust his head into the door and sang out in shrill tones:

"Good night, lovey!"

Then the cab started off again, followed by a burst of laughter.

VI. A Long Step Forward

Duroy woke up crestfallen the next morning. He dressed himself slowly, and then sat down at his window and began to reflect. He felt a kind of aching sensation all over, just as though he had received a drubbing over night. At last the necessity of finding some money spurred him up, and he went first to Forestier.

His friend received him in his study, sitting before the fire.

"What has brought you out so early?" said he.

"A very serious matter, a debt of honor."

"At play?"

He hesitated a moment, and then said: "At play."

"Heavy?"

"Five hundred francs."

He only owed two hundred and eighty.

Forestier, skeptical on the point, inquired: "Whom do you owe it to?"

Duroy could not answer right off. "To—to—a Monsieur de Carleville."

"Ah! and where does he live?"

"At—at——"

Forestier began to laugh. "Number naught, Nowhere Street, eh? I know that gentleman, my dear fellow. If you want twenty francs, I have still that much at your service, but no more."

Duroy took the proffered louis. Then he went from

house to house among the people he knew, and wound up by having collected at about five o'clock the sum of eighty francs. As he still needed two hundred more, he came to a decision, and keeping for himself what he had thus gleaned, murmured: "Bah! I am not going to put myself out. I will pay her when I can."

For a fortnight he lived regularly, economically, and chastely, his mind filled with good resolves. This sudden reformation did not last long, and he went one evening to the Folies-Bergère, in the hope of finding Rachel. He caught sight of her directly he entered, for she scarcely went anywhere else. He went up to her, smiling, with outstretched hand; but she merely looked him down from head to foot, saying: "What do you want with me?"

He tried to laugh it off, with: "Come, don't be stuck up."

She turned on her heel, saying: "I don't associate with men of your stamp."

She had picked out the bitterest insult. He felt the blood rush to his face, and went home alone.

Forestier, ill, weak, always coughing, led him a hard life at the paper, and seemed to rack his brain to find him tiresome jobs. One day, even, in a moment of nervous irritation, and after a long fit of choking, as Duroy had not brought him a piece of information he wanted, he growled out: "Confound it! You are a bigger fool than I thought."

The other almost struck him, but restrained himself, and went away muttering: "I'll manage to pay you out some day." An idea occurred to him, and he added: "I'll make a fool of you, old fellow!" And he took himself off, rubbing his hands, delighted at this project.

He resolved to pay Madame Forestier a visit, to spy out the land. He found her reclining on a couch, reading a book. She held out her hand, without rising, merely turning her head, and said: "Good day, Bel-Ami!"

He felt as though he had received a blow. "Why do you call me that?" he said.

She replied, with a smile: "I saw Madame de Marelle the other day, and learned how you had been baptized at her place."

He felt reassured by her amiable air. Besides, what was there for him to fear?

She resumed: "You spoil her. As to me, people come to see me when they think of it—the thirty-sixth of the month, or thereabout."

He sat down near her, and regarded her with a new species of curiosity, the curiosity of the amateur who is bargain-hunting.

He said resolutely: "I did not come to see you because it was better so."

She asked, without understanding: "What? Why?"

"Why? Cannot you guess?"

"No, not at all."

"Because I am afraid that I might fall in love with you."

She seemed neither astonished, nor shocked, nor flattered; she went on smiling the same indifferent smile, and replied with the same tranquillity: "Oh, you can come, all the same. No one is in love with me long."

He was surprised more by the tone than the words, and asked: "Why not?"

"Because it is useless. I let this be understood at once. If you had told me of your fear before, I should have reassured you, and invited you, on the contrary, to come as often as possible."

He exclaimed, in a pathetic tone: "Can we command our feelings?"

She turned toward him: "My dear friend, for me a

man in love is struck off the list at once. He becomes
idiotic, and not only idiotic, but dangerous. I cease all
relations with people who are in love with me, or who
pretend to be so—because they bore me, in the first
place; and, secondly, because they are as much objects
of suspicion to me as a mad dog, which may have a fit of
biting. I therefore put them into a kind of moral quaran-
tine until the attack is over. Do not forget this. I know
very well that in your case love is only a species of
appetite, while with me it would be, on the contrary, a
kind of—of—of communion of souls which does not
enter into a man's religion. You understand its letter, I
its spirit. But look me well in the face." She no longer
smiled. Her face was calm and cold, and she continued
emphatically: "And now that we understand each other,
will you agree to be friends—good friends—real friends,
I mean, without any mental reservation?"

He made up his mind at once, and, delighted at being
able to secure this ally in the battle of life, held out
both hands, saying: "I am yours, Madame—Bel-Ami."

She read the sincerity of his intention in his voice, and
gave him her hands. He kissed them both, one after the
other, and then said simply, as he raised his head: "Ah!
if I had found a woman like you, how gladly I would
have married her."

She was touched this time—soothed by this phrase as
women are by the compliments which reach their hearts,
and she gave him one of those rapid and grateful looks
which make us their slaves. Then, as he could find no
change of subject to renew the conversation, she said
softly, laying her finger on his arm: "And I am going
to play my part of a friend at once. You are clumsy."
She hesitated a moment, and then asked: "May I speak
plainly?"

"Yes."

"Quite plainly?"

"Quite."

"Well, go and see Madame Walter, who greatly appreciates you, and do your best to please her. You will find a place there for your compliments, although she is, you understand me, a perfectly virtuous woman. Oh, there is no hope for poachers there. You may find something better, though, by going about more. I know that you still hold a subordinate position on the paper. But do not be afraid; they receive all their staff with the same kindness. Go there, take my advice."

He said, with a smile: "Thank you; you are an angel, a guardian angel."

They spoke of one thing and another. He stayed some time, wishing to prove that he took pleasure in being with her, and on leaving, remarked: "It is understood, then, that we are friends."

"It is understood."

As he had noted the effect of the compliment he had paid her shortly before, he seconded it by adding: "And if ever you become a widow, I enter the lists."

Then he hurried away, so as not to give her time to get angry.

A visit to Madame Walter was rather awkward for Duroy, for he had not been invited to call, and he did not want to commit a blunder.

One day, however, having risen early, he went to the market, and for ten francs obtained a score of splendid pears. Having carefully packed them in a hamper to make it appear that they had come from a distance, he left them with the concierge at Madame Walter's, with his card, on which he had written: "George Duroy begs Madame Walter to accept a little fruit which he received this morning from Normandy."

He found the next morning, among his letters at the

office, an envelope in reply, containing the card of Madame Walter, who "thanked Monsieur George Duroy, and was at home every Saturday."

On the following Saturday he called. Monsieur Walter lived on the Boulevard Malesherbes, in a double house, which he owned, part of which he rented to another family.

Two footmen were dozing on benches. One of them took Duroy's overcoat and the other relieved him of his cane, opened a door, advanced a few steps in front of his visitor, and then, drawing aside, let him pass, calling out his name, into an empty room.

The young fellow, somewhat embarrassed, looked around on all sides, when he perceived in a mirror some people sitting down, who seemed very far off. He passed through two empty reception rooms, and reached a sort of small boudoir hung with blue silk, where four ladies were chatting round a table on which were cups of tea. In spite of the assurance he had acquired during his residence in Paris, and, above all, in his career as a reporter, which constantly brought him in contact with important personages, Duroy felt somewhat abashed at the elegance of the house and at having to walk through the deserted drawing-rooms. He stammered: "Madame, I have ventured," as his eyes sought the mistress of the house.

She held out her hand, which he took with a bow, and having remarked: "You are very kind, sir, to call and see me," she pointed to a chair, into which he almost fell, being deceived as to its height.

They had become silent. One of the ladies began to talk again.

Madame Walter noticed that Duroy had not said anything, that he had not been spoken to, and that he seemed slightly ill at ease; and as the ladies were still conversing about the Academy, that favorite subject always occupying them some time, she said: "And you, who should be better informed than any one, Monsieur Duroy, who is your favorite?"

He replied unhesitatingly: "In this matter, Madame, I should never consider the merit, always disputable of the candidates, but their age and their state of health. I should not ask about their credentials, but their disease. I should not seek to learn whether they have made a metrical translation of Lope de Vega, but I should take care to obtain information as to the state of their liver and other organs. For me, a good hypertrophy, a good aneurism, and, above all, a good beginning of locomotor ataxia, would be a hundred times more valuable than forty volumes of digressions on the idea of patriotism as embodied in barbaric poetry."

An astonished silence followed this opinion, and Madame Walter asked, with a smile: "But why?"

He replied: "Because I never look for anything but the enjoyment that ladies derive from a subject. Now, Madame, the Academy only has any real interest for you when an Academician dies. The more of them that die the happier you are. But in order that they may die quickly, they must be elected when they are infirm or old." As they all seemed somewhat surprised, he continued: "I am like you; I like to read of the death of an Academician. I at once ask myself: 'Who will replace him?' And I draw up my list. It is a game, a very pretty little game that is played in all Parisian salons at the decease of each of the Immortals, the game of 'Death and the Forty Ancients.' "

The ladies, still slightly disconcerted, began, however, to smile, so true were his remarks. He concluded, as he rose: "It is you who really elect them, ladies, and you only elect them to see them die. Choose them old, therefore, very old, as old as possible, and do trouble yourselves about anything else."

He then retired very gracefully. As soon as he was gone, one of the ladies said: "He is very comical, that young fellow. Who is he?"

Madame Walter replied: "One of our staff who attends to minor work, but I feel sure that he will get on."

Duroy strode gayly down the Boulevard Malesherbes, pleased at his first attempt, and murmuring: "A capital start."

He made it up with Rachel that evening.

The following week two things happened to him. He was made news editor-in-chief, and invited to dinner at Madame Walter's. He traced at once a connection between these things.

Monsieur Walter, who thoroughly appreciated him, had, however, often wished for another man to whom to intrust the "Echoes," which he held to be the very marrow of the paper. It is through them that rumors are set afloat, and the public and the funds influenced. It is necessary to know how to slip the all-important matter, rather hinted at than said right out, in between the description of two fashionable entertainments, without appearing to intend it. Things should be hinted at in such a manner as to allow of any construction being placed on them, refuted in a manner that confirms the rumor, or affirmed in such a way that no one believes them.

Monsieur Boisrenard, who had the skill acquired by long practice, nevertheless lacked virility and elegance; he lacked, above all, the inborn tact required in order to read the manager's mind day by day. Duroy could do it to perfection, and was an admirable addition to the staff. The wire-pullers and real editors of the *Vie Française* were half a dozen deputies, interested in all the speculations brought out or backed up by the manager. They were known in the Chamber as "Walter's gang," and envied because they gained money with him and through him. Forestier, the political editor, was only the man of straw of these men of business, the worker-out of ideas suggested by them. They prompted his editorials on the money markets, which he always wrote at home, where he could be quiet, he said.

Duroy was jubilant at his appointment as editor of the "Echoes," when he received a printed card on which he read: "Monsieur and Madame Walter request the pleasure of Monsieur George Duroy's company at dinner on Thursday, January 20." This new mark of favor, following on the other, filled him with such joy that he kissed the invitation as he would have kissed a love letter. Then he went in search of the cashier, to deal with the important question of money. The news editor on a Paris paper generally has his budget out of which he pays his reporters for the intelligence, important or trifling, brought in by them, as gardeners bringing in their fruits to a dealer. Twelve hundred francs a month were alloted at the outset to Duroy, who proposed to himself to retain a considerable share of it. The cashier, on his urgent representation, ended by advancing him four hundred francs. He had at first intended to send Madame de Marelle the two hundred and eighty francs he owed her, but he almost immediately reflected that he would only have a hundred and twenty left, a sum utterly insufficient to carry on his new duties in suitable fashion, and so put off this restitution to a future day.

It took him a couple of days to settle down in his new position, for he had inherited a table to himself, and a set of pigeonholes in the large room occupied by the entire editorial staff. He occupied his spare time playing cup and ball. Duroy had acquired a taste for this amusement, and was beginning to get expert at it, under the guidance, and thanks to the advice of, Saint-Potin.

"One—two—three—four—five—six." It happened that,

for the first time, he spiked the ball twenty times running, the very day that he was to dine at Madame Walter's. "A good day," he said and was going up the Rue de Londres, when he saw, trotting along in front of him, a little woman whose figure recalled that of Madame de Marelle. He felt his cheeks flush, and his heart began to beat. He crossed the road to get a view of her. She stopped, in order to cross over, too. He had made a mistake, and breathed again. He had often asked how he ought to behave if he met her face to face. Should he bow, or should he appear not to have seen her? "I would not see her," he thought.

When he got home he thought: "I must change my lodgings; this is no longer good enough for me." He felt nervous and lively, capable of anything; and he said aloud, as he walked from his bed to the window: "Fortune is here at last! Fortune is here! I must write to father." From time to time he wrote to his father, and the letter always brought thought; "I am successful in everything." For skill at cup and ball really conferred a kind of superiority in the office of the *Vie Française*.

He left the office early, to have time to dress, happiness to the little Norman inn by the roadside, at the summit of the slope overlooking Rouen and the broad valley of the Seine. From time to time, too, he received a blue envelope, addressed in a large, shaky hand, and read the same unvarying lines at the beginning of the paternal epistle: "My dear son, this leaves your mother and myself in good health. There is not much news here. I must tell you, however," etc. In his heart he retained a feeling of interest for the village matters, for the news of the neighbors and the condition of the crops.

He repeated to himself, as he tied his white tie before his little looking-glass: "I must write to father to-morrow. If the old fellow could see me this evening in the house I am going to, wouldn't he be astonished! By Jove! I am going to have such a dinner as he has never tasted." And he suddenly saw the dark kitchen behind the empty café, the copper stewpans casting their yellow reflections on the wall; the cat on the hearth, with her nose to the fire, in sphinx-like attitude; the wooden table, greasy with time and spilled liquids, a soup tureen smoking upon it, and a lighted candle between two plates. He saw them, too—his father and mother, two slow-moving peasants, eating their soup. He knew the smallest wrinkles on their old faces, the slightest movements of their arms and heads. He knew even what they talked about every evening as they sat at supper. He thought, too: "I must really go and see them." But, his toilet being ended, he blew out his light and went downstairs.

He entered the anteroom, lighted by tall bronze candelabra, with confidence, and handed his cane and overcoat quite naturally to two valets who approached. All the drawing-rooms were illuminated. Madame Walter received her guests in the second, the largest. She welcomed him with a charming smile, and he shook hands with two gentlemen who had arrived before him—Monsieur Firmin and Monsieur Laroche-Mathieu, deputies and anonymous editors of the *Vie Française*. Monsieur Laroche-Mathieu had special authority at the office, due to his influence in the Chamber. No one doubted his being a minister some day. Then came the Forestiers, the wife in pink and looking charming. Duroy was astonished to see her on terms of intimacy with the two deputies. She chatted in low tones with Monsieur Laroche-Mathieu for more than five minutes beside the fireplace. Charles seemed worn out. He had grown much thinner during the past month, and coughed incessantly as he repeated: "I should make up my mind to finish the winter in the south." Norbert de Varenne and Jacques Rival made their appearance together. Then, as a door

opened at the farther end of the room, Monsieur Walter
came in with two tall young girls, of from sixteen to
eighteen, one ugly, the other pretty.

Duroy knew that the chief was the father of a family,
but he was struck with astonishment. He had never
thought of his daughters, save as one thinks of distant
countries which one will never see. And then he had
fancied them quite young; and here they were, grown-up
women. They held out their hands to him after being
introduced, and then went and sat down at a little table,
without doubt reserved for them. Some one was still
expected, and all were silent with that sense of oppres-
sion preceding dinner among people whose mental atmos-
phere differs at the close of their various daily occupa-
tions.

Duroy having aimlessly raised his eyes toward the
walls, Monsieur Walter called to him from a distance,
with an evident wish to show off his property: "Are you
looking at my pictures? I will show them to you;" and
he took a lamp, so that the details might be distinguished.

Stopping before the next wall, he announced in a
grave tone, like a master of ceremonies: "High art."
There were four: "A Hospital Visit," by Gervex; "A
Harvester," by Bastien-Lepage; "A Window," by Bou-
guereau; and "An Execution," by Jean Paul Laurens.
Then the governor showed a Detaille, "The Lesson,"
which represented a soldier in a barrack room teaching
a poodle to play the drum, and said: "That is very
witty."

Duroy laughed, and exclaimed:

"It is charming, charm——" He stopped short on
hearing behind him the voice of Madame de Marelle,
who had just come in.

M. Walter continued to light up the pictures as he
explained them. But Duroy saw nothing, and heard with-

out understanding. Madame de Marelle was there behind him. What ought he to do? If he spoke to her, might she not turn her back on him, or treat him with insolence? If he did not approach her, what would people think? He said to himself: "I will gain time, at any rate." He was so upset that for a moment he thought of feigning a sudden indisposition, which would allow him to withdraw.

The examination of the walls was over. M. Walter went to put down his lamp and welcome the last comer, while Duroy began to re-examine the pictures, as if he could not tire of admiring them. He was quite overcome. What should he do? Madame Forestier called to him: "Monsieur Duroy!" He went to her. It was to speak to him of a friend of hers who was about to give a fête, and who would like to have a line to that effect in the *Vie Française*. He gasped out: "Certainly, Madame, most certainly."

Madame de Marelle was now quite close to him. He dared not turn round to go away. All at once he thought he was going crazy; she had said aloud: "Good evening, Bel-Ami. So you no longer recognize me."

He immediately turned round. She stood before him, smiling, her eyes beaming with sprightliness and affection, and held out her hand. He took it tremblingly, still fearing some trick, some perfidy. She added calmly: "What has become of you? One no longer sees anything of you."

He stammered, without recovering his presence of mind: "I have a great deal to do, Madame, a great deal to do. Monsieur Walter has intrusted me with new duties which keep me very busy."

She replied, still looking him in the face, but without his being able to discover anything save good will in her glance: "I know it. But that is no reason why you should forget your friends."

They were separated by a stout lady with red arms and red face, who just came in, with an elaborate dress cut very low, and walking so heavily that one guessed by her motions the size and weight of her legs. As she seemed to be treated with great attention, Duroy asked Madame Forestier: "Who is that lady?"

"The Vicomtesse de Percemur, who signs her articles 'Lily Fingers.'"

He was astounded and felt inclined to laugh. "'Lily Fingers,' 'Lily Fingers.' And I, who imagined her young like yourself. So that is 'Lily Fingers.' That is very funny, very funny."

A servant appeared in the doorway and announced dinner. The dinner was commonplace and lively, one of those dinners at which people talk about everything without saying anything. Duroy found himself between the elder daughter of the master of the house, the ugly one, Mademoiselle Rose, and Madame de Marelle. The vicinity of the latter embarrassed him somewhat, although she seemed very much at her ease, and chattered with her usual vivacity. He was disturbed at first, constrained, hesitating like a musician who has lost the keynote. By degrees, however, he recovered his assurance, and their eyes continually meeting, questioned one another, exchanging looks in an intimate fashion as of old. What did they say then? Not much, but their lips quivered every time that they looked at each other.

The young fellow, however, wishing to do the amiable to his employer's daughter, spoke to her from time to time. She replied as the mother would have done, never hesitating as to what she should say. On the right of Monsieur Walter, the Vicomtesse de Percemur gave herself the airs of a princess, and Duroy, amused at watching her, said in a low voice to Madame de Marelle: "Do you know the other, the one who signs her articles 'Pink Domino'?"

"Yes, very well; the Baroness de Livar."

"Is she of the same variety?"

"No, but quite as funny. A tall, dried-up woman of sixty, false curls, projecting teeth, ideas dating from the Restoration, and toilets of the same epoch."

"Where did they unearth these literary phenomena?"

"Waifs of the nobility are always lionized by *bourgeois parvenus.*"

"No other reason?"

"None."

Then a political discussion began between the master of the house, the two deputies, Norbert de Varenne, and Jacques Rival, and lasted till dessert.

When they returned to the drawing-room, Duroy again approached Madame de Marelle, and looking her in the eyes, said: "Shall I see you home tonight?"

"No."

"Why not?"

"Because Monsieur Laroche-Mathieu, who is my neighbor, sees me to my door every time I dine here."

"When shall I see you?"

"Come and lunch with me to-morrow."

And they separated without saying anything more.

Duroy did not remain late, finding the evening dull. As he went downstairs he overtook Norbert de Varenne, who was also leaving. The old poet took him by the arm. No longer having to fear any rivalry in the paper, their work being essentially different, he now manifested a fatherly kindness toward the young fellow.

"Well, will you walk home a bit of my way with me?" said he.

"With pleasure," replied Duroy.

And they went out, walking slowly along the Boulevard Malesherbes. Paris was almost deserted that night— a cold night; one of those nights in which space seems vaster than on others, when the stars seem higher and the air bears on its icy breath something coming from beyond the stars. The two men did not speak at first. Then Duroy, in order to say something, remarked: "You are gloomy to-day, dear master."

The poet replied: "I am always so, my lad; so will you be in a few years. Life is a hill. As long as one is climbing up one looks toward the summit and is happy, but when one reaches the top one suddenly perceives the descent before one, and its end, which is death. One climbs up slowly, but one goes down quickly. At your age one is happy. One hopes for many things which, however, never come to pass. At my age one no longer expects anything—but death."

Duroy began to laugh: "You make chills run down my back."

Norbert de Varenne went on: "No, you do not understand me now, but later on you will remember what I am saying to you at this moment. A day comes, and it comes early for many, when there is an end to mirth, for behind everything one looks at one sees death. You do not even understand the word. At your age it means nothing; at mine it is terrible. Yes, one understands it all at once, one does not know how or why, and then everything in life changes its aspect. To live, in short, is to die. I now see death so near that I often want to stretch out my arms to push it back. I see it everywhere. The insects crushed on the path, the falling leaves, the white hair in a friend's head, rend my heart and cry to me: 'Behold it!' It spoils for me all I do, all I see, all that I eat and drink, all that I love; the bright moonlight, the sunrise, the broad ocean, the noble rivers, and the soft summer evening air so sweet to breathe."

He stopped, reflected for a few moments, and then, with a look of resignation, said: "I am a lost creature. I have neither father nor mother, nor sister nor brother; no wife, no children, no God."

He added, after a pause: "I have only poetry."

They reached the Pont de la Concorde, crossed it in silence, and walked past the Palais Bourbon. Norbert de Varenne began to speak again, saying: "Get married, my friend; you do not know what it is to live alone at my age. Solitude now fills me with horrible agony—solitude at home by the fireside of a night. It is so profound, so sad; the silence of the room in which one dwells alone. It is not alone the silence that surrounds the body, but the silence around the soul; and when the furniture creaks, I tremble all over, for no sound is expected in my gloomy dwelling." He was silent again for a moment, and then added: "When one is old it is good to have children."

They had got halfway down the Rue de Bourgogne. The poet stopped in front of a high house, rang the bell, shook Duroy by the hand, and said:

"Forget all this old man's doddering, young man, and live as befits your age. Good night."

And he disappeared in the dark passage.

Duroy resumed his route with a pain at his heart. It seemed to him as though he had been shown a hole filled with bones, an unavoidable gulf into which all must fall one day. He muttered: "By Jove! it can't be very lively in his place. I should not care for a front seat to see the procession of his thoughts. The deuce, no!"

But having paused to allow a perfumed lady to alight from her carriage and enter her house, he drew in with eager breath, as she passed him, the scent of verbena and orris floating in the air. His lungs and heart throbbed suddenly with hope and joy, and the recollection of Madame de Marelle, whom he was to see the next day, came vividly to mind. Everything smiled on him, life welcomed him with kindness. How sweet is the realization of one's hopes!

Madame de Marelle received him as though no rupture had taken place. Then she said: "You don't know what a vexation has happened to me, darling. My husband is home for six weeks. He has obtained leave. But I won't remain six weeks without seeing you, especially after our little tiff, and this is how I have arranged matters. You are to come and dine with us on Monday. I have already spoken to him about you, and I will introduce you."

Duroy hesitated, somewht perplexed. He was afraid lest something might betray him—a slight embarrassment, a look, no matter what. He stammered out: "No, I would rather not make your husband's acquaintance."

She insisted, very much astonished, standing before him with wide-open, wondering eyes. "But why? What a funny thing. I should not have thought you such a goose."

He was hurt, and said: "Very well, then, I will come to dinner on Monday."

She went on: "In order that it may seem more natural, I will ask the Forestiers, though I really do not like entertaining people at home."

Until Monday, Duroy scarcely thought any more about the interview, but on mounting the stairs at Madame de Marelle's he felt strangely uneasy, not that it was so repugnant to him to take her husband's hand, to drink his wine, and eat his bread, but because he apprehended something, without knowing what. He was shown into the drawing-room and waited as usual. Soon the door of the inner room opened, and he saw a tall, white-bearded man, wearing the ribbon of the Legion of Honor, grave and correct, who advanced toward him with punctilious politeness, saying: "My wife has often spoken to me of you, sir, and I am delighted to make your acquaintance."

Duroy stepped forward, assuming an expression of excessive cordiality, and grasped his host's hand with exaggerated energy. Then, sitting down, he could find nothing to say.

Monsieur de Marelle placed a log upon the fire, and inquired: "Have you been long engaged in journalism?"

"Only a few months."

"Ah! You have got on quickly?"

"Yes, fairly so;" and he began to chat at random, without thinking very much about what he was saying, talking of all the trifles customary among men who do not know one another.

Madame de Marelle came in suddenly, and having taken in matters with a smiling, impenetrable glance, went toward Duroy, who dared not, in the presence of her husband, kiss her hand as he always did. She was calm and light-hearted as a woman of the world, this meeting seeming quite natural to her frank and inborn trickiness. Laurine appeared, and went and held up her forehead to George more quietly than usual, her father's presence intimidating her. Her mother said to her: "Well, you don't call him Bel-Ami to-day." And the child blushed as if a serious indiscretion had been committed, a thing revealed that ought not to have been mentioned, an intimate and, so to say, guilty secret of her heart laid bare.

When the Forestiers arrived, all were alarmed at the condition of Charles. He had grown frightfully thin and pale within a week, and coughed incessantly. He told them that he was leaving for Cannes on the following Thursday, by the doctor's imperative orders. They left early, and Duroy said, shaking his head: "I think he is very bad. He will never make old bones."

Madame de Marelle said calmly: "Oh, he is done for. There is a man who was lucky in finding the wife he did."

Duroy asked: "Does she help him much?"

"She does everything. She is acquainted with everything that is going on; she knows every one without seeming to go and see anybody; she gets what she wants as she wants it, and when she wants it. Oh, she is keen, clever, and intriguing as no one else is. She would be a treasure for any one wanting to get on."

George said: "She will marry again very quickly, no doubt?"

Madame de Marelle replied: "Yes. I should not be surprised if she had some one in view—a deputy, unless, indeed, he objects—for—for—there may be serious—moral—obstacles. But then—I don't really know."

Monsieur de Marelle grumbled, with slow impatience: "You are always suspecting a number of things, and I do not like it. Do not let us meddle with the affairs of others. We have enough to do to guide our own conscience. That should be a rule with every one."

Duroy withdrew, uneasy at heart, and with his mind full of vague plans. The next day he paid a visit to the Forestiers, and found them finishing their packing. Charles, stretched on a sofa, exaggerated his difficulty of breathing, and repeated: "I ought to have been off a month ago."

Then he gave George a series of orders concerning the paper, although everything had been agreed upon and settled with Monsieur Walter. As George left, he energetically squeezed his old comrade's hand, saying: "Well, old man, we shall have you back soon." But as Madame Forestier was showing him out, he said to her quickly: "You have not forgotten our agreement? We are friends and allies, are we not? So if you have need of me, for no matter what, do not hesitate to call on me. Send a letter or a telegram, and I will obey."

She murmured: "Thank you, I will not forget." And her eye, too, said: "Thank you," in a deeper and tenderer fashion.

As Duroy went downstairs, he met, slowly coming up, Monsieur de Vaudrec, whom he had met there once before. The comte appeared sad, and at this departure perhaps. Wishing to show his good breeding, the journalist eagerly bowed. The other returned the salutation courteously, but in a somewhat dignified manner.

The Forestiers left on Thursday evening.

VII. A Means to an End

Charles's absence gave Duroy an increased importance in the editorial department of the *Vie Française*. He signed several editorials, besides his "Echoes," for the manager insisted on every one assuming the responsibility of his own "copy." He became engaged in several newspaper controversies, in which he acquitted himself creditably, and his constant relations with different statesmen were gradually preparing him to become in his turn a clever and discriminating political editor. There was only one cloud on his horizon. It came from a little free-lance newspaper which continually assailed him, or, rather, in him assailed the editor of "Echoes" in the *Vie Française*, the editor of "Monsieur Walter's startlers," according to the anonymous writer of the *Plume*. Day by day cutting paragraphs, insinuations of every kind, appeared in it.

One day Jacques Rival said to Duroy: "You are very patient."

Duroy replied: "What can I do? There is no direct attack."

But one afternoon, as he entered the editor's room,

Boisrenard held out the current number of the *Plume*, saying: "Here's another spiteful dig at you."

"Ah! what about?"

"Oh, a mere nothing—the arrest of a Madame Aubert by the Society for the Prevention of Vice."

George took the paper, and read, under the heading, "Duroy's latest":

"The illustrious reporter of the *Vie Française* to-day informs us that Madame Aubert, whose arrest by an agent of the odious S. P. V. we announced, exists only in our imagination. Now, the person in question lives at 18 Rue de l'Ecureuil, Montmartre. As to the reporter of whom it is a question, he would do better to give us one of those good sensational bits of news of which he has the secret—news of deaths contradicted the following day, news of battles which have never taken place, announcements of important utterances by sovereigns who have not said anything—all the news, in short, which constitutes Walter's profits, or even one of those little indiscretions concerning entertainments given by would-be fashionable ladies, or the excellence of certain articles of consumption which are a means of income to some of our colleagues of the press."

The young fellow was more astonished than annoyed, only understanding that there was something very disagreeable for him in all this.

Boisrenard went on: "Who gave you that piece of gossip?"

Duroy thought for a moment, having forgotten. Then all at once the recollection occurred to him, "Saint-Potin." He reread the paragraph in the *Plume* and reddened, roused by the accusation of graft. He exclaimed: "What! Do they mean to assert that I am paid——"

Boisrenard interrupted him: "Why, yes. It is very annoying for you. The governor is very strict about that sort of thing. It might so often occur in the 'Echoes.'"

Saint-Potin came in at that moment. Duroy went to meet him. "Have you seen the paragraph in the *Plume?*"

"Yes, and I have just come from Madame Aubert. She does exist, but she was not arrested. That much of the report has no foundation."

Duroy hastened to the room of the manager, whom he found somewhat cool and with a look of suspicion in his eye. After having listened to the statement of the case, Monsieur Walter said: "Go and see the woman yourself, and contradict the paragraph in such terms as will put a stop to such things being written about you any more. I mean the latter part of the paragraph. It is very annoying for the paper, for yourself, and for me. A journalist should no more be suspected than Cæsar's wife."

Duroy got into a cab, with Saint-Potin as his guide, and called out to the driver: "Number 18 Rue de l'Ecureuil, Montmartre."

It was a huge house, and he had to scale six flights of stairs. An old woman in a woolen jacket opened the door to them. "What is it you want with me now?" said she, on catching sight of Saint-Potin.

He replied: "I have brought this gentleman, who is an inspector of police, and who would like to hear your story."

Then she let them in, saying: "Two more have been here since you, from some paper or other, I don't know which." Then, turning toward Duroy, she added: "So this gentleman wants to know about it?"

"Yes. Were you arrested by the society?"

She raised her arms in the air. "Never in my life, sir, never in my life. This is what it was all about. I have a butcher who sells good meat, but who gives bad weight. I have often noticed it without saying anything; but the other day, when I asked him for two pounds of chops, as I had my daughter and my son-in-law to dinner, I caught him weighing in bits of trimmings—trimmings of chops, it is true, but not of mine. I could have made a stew of them, it is true, but when I ask for chops it is not to get other people's trimmings. I refused to take them, and he calls me an old shark. I call him an old rogue, and from one thing to another, we raised such a row that there were over a hundred people round the shop, some of them laughing to kill themselves. So that at last a police officer came up and asked us to settle it at the police station. We went, and the captain dismissed the case. Since then I get my meat elsewhere, and don't even pass his door, in order to avoid any disturbance."

She ceased talking, and Duroy asked: "Is that all?"

"It is the whole truth, sir," and having offered him a glass of liqueur, which he declined, the old woman insisted on the short weight of the butcher being spoken of in the report.

On his return to the office, Duroy wrote his reply:

"An anonymous scribbler in the *Plume* seeks to pick a quarrel with me on the subject of an old woman whom he states was arrested by an *agent des moeurs,* which fact I deny. I have myself seen Madame Aubert—who is at least sixty years of age—and she told me in detail her quarrel with the butcher over the weighing of some chops, which led to an explanation before the commissary of police. This is the whole truth. As to the other insinuations of the writer in the *Plume,* I despise them. Besides, a man does not reply to such things when they are written under a mask.

"GEORGE DUROY."

Monsieur Walter and Jacques Rival, who had come in, thought this note satisfactory, and it was settled that it should go in at once.

Duroy went home early, somewhat agitated and slightly uneasy. What reply would the other man make? Who was he? Why this brutal attack? With the rough manners of journalists, this affair might go very far. He slept badly. When he read his reply in the paper next morning, it seemed to him more aggressive in print than in manuscript. He might, it seemed to him, have softened certain phrases. He felt feverish all day, and slept badly again at night. He rose at dawn to get the number of the *Plume* that must contain a reply to him.

The weather had turned cold again; it was freezing hard. The gutters, frozen while still flowing, showed like two ribbons of ice alongside the pavement. The morning papers had not yet come in, and Duroy recalled the day of his first article, "Souvenirs d'un Chasseur d'Afrique." At length the newspapers were passed in at the window of the kiosk, and the woman vendor held out to Duroy an unfolded copy of the *Plume*.

He glanced through it in search of his name, and at first saw nothing. He was breathing again, when he saw between two dashes:

"Monsieur Duroy, of the *Vie Française*, contradicts us, and, in contradicting us, lies. He admits, however, that there is a Madame Aubert, and that an agent took her before the commissary of police. It only remains, therefore, to add two words, '*des moeurs,*' after the word '*agent,*' and he is right. But the conscience of certain journalists is on a level with their talent. And I sign,

"LOUIS LANGREMONT."

George's heart began to beat violently, and he went home to dress without being too well aware of what he was doing.

He dressed quickly, and went to see Monsieur Walter, although it was barely eight o'clock. Monsieur Walter, already up, was reading the *Plume*. "Well," said he, with a grave face, on seeing Duroy, "you cannot draw back now." The young fellow did not answer, and the other went on: "Go at once and see Rival, who will act for you."

Duroy stammered a few vague words, and went out in

quest of the descriptive writer, who was still asleep. He jumped out of bed, and having read the paragraph, said: "By Jove! you will have to fight! Whom do you think of for the other second?"

"I really don't know."

"Boisrenard? What do you think of him?"

"Yes. Boisrenard."

"Are you a good swordsman?"

"Not at all."

"The devil! And with the pistol?"

"I can shoot a little."

"Good. You shall practice while I look after everything else. Wait for me a moment."

He went into his dressing-room and soon reappeared, washed, shaved, correct-looking.

"Come with me," said he.

He lived on the ground floor of a small house, and he led Duroy to the cellar, an enormous cellar, converted into a fencing room and shooting gallery, all the openings to the street being closed. After having lit a row of gas jets running the whole length of the second cellar, at the end of which was an iron man painted red and blue, he placed on a table two pairs of breech-loading pistols and began to give the word of command in a sharp tone as though on the ground: "Ready! Fire—one—two—three."

Duroy, dumfounded, obeyed, raising his arm, aiming and firing, and as he often hit the mark fair on the body, having frequently made use of an old horse pistol of his father's when a boy against the birds, Jacques Rival, well satisfied, exclaimed: "Good—very good—very good—you will do—you will do."

Then he left George, saying: "Go on shooting till noon. Here is plenty of ammunition; don't be afraid to use it. I will come back to take you to lunch and tell you how things are going."

Left to himself, Duroy fired a few more shots, and then

sat down and began to reflect. How absurd these things were, all the same! What did a duel prove? Was a rascal less of a rascal after going out? What did an honest man who had been insulted gain by risking his life against a scoundrel? And his mind, gloomily inclined, recalled the words of Norbert de Varenne.

Then he felt thirsty, and, having heard the sound of water dropping behind him, found that there was a hydrant with a hose attached, and he drank from the nozzle of the hose. Then he began to think again. It was gloomy in this cellar, as gloomy as a tomb. The dull and distant rumbling of vehicles sounded like the rumblings of a far-off storm. What o'clock could it be? The hours passed by there as they must pass in prisons, without anything to indicate or mark them save the visits of the warden. He waited a long time. Then all at once he heard footsteps and voices, and Jacques Rival reappeared accompanied by Boisrenard. He called out as soon as he saw Duroy: "It's all settled."

The latter thinking the matter was settled by a letter of apology, his heart beat and he stammered, "Ah! thanks!"

The descriptive writer continued: "That fellow Langremont is very square; he accepted all our conditions. Twenty-five paces, one shot, raising the pistol at the word of command. The hand is much steadier that way than in bringing it down. See here, Boisrenard, this is what I mean."

And taking a pistol he fired, pointing out how much better one could aim by raising the arm. Then he said: "Now, let's go and lunch; it is past twelve o'clock."

They went to a neighboring restaurant. Duroy scarcely spoke. He ate in order not to appear afraid, and then, in course of the afternoon, accompanied Boisrenard to the office, where he got through his work mechanically and in a distracted fashion. They considered him game.

Jacques Rival dropped in in the course of the afternoon, and it was settled that his seconds should call for him in a landau at seven o'clock the next morning, and drive to the Bois du Vesinet, where the duel was to take place. All this had been done so unexpectedly, without his taking part in it, without his saying a word, without his giving his opinion, without his accepting or refusing, and with such rapidity, too, that he was bewildered, scared, and scarcely able to understand what was going on.

He found himself at home at nine o'clock, after having dined with Boisrenard, who out of self-devotion had not left him all day. As soon as he was alone, he sat down and began to reflect. He had thrown upon his little table one of his adversary's cards, given him by Rival in order to retain his address. He read, as he had already done a score of times during the day, "Louis Langremont, 176 Rue Montmartre." Nothing more. He examined these assembled letters, which seemed to him mysterious and full of some disturbing import! Louis Langremont. Who was this man? What was his age, his height, his appearance? Was it not disgusting that a stranger, an unknown, should thus come and suddenly disturb one's existence without cause and from sheer caprice, on account of an old woman who had had a quarrel with her butcher? What a brute!

And he stood lost in thought, his eyes fixed on the card. Anger was aroused in him against this bit of paper, an anger with which was blended a strange sense of uneasiness. What a stupid business it was! He took a pair of nail scissors which were lying about, and stuck their points into the printed name as though he were stabbing some one.

The sound of his own voice made him shudder, and he glanced about him. He began to feel very nervous. He drank a glass of water and went to bed.

As soon as he was in bed he blew out his candle and closed his eyes. He was warm between the sheets, though it was very cold in his room, but he could not manage to doze off.

A strange desire to get up and look at himself in the glass suddenly seized him. He relit his candle. When he saw his face so reflected, he scarcely recognized himself, and it seemed to him that he had never seen himself before. His eyes appeared enormous, and he was pale, yes, he was certainly pale, very pale. Suddenly the thought shot through his mind, "By this time to-morrow I may be dead." And his heart began to beat again furiously.

The thought occurred to him to make a fire. He built it up slowly without looking round. His hands shook slightly with a kind of nervous tremor when he touched anything. His head wandered, his disjointed, drifting thoughts became fleeting and painful, an intoxication invaded his mind as though he had been drinking. And he kept asking himself: "What shall I do? What will become of me?"

He began to walk up and down, repeating mechanically: "I must pull myself together, I must pull myself together." Then he added: "I will write to my parents in case of accident." He sat down again, did not dare write, and sprang up with a jump. From time to time his teeth absolutely chattered, and he asked himself: "Has my opponent been out before? Is he a frequenter of the shooting galleries? Is he known and classed as a shot?" He had never heard his name mentioned. And yet if this man had not been a remarkably good pistol shot, he would scarcely have accepted that dangerous weapon without discussion or hesitation.

Day was breaking, and he set about his toilet. He had another moment of weakness while shaving, in thinking that it was, perhaps, the last time he should shave his face. But he swallowed a mouthful of brandy, and finished dressing. The hour which followed was difficult to get through. He paced up and down, trying to keep from thinking. When he heard a knock at the door he almost fell over backward, so startled was he. It was his seconds. Already!

They were wrapped up in furs, and Rival, after shaking his principal's hand, said: "It is as cold as Siberia." Then he added: "Well, how goes it?"

"Very well."

"You are quite steady?"

"Quite."

"That's all right. Have you had something to eat and drink?"

"Yes; I don't need anything."

Boisrenard, in honor of the occasion, sported the ribbon of a foreign order, yellow and green, that Duroy had never seen him display before.

They went downstairs. A gentleman was awaiting them in the carriage. Rival introduced him as "Dr. Le Brument." Duroy shook hands, saying: "I am very much obliged to you;" and sought to take his place on the front seat. He sat down on something hard that made him jump up again, as though impelled by a spring. It was the pistol-case.

Rival observed: "No, the back seat for the doctor and the principal, the back seat."

Duroy ended by understanding him, and sank down beside the doctor. The two seconds got in in their turn, and the driver started. He knew where to go. But the pistol case was in the way of every one, above all of Duroy, who would have preferred it out of sight. They tried to put it behind them, but it hurt their backs; they stuck it upright between Rival and Boisrenard, and it kept falling all the time. They finished by stowing it away under their feet. Conversation languished, although the doctor related some anecdotes. Rival alone replied to him. Duroy would have liked to say something witty, but he was afraid of losing the thread of his ideas, of showing the troubled state of his mind, and was haunted, too, by the fear that he might begin to tremble.

The carriage was soon right out in the country. It was about nine o'clock. It was one of those sharp winter mornings when everyhing is bright and brittle as glass. The trees, coated with hoar frost, seemed to have been sweating ice; the earth rang beneath one's steps, the dry air carried the slightest sound to a distance, the blue sky seemed to shine like a mirror, and the sun, dazzling and cold itself, shed upon the frozen universe rays which did not warm anything.

Rival observed to Duroy: "I got the pistols at Gastine Renet's. He loaded them himself. The box is sealed. We shall toss up, besides, to see whether we use them or those of our adversary."

Duroy mechanically replied: "I am very much obliged to you."

Then Rival gave him some special directions, for he was anxious that his principal should not make any mistake. He emphasized each point several times, saying: "When they say, 'Are you ready, gentlemen?' you must answer, 'Yes,' in a loud tone. When they give the word 'Fire!' you must raise your arm quickly, and you must fire before they say 'three.'"

And Duroy kept repeating to himself—"When they give the word to fire, I must raise my arm. When they give the word to fire, I must raise my arm." He learned it as children learn their lessons, by murmuring them to satiety in order to fix them on their minds. "When they give the word to fire, I must raise my arm."

The carriage entered a wood, turned down an avenue

on the right, and then to the right again. Rival suddenly opened the door to cry to the driver: "That way, down that narrow road."

Duroy caught sight, at the farther side of the clearing, of another carriage drawn up, and four gentlemen stamping to keep their feet warm, and he was obliged to open his mouth, so difficult did his breathing become.

The seconds got out first, and then the doctor and the principal. Rival had taken the pistol case and had walked away with Boisrenard to meet two of the strangers who came toward them. Duroy watched them salute one another ceremoniously, and then walk up and down the clearing, looking now on the ground and now at the trees, as though they were looking for something that had fallen down or might fly away. Then they measured off a certain number of paces, and with great difficulty stuck two walking sticks into the frozen ground. Then they reassembled in a group and went through the action of tossing, like children playing heads or tails.

Doctor Le Brument said to Duroy: "Do you feel all right? Do you want anything?"

"No, nothing, thanks."

It seemed to him that he was mad, that he was asleep, that he was dreaming, that a supernatural influence enveloped him. Was he afraid? Perhaps. But he did not know. Everything about him had altered.

Jacques Rival returned and announced in low tones of satisfaction: "It is all ready. Luck has favored us as regards the pistols."

That, so far as Duroy was concerned, was a matter of profound indifference.

They took off his overcoat, which he let them do mechanically. They felt the breast pocket of his frock coat to make certain that he had no pocketbook or papers likely to deaden a ball. He kept repeating to himself like a prayer: "When the word is given to fire, I must raise my arm."

They led him up to one of the sticks stuck in the ground, and handed him his pistol. Then he saw a man standing just in front of him—a short, stout, bald-headed man, wearing spectacles. It was his adversary. He saw him very plainly, but he could not think. "When the word to fire is given, I must raise my arm and fire at once."

A voice rang out in the deep silence, a voice that seemed to come from a great distance, saying: "Are you ready, gentleman?"

George exclaimed: "Yes."

The same voice gave the word: "Fire!"

He heard nothing more, he saw nothing more, he took note of nothing more, he only knew that he raised his arm, pressing strongly on the trigger. And he heard nothing. But he saw all at once a little smoke at the end of his pistol barrel, and as the man in front of him still stood in the same position, he perceived, too, a little cloud of smoke drifting off over his head.

They had both fired. It was over.

His seconds and the doctor touched him, felt him, and unbuttoned his clothes, asking anxiously: "Are you hit?"

He replied at haphazard: "No, I do not think so."

Langremont, too, was as unhurt as his enemy, and Jacques Rival murmured in a discontented tone: "It is always so with those damned pistols. You either miss or kill. What a filthy weapon!"

Duroy did not move, paralyzed by surprise and joy. It was over. They had to take away his pistol, which he still held clinched in his hand. It seemed to him now that he could have done battle with the whole world. It was over. What happiness! He felt suddenly brave enough to defy no matter whom.

All the seconds conversed together for a few moments, making an appointment to draw up their report of the proceedings in the course of the day. Then they got into the carriage again, and the driver, who was laughing on the box, started off, cracking his whip. They breakfasted together on the boulevards, and in chatting over the event, Duroy narrated his impressions.

"I felt quite unconcerned, quite. You must, however, have noticed it yourselves."

Rival replied: "Yes, you bore yourself very well."

When the report was drawn up it was handed to Duroy, who was to insert it in the paper. He was astonished to read that he had exchanged a couple of shots with Monsieur Louis Langremont, and rather uneasily interrogated Rival, saying: "But we only fired once."

The other smiled. "Yes, one shot apiece, that makes a couple of shots."

Duroy, deeming the explanation satisfactory, did not persist. Daddy Walter embraced him, saying: "Bravo, bravo! You have defended the colors of the *Vie Française*. Bravo!"

George showed himself in the course of the evening at the principal newspaper offices, and at the chief cafés on the boulevards. He twice encountered his adversary, who was also showing himself. They did not bow to each other. If one of them had been wounded they would have shaken hands. Each of them, moreover, swore with conviction that he had heard the whistling of the other's bullet.

The next day, about eleven, Duroy received a telegram.

"Awfully worried. Come at once. Rue de Constantinople.   Clo."

When he met her, he gave a dramatic account of the duel, which aroused her sympathy, and she murmured:

"Oh, my poor darling, my poor darling!"

Suddenly an idea came to him, and he asked: "What is the rent here?"

"A hundred francs a month."

"Well, I will take the rooms on my own account. Mine are no longer good enough for my new position."

After a few moments' reflection, she said:

"No, I do not wish it."

"Why not?" he asked, in astonishment.

"Because."

It was agreed on, however, that he should take the rooms, and, as they parted, she said:

"Come and dine with us on Sunday. My husband thinks you are charming."

"What a strange being! What a feather-brain! How came that old man to marry that madcap!" thought Duroy, as he made his way to the office.

VIII. Duroy Proposes

His duel had given Duroy a position among the leader writers of the *Vie Française;* but as he had great difficulty in finding ideas, he made a specialty of diatribes on the decadence of morality, the lowering of the standard of character, the weakening of the patriotic fibre and the anæmia of French honor. He had discovered the word anæmia, and was very proud of it. And when Madame de Marelle, filled with that skeptical, mocking, and incredulous spirit characteristic of the Parisian, laughed at his tirades, which she demolished with an epigram, he replied with a smile:

"Bah! this sort of thing will give me a good reputation later on."

He now resided in the Rue de Constantinople, whither he had moved his portmanteau, his hair-brush, his razor, and his soap, which was all his moving amounted to.

February was drawing to a close. There was an odor of violets in the street, as one passed the barrows of the flower sellers of a morning. Duroy was living beneath a sky without a cloud.

One night, on returning home, he found a letter that had been slipped under the door. He glanced at the postmark and read "Cannes." Having opened it, he read:

> "VILLA JOLIE, CANNES.
>
> "DEAR SIR AND FRIEND: You told me, did you not, that I could reckon upon you for anything? Well, I have a very painful service to ask of you; it is to come and help me, so that I may not be left alone during the last moments of Charles, who is dying. He may not last the week out, as the doctor forewarned me, although he has not taken to his bed. I have no longer strength nor courage to witness this hourly death, and I think with terror of those last moments which are drawing near. You are the only one of whom I can ask such a service, as my husband has no relatives. You were his comrade; he opened the door of the paper to you. Come, I beg of you; I have no one else to ask. Believe me, your very sincere friend,
>
> MADELEINE FORESTIER."

A strange feeling filled George's heart, a sense of freedom and of space opening before him, and he murmured: "To be sure I'll go. Poor Charles! What are we, after all?"

Monsieur Walter, to whom he read the letter, grumblingly granted permission, repeating: "But be back soon; you are indispensible to us."

George left for Cannes next day by the seven o'clock express, after letting the Marelles know of his departure by telegram. He arrived the following evening about four o'clock. A commissionaire guided him to the Villa Jolie, built halfway up the slope of the pine forest clothed with white houses, which extends from Cannes to the Golfe Juan. The house—small, low, and in the Italian style—was built beside the road which winds zigzag fashion up through the trees, revealing a succession of charming views at every turn.

The manservant opened the door, and exclaimed: "Oh! sir, Madame is expecting you most impatiently."

"How is your master?" inquired Duroy.

"Not at all well, sir. He cannot last much longer."

The drawing-room, into which George was shown, was hung with pink and blue chintz. The tall and wide windows overlooked the town and the sea. Duroy muttered: "By Jove! this is swell for a country house. Where the deuce do they get the money from?"

The rustle of a dress made him turn round. Madame Forestier held out both hands to him. "How good of you to come! How good of you to come!" said she.

She was somewhat paler and thinner, but still fresh-complexioned, and, perhaps, still prettier for her additional delicacy. She murmured: "He is dreadful, do you know; he knows that he is doomed, and he leads me a fearful life. But where is your portmanteau?"

"I have left it at the station, not knowing what hotel you would like me to stop at in order to be near you."

She hesitated a moment, and then said: "You must stay here. Besides, your room is all ready. He might die at any moment, and if it were to happen during the night, I should be alone. I will send for your baggage."

He bowed, saying: "As you please."

"Now, let us go upstairs," she said.

He followed her. She opened a door on the first floor, and Duroy saw, wrapped in rugs and seated in an armchair near the window, a kind of living corpse, livid even under the red light of the setting sun, and looking toward him. He scarcely recognized, but rather guessed, that it was his friend. The room reeked of fever, medicated drinks, ether, tar, the nameless and oppressive odor of a consumptive's sick room. Forestier held out his hand slowly and with difficulty. "So here you are. You have come to see me die, then! Thank you."

Duroy affected to laugh. "To see you die? That would not be a very amusing sight, and I should not select such an occasion to visit Cannes. I came to look in upon you, and to rest myself a bit."

Forestier murmured: "Sit down," and then bent his head as though lost in painful thoughts. He breathed hurriedly and pantingly, and from time to time gave a kind of groan, as if he wanted to remind the others how ill he was.

Seeing that he would not speak, his wife came and leaned against the window sill, and indicating the view with a motion of her head, said: "Look! Is not that beautiful?"

The void beyond the dark hilltops was red, a glowing red that the eye would not bear, and Duroy, despite himself, felt the majesty of the close of the day. He murmured, finding no other term strong enough to express his admiration: "It is stunning."

Forestier raised his head, and, turning to his wife, said: "Let me have some fresh air."

She opened the window quite wide. The air that entered surprised all three like a caress. It was a soft, warm breeze, a breeze of spring, already laden with the breath of the fragrant shrubs and flowers which grow on these coasts. A powerful odor of turpentine and the pungent smell of the eucalyptus could be distinguished.

Forestier drank it in with short and fevered gasps. He clutched the arms of the chair with his nails, and said in low, hissing, and savage tones: "Shut the window. It hurts me. I would rather die in a cellar."

His wife slowly closed the window, and then looked out into space, her forehead against the pane. Duroy, feeling very ill at ease, would have liked to have chatted with the invalid and reassured him. But he could think of nothing to comfort him. At length he said:

"Then you have not improved since you have been here?"

Forestier shrugged his shoulders with low-spirited impatience. "You see very well I have not," he replied, and again lowered his head.

Duroy went on: "By heavens! it is ever so much nicer here than in Paris. We are still in the middle of winter there. It snows, it freezes, it rains, and it is dark enough for the lamps to be lit at three in the afternoon."

"Anything new at the office?" asked Forestier.

"Nothing. They have taken on young Lacrin, who left the *Voltaire,* to do your work, but he is not up to it. It is time that you came back."

The invalid muttered: "I—I shall do all my work six feet under the sod now."

This fixed idea recurred like a knell *àpropos* of everything, continually cropped up in every idea, every sentence.

Forestier began to speak in a broken, breathless voice, heartrending to listen to. "How many more sunsets shall I see? Eight, ten, fifteen, or twenty, perhaps thirty—no more. You have time before you; for me it is all over. And it will go on all the same, after I am gone, as if I was still here." He was silent for a few moments, and then continued: "All that I see reminds me that in a few days I shall see it no more. It is horrible." Duroy suddenly recalled what Norbert de Varenne had said to him some weeks before: "I now see death so near that I often want to stretch out my arms to push it back. I see it everywhere. The insects crushed on the path, the falling leaves, the white hair in a friend's beard, rend my heart and cry to me, 'Behold it!' "

He had not understood all this at the time; but did so now, on seeing Forestier. An unknown anguish seized him as if he himself were sensible of the presence of death, hideous death, hard by, within reach of his hand, on the chair in which his friend lay gasping.

He longed to get up, to go away, to fly, to return to Paris at once. Oh! if he had known he would not have come.

Darkness had now spread over the room, like premature mourning for this dying man. The window alone remained still visible, showing, within the lighter square formed by it, the motionless outline of the young wife.

Forestier remarked, with irritation: "Well, are they going to bring in the lamp to-night? This is what they call looking after an invalid."

The shadow against the window panes disappeared, and the sound of an electric bell rang through the house. A servant shortly entered, and placed a lamp on the mantelpiece. Madame Forestier said to her husband: "Will you go to bed, or would you rather come down to dinner?"

He murmured: "I will come down."

Waiting for this meal kept them all three sitting still for nearly an hour, only uttering from time to time some useless, commonplace remark, as if there were some danger, some mysterious danger, in letting silence endure too long, in letting the air congeal in this room where death was prowling.

At length dinner was announced. The meal seemed

interminable to Duroy. They did not speak, but ate noiselessly, and then crumbled their bread with their fingers.

As soon as dinner was over, Duroy, on the plea of fatigue, retired to his room, and strove to find some reason to justify a swift departure, inventing plans, telegrams he was to receive, a recall from Monsieur Walter.

But his resolves to fly appeared more difficult to realize on awakening the next morning.

It was a bright day, one of those bright Southern days that make the heart feel light, and Duroy walked down to the sea, thinking that it would be soon enough to see Forestier some time in course of the afternoon. When he returned to lunch, the servants remarked: "Master has already asked for you two or three times, sir. Will you please step up to his room, sir?"

He went upstairs. Forestier appeared to be dozing in his armchair. His wife was reading, stretched out on the sofa.

The invalid raised his head, and Duroy said: "Well, how do you feel? You seem quite fresh this morning."

"Yes, I am better. I have recovered some of my strength. Get through your lunch with Madeleine as soon as you can, for we are going for a drive."

As soon as she was alone with Duroy, the young wife said to him: "There, to-day he thinks he is all right again. He has been making plans all the morning. We are going to the Golfe Juan now to buy some pottery for our rooms in Paris. He is determined to go out, but I am horribly afraid of some mishap. He cannot bear the shaking of the drive."

When the landau arrived, Forestier came downstairs a step at a time, supported by his servant. But as soon as he caught sight of the carriage, he ordered the hood to be put down. His wife opposed this, saying: "You will catch cold. It is madness."

He persisted, repeating: "Oh, I am much better. I feel it."

They passed at first along some of those shady roads, bordered by gardens, which make Cannes resemble a kind of English park, and then reached the highway to Antibes, running along the seashore.

The carriage stopped opposite a kind of large pavilion, on the front of which was the inscription, "Art Pottery of the Golfe Juan." Forestier wanted to buy a couple of vases for his study. As he felt unequal to getting out of the carriage, specimens were brought out to him one after the other. He was a long time in making a choice, and consulted his wife and Duroy.

"You know," he said, "it is for the cabinet at the end of my study. Sitting in my chair, I have it before my eyes all the time. I want an antique form, a Greek outline." He examined the specimens, had others brought, and then turned again to the first ones. At length he made up his mind, and, having paid, insisted upon the articles being sent on at once. "I shall be going back to Paris in a few days," he said.

They drove home, but as they skirted the bay a rush of cold air, from one of the valleys, suddenly met them, and the invalid began to cough. It was nothing at first, but it grew worse and became an unbroken fit of coughing, and then a kind of gasping hiccough.

Forestier was choking, and every time he tried to draw breath the cough seemed to tear his chest. Nothing would soothe or check it. He had to be borne from the carriage to his room, and Duroy, who supported his legs, felt the jerking of his feet at each spasm of his lungs. The warmth of the bed did not check the attack, which lasted till midnight, when, at length, it was lulled with narcotics. The sick man remained till morning sitting up in bed, with his eyes open.

The first words he uttered were to ask for the barber, for he insisted on being shaved every morning. He got up for this operation, but had to be helped back into bed at once, and his breathing grew so short, so hard, and so difficult, that Madame Forestier, in alarm, had Duroy, who had just turned in, roused up again in order to beg him to go for the doctor.

He came back almost immediately with Dr. Gavaut, who prescribed a soothing drink and gave some advice; but when the journalist saw him to the door, in order to ask his real opinion, he said: "It is the end. He will be dead to-morrow morning. Break it to his poor young wife, and send for a priest. I, for my part, can do nothing more. I am, however, entirely at your service."

Duroy sent for Madame Forestier. "He is dying," said he. "The doctor advises a priest being sent for. What would you like done?"

She hesitated for some time, and then, in low tones, as though she had thought of everything, replied: "Yes, that will be best—in many respects. I will break it to him—tell him the vicar wants to see him, or something or other; I really don't know what. You would be very kind if you would go and find a priest for me and pick one out, one who won't raise too many difficulties over confession."

The young fellow returned with a complaisant old ecclesiastic, who accommodated himself to the state of affairs. As soon as he had gone into the dying man's room, Madame Forestier came out of it, and sat down with Duroy in the one adjoining.

"It has quite upset him," said she. "When I spoke to him about a priest his face assumed a frightful expression as if he had felt the breath—the breath of—you know. He understood that it was all over at last, and that his hours were numbered." She was very pale as she continued: "I shall never forget the expression of his face. He certainly saw death face to face at that moment. He saw him."

They could hear the priest, who spoke in somewhat loud tones, being slightly deaf, and who was saying: "No, no; you are not so bad as all that. You are ill, but in no danger. And the proof is that I have called in as a friend, as a neighbor."

They could not make out Forestier's reply, but the old man went on: "No, I will not administer the sacrament. We will talk of that when you are better. If you wish to profit by my visit—to confess, for instance—I ask nothing better. I am a shepherd, you know, and seize every occasion to bring my lambs back to the fold."

A long silence followed. Forestier must have said something in a feeble tone. Then all at once the priest uttered in a different tone, the tone of one officiating at the altar: "The mercy of God is infinite. Repeat the *Confiteor*, my son. You have perhaps forgotten it; I will help you. Repeat after me: '*Confiteor Deo omnipotenti—Beatae Mariae semper virgini.*'"

He paused from time to time to allow the dying man to follow him. Then he said: "And now confess."

The young wife and Duroy sat still, filled with a strange emotion, stirred by anxious expectation. The invalid had murmured something. The priest repeated: "You have given way to guilty pleasures—of what kind, my son?"

Madeleine rose and said: "Let us go into the garden. We must not listen to his secrets."

And they went out and sat on a bench before the door, beneath a rose tree in bloom, and beside a bed of pinks, which shed their sweet, strong fragrance abroad in the pure air. Duroy, after a few moments' silence, inquired: "Will you delay your return to Paris?"

"Oh, no," she replied. "As soon as it is all over I shall go back there."

The servant came to inform them that "M. le Curé had finished," and they went upstairs together.

Forestier seemed to have grown thinner since the previous day. The priest held out his hand to him, saying: "Good day, my son; I will call in again to-morrow morning," and took his departure.

As soon as he had left the room the dying man, who was panting for breath, strove to hold out his two hands to his wife, and gasped: "Save me—save me, darling. I don't want to die—I don't want to die. Oh! save me—tell me what I had better do; send for the doctor. I will take whatever you like. I won't die—I won't die."

He wept. Big tears streamed from his eyes down his fleshless cheeks, and the corners of his mouth contracted like those of a vexed child.

His wife, who began to cry, too, said: "No, no, it is nothing. It is only a passing attack; you will be better to-morrow; you tired yourself too much going out yesterday."

He kept repeating: "I don't want to die. Oh! God— God—God; what is to become of me? I shall no longer see anything—anything any more! The cemetery—I—— Oh! God!"

He said no more, but lay motionless, haggard, and gasping.

Time sped on; noon struck by the clock of a neighboring convent. Duroy left the room to eat a mouthful or two. He came back an hour later. Madame Forestier refused to take anything. The invalid had not stirred. He still continued to draw his thin fingers along the sheet as though to pull it up over his face.

His wife was seated in an armchair at the foot of the bed. Duroy took another beside her, and they waited in silence. A nurse had come, sent by the doctor, and was dozing near the window.

Duroy himself was beginning to doze off when he felt that something was taking place. He opened his eyes just in time to see Forestier close his, like two lights suddenly extinguished. A faint rattle stirred in the throat of the dying man, and two streaks of blood appeared at the corners of his mouth, and then flowed down into his shirt. His hands ceased their hideous motion. He had ceased to breathe.

His wife understood this, and, uttering a kind of shriek she fell on her knees, sobbing, with her face buried in the bedclothes. George, surprised and terrified, mechanically made the sign of the cross. The nurse, having awoke, drew near the bed. "It is all over," said she.

Duroy, who was recovering his self-possession, murmured, with a sigh of relief: "It was over sooner than I expected."

When the first shock was over and the first tears shed, they had to busy themselves with the necessary care for the dead. Duroy was running errands till nightfall. He was very hungry when he got back. Madame Forestier ate a little, and then they both sat down in the chamber of death to watch beside the body. Two candles burned on the night table beside a plate filled with holy water, in which lay a sprig of mimosa, for they had not been able to get the required twig of consecrated box.

They were alone, the young man and the young wife, beside him who was no more. They sat, without speaking, thinking and watching.

An enormous, confused, and crushing sense of terror weighed down the soul of Duroy, the terror of that boundless and inevitable annihilation that destroys our wretched, fleeting lives. He already bowed his head before its menace. He thought of the flies who live a few hours, the beasts who live a few days, the men who live a few years, the worlds which live a few centuries. What was the difference between one and the other? A few more dawns, that was all.

He turned away his eyes that he might no longer see the corpse. Madame Forestier, with bent head, seemed also absorbed in painful thoughts. Her fair hair was so pretty around her pale face that a feeling, sweet as the touch of hope, flitted through the young fellow's breast. Why grieve, when he had still so many years before him? And he began to observe her. Lost in thought she did not notice him. He said to himself:

What luck the dead man had to meet such an intelligent and charming companion! How had they become acquainted? However had she agreed on her part to marry that poor, commonplace young fellow? How had she succeeded in making something of him? He remembered what had been whispered about the Comte de Vaudrec, who had dowered and married her off, it was said.

What would she do now? Whom would she marry? A deputy, as Madame de Marelle fancied, or some young fellow with a future before him, a higher class Forestier? Had she any projects, any plans, any settled ideas? How he would have liked to know that. But why this anxiety as to what she would do? He asked himself this, and perceived that his uneasiness was due to one of those half-formed and secret ideas which one hides even from one's self, and only discovers when fathoming one's self to the very bottom.

Yes, why should he not attempt this conquest himself? How strong and redoubtable he would be with her beside him!

An impatient desire to know this, to question her, to learn her intentions, took possession of him. He would have to leave on the next day but one, as he could not remain alone with her in the house. So it was necessary to be quick; it was necessary before returning to Paris to become acquainted, cleverly and delicately, with her projects, and not to allow her to retract, to yield, perhaps, to the solicitations of another, and pledge herself irrevocably.

He did not know how to give her to understand that he would be happy, very happy, to have her for his wife in his turn. Certainly he could not tell her so at that hour, in that place, before that corpse.

"Cannot we open the window a little?" said Duroy. "It seems to me that the air is tainted."

"Yes," she replied, "I have just noticed it, too."

He went to the window and opened it, and, turning round, said: "Come and get a little fresh air. It is delightful."

She came quietly, and leaned on the window sill beside him. Then he murmured in a low tone: "Listen to me, and try to understand what I want to tell you. Above all, do not be indignant at my speaking to you of such a matter at such a moment, for I shall leave you the day after to-morrow, and when you return to Paris it may be too late. I am only a poor devil without fortune, and with a position yet to make, as you know. But I have a firm will, some brains I believe, and I am well on the right track. In short, I told you one day at your house that my brightest dream would have been to have married a woman like you. I repeat this wish to you now. Do not answer, let me continue. It is not a proposal I am making to you. The time and the place would render that odious. I wish only not to leave you ignorant that you can make me happy with a word, that you can make of me either a friend and brother or a husband at your will; that my heart and myself are yours. I do not want you to answer me now. I do not want us to speak any more about the matter here. When we meet again in

Paris you will let me know what you have resolved upon. Until then, not a word. Is it not so?"

He had uttered all this without looking at her, as though scattering his words abroad in the night before him. She seemed not to have heard them, so motionless had she remained, looking also straight before her with a fixed and vague stare at the vast landscape lit up by the moon. They remained for some time side by side, elbow touching elbow, silent and reflecting. Then she murmured: "It is rather cold," and turning round, returned to her chair.

Toward midnight Duroy dozed off first. When he woke up he saw that Madame Forestier was also slumbering, and, having shifted to a more comfortable position, he reclosed his eyes, growling: "Confound it all, it is more comfortable between sheets, all the same."

A sudden noise made him start up. The nurse was entering the room. It was broad daylight. The young wife in the armchair in front of him seemed as surprised as himself. She was somewhat pale, but still pretty, fresh-looking, and attractive, in spite of this night passed in a chair.

Madame Forestier suggested a stroll in the garden to Duroy, and they began to walk slowly round the little lawn, inhaling with pleasure the balmy air, laden with the scent of pine and eucalyptus. Suddenly she began to speak, without turning her head toward him, as he had done during the night upstairs. She uttered her words slowly in a low and serious voice:

"Look here, my dear friend, I have deeply reflected, already, on what you proposed to me, and I do not want you to go away without an answer. Besides, I am going to say neither yes nor no. It is necessary, after what you have said to me, that you should thoroughly understand what sort of a woman I am, in order that you may no longer cherish the wish you expressed to me, in case you are not of a—of a—disposition to comprehend and bear with me. Understand me well. Marriage for me is not a charm but a partnership. I mean to be free, perfectly free, as to my ways, my acts, my going and coming. I could neither tolerate supervision, nor jealousy, nor discussion of my behavior. I should undertake, be it understood, never to compromise the name of the man who takes me as his wife, never to render him hateful and ridiculous. But this man must also undertake to see in me an equal, an ally, and not an inferior or an obedient and submissive wife. My notions, I know, are not those of every one, but I shall not change them. There you are. I will also add, do not answer me; it would be useless and unsuitable. We shall see each other again, and shall perhaps speak of all this again later on. Now, go for a stroll. I shall return to watch beside him. I shall see you this evening."

He printed a long kiss on her hand, and went away without uttering a word. That evening they only saw each other at dinner time. Then they retired to their rooms, both exhausted with fatigue.

Charles Forestier was buried the next day, without any funeral display, in the cemetery at Cannes. George Duroy wished to take the Paris express, which passed through the town at half-past one.

Madame Forestier drove with him to the station. They walked quietly up and down the platform pending the time for his departure, speaking of trivial matters.

The train rolled into the station. The journalist took his seat, and then got out again to have a few more moments' conversation with her, suddenly seized as he was with sadness and a strong regret at leaving her, as though he were about to lose her forever.

A porter shouted: "Take your seats for Marseilles, Lyons, and Paris." Duroy got in and leaned out of the window to say a few words. The engine whistled, and the train began to move slowly on.

The young fellow, leaning out of the carriage, watched the woman standing still on the platform and following him with her eyes. Suddenly, as he was about to lose sight of her, he put his hand to his mouth and threw a kiss toward her. She returned it with a discreet and hesitating gesture.

IX. A Wedding

Duroy returned to all his old habits.

Installed at present in the little ground-floor suite of rooms in the Rue de Constantinople, he lived soberly, like a man preparing a new existence for himself. His relations with Madame de Marelle had even assumed a conjugal aspect, as if he were practicing in advance for the coming event, and his mistress, often annoyed at the calm regularity of their union, repeated with a laugh: "You are still more domesticated than my husband; it was not worth while changing."

Madame Forestier had not yet returned. She was lingering at Cannes. He received a letter from her merely announcing her return about the middle of April, without a word of allusion to the farewell. He was waiting. His mind was thoroughly made up now to employ every means in order to marry her, if she seemed to hesitate. But he had faith in his luck, confidence in that power of seduction which he felt within him, a vague and irresistible power of which all women felt the influence.

A short note informed him that the decisive hour was at hand.

"I am in Paris. Come and see me.
                    "MADELEINE FORESTIER."

Nothing more. He received it by the nine-o'clock mail. He was at her residence at three on the same day. She held out both her hands to him, smiling with her pleasant smile, and they looked into each other's eyes for a few seconds. Then she said: "How good you were to come to me there under those terrible circumstances."

"I should have done anything you told me," he replied.

And they sat down. She asked the news, inquired about the Walters, about all the staff, about the paper. She had often thought about the paper.

"I miss it very much," she said, "really very much. I had become at heart a journalist. I cannot help it, I love the profession."

Then she paused. He thought he understood, he thought he divined in her smile, in the tone of her voice, in her words themselves a kind of invitation, and, although he had promised to himself not to precipitate matters, he stammered out. "Well then, why—why—why should you not resume—this occupation—under—under the name of Duroy?"

She suddenly became serious again, and, placing her hand on his arm, murmured: "Do not let us speak of that yet a while."

But he divined that she accepted, and, falling at her knees, began to passionately kiss her hands, repeating: "Thanks, thanks; oh! how I love you."

"Listen," she said, in a serious tone, "I have not yet

made up my mind to anything. However, it may be—
Yes. But you must promise me the most absolute secrecy
until I give you leave to speak."

He swore this and left, his heart overflowing with joy.

He was from that time on very discreet as regards the
visits he paid her, and did not ask for any more definite
consent on her part, for she had a way of speaking of the
future, of saying "by and by," and of shaping plans in
which these two lives were blended, which answered him
better and more delicately than a formal acceptation.

Duroy worked hard and spent little, trying to save
money so as not to be without a penny at the date fixed
for his marriage, and becoming as close as he had been
prodigal. The summer went by, and then the autumn,
without any one suspecting anything, for they met very
little, and only in the most natural way in the world.

One evening Madeleine, looking him straight in the
eyes, said: "You have not yet announced our intentions
to Madame de Marelle?"

"No, dear. Having promised you to be secret, I have
not opened my mouth to a living soul."

"Well, it is about time to tell her. I will undertake to
inform the Walters. You will do so this week, will you
not?"

He blushed as he said: "Yes, to-morrow."

She had turned away her eyes in order not to notice
his confusion, and said: "If you like, we will be married
in the beginning of May. That will be a very good time."

"I obey you in all things joyfully."

"I had thought about one matter," she continued, "but
it is rather difficult to explain."

"What is it?" he asked.

"Well, it is this, my dear boy. I am like all women.
I have my weaknesses, my pettinesses. I love all that glit-
ters, that catches the ear. I should have so delighted to

have borne a noble name. Could you not, on the occasion of our marriage, enoble yourself a little?"

She had blushed in her turn, as if she had proposed something indelicate.

He replied, simply enough: "I have often thought about it, but it did not seem to me so easy."

"Your native place is Canteleu?" she queried.

"Yes."

She hesitated, saying: "No, I do not like the termination. Come, cannot we modify this word Canteleu a little."

She had taken up a pen from the table, and was scribbling names and studying their physiognomy. All at once she exclaimed: "There! there it is!" and held out to him a paper, on which he read: "Madame Duroy de Cantel."

He reflected a few moments, and then said gravely: "Yes, that does very well."

She was delighted, and kept repeating: "Duroy de Cantel, Duroy de Cantel, Madame Duroy de Cantel. It is capital, capital." She went on with an air of conviction: "And you will see how easy it is to get every one to accept it. But one must know how to seize the opportunity, for it will be too late afterward. You must from to-morrow sign your descriptive articles D. de Cantel, and your 'Echoes' simply Duroy. It is done every day in the press, and no one will be astonished to see you take a pseudonym. At the moment of our marriage we can modify it a little more, and tell our friends that you had given up the 'du' out of modesty on account of your position, or even say nothing about it. What is your father's Christian name?"

"Alexander."

She murmured: "Alexander, Alexander," two or three times, listening to the sonorous roll of the syllables, and then wrote on a blank sheet of paper:

"Monsieur and Madame Alexander du Roy de Cantel have the honor to inform you of the marriage of Monsieur George du Roy de Cantel, their son to Madame Madeleine Forestier."

She looked at her writing, holding it at a distance, charmed by the effect, and said: "With a little method we can manage whatever we wish."

When he found himself once more in the street, firmly resolved to call himself in future Du Roy, and even Du Roy de Cantel, it seemed to him that he had acquired fresh importance. He walked with more swagger, his head higher, his mustache fiercer, as a gentleman should walk. He felt in himself a species of joyous desire to say to the passers-by: "My name is Du Roy de Cantel."

He received a telegram from Madame de Marelle next morning saying that she would call at one o'clock. He waited for her somewhat feverishly, his mind made up to bring things to a point at once, to say everything right out, and then, when the first emotion had subsided, to argue cleverly in order to prove to her that he could not remain a bachelor forever, and that as Monsieur de Marelle insisted on living, he had been obliged to think of another than herself as a life companion. He felt moved, though, and when he heard her ring, his heart began to beat.

She entered the room, exclaiming: "Good morning, Bel-Ami." Then finding his manner cold, she looked at him and said: "What is the matter with you?"

"Sit down," said he; "we have to talk seriously."

She sat down without taking her hat off, only turning back her veil, and waited.

He had lowered his eyes, and was preparing the beginning of his spech. He commenced in a low tone of voice: "My dear one, you see me very uneasy, very sad, and very much embarrassed at what I have to admit to you. I really love you from the bottom of my heart, so that the fear of causing you pain afflicts me more than even the news I am going to tell you."

She grew pale, felt herself tremble, and stammered out: "What is the matter? Tell me at once."

He said in sad but resolute tones, with that feigned sorrow which we make use of to announce fortunate misfortunes: "I am going to be married."

She gave a sigh as of a woman about to faint, a painful sigh from the very depths of her bosom, and then began to choke and gasp without being able to speak.

He knelt down before her, without daring to touch her, however, and, more deeply moved by this silence than he would have been by a fit of anger, stammered out: "Clo! my darling Clo! just consider my situation, consider what I am. Oh, if I had been able to marry you, what happiness it would have been. But you are married. What could I do? Come, think of it now. I must take a place in society, and I cannot do it so long as I have not a home. If you only knew. There are days when I have felt a longing to kill your husband."

He spoke in his soft, subdued, seductive voice, a voice which fell on the ear like music. He saw two tears slowly gather in the fixed and staring eyes of his mistress and then roll down her cheeks, while two more were ready to fall.

He murmured: "Do not cry, Clo; do not cry, I beg of you. You wring my heart."

Then she made an effort, a strong effort, to be proud and dignified, and asked, in the quivering tone of a woman about to burst into sobs: "Who is it?"

He hesitated a moment, and then, understanding that it was necessary, said: "Madeleine Forestier."

She rose. Duroy guessed that she was going away without saying a word, without reproach or forgiveness, and he felt hurt and humiliated to the bottom of his soul.

Wishing to stay her, he threw his arms about her, saying: "I beg of you, do not go away like that."

Then she looked down on him from above with that moistened and despairing eye, at once so charming and so sad, which shows all the grief of a woman's heart, and gasped out: "I—I have nothing to say. I can do nothing. You—you are right. You—you have chosen well."

And, freeing herself by a backward movement, she left the room without his trying to detain her further.

Left to himself, he rose as bewildered as if he had received a blow on the head. Then, making up his mind, he muttered: "Well, it is all for the worse, or the better. It is over, and without a scene. It is just as well." And relieved from an immense weight, suddenly feeling himself free, delivered, at ease as to his future life, he began to spar at the wall, hitting out with his fists in a kind of intoxication of strength and triumph as if he had been fighting Fate.

When Madame Forestier asked: "Have you told Madame de Marelle?" he quietly answered: "Yes."

She scanned him closely with her bright eyes, saying: "And did it not cause her any emotion?"

"No, not at all. She thought it, on the contrary, a very good idea."

The news was soon known. Some were astonished, others asserted that they had foreseen it; others, again, smiled, and let it be understood that they were not surprised.

The young man, who now signed his descriptive articles D. de Cantel, his "Echoes" Duroy, and the political articles which he was beginning to write from time to time Du Roy, passed half his time with his betrothed. She had decided that the marriage should be quite private, only the witnesses being present, and that they should leave the same evening for Rouen. They would go the next day to see the journalist's parents, and remain with them some days. Duroy had striven to get her to renounce this project, but not having been able to do so, had ended by giving in to it.

So the tenth of May having come, the newly married couple, having considered the religious ceremony useless since they had not invited any one, returned to finish packing their boxes after the brief civil ceremony at the Town Hall. They took the six o'clock train, which bore them away toward Normandy. They had scarcely exchanged twenty words up to the time that they found themselves alone in the railway carriage. As soon as they were on their way they looked at each other and began to laugh, to hide a certain feeling of awkwardness which they did not want to manifest.

The train slowly passed through the long station of Batignolles, and then crossed the mangy-looking plain extending from the fortifications to the Seine. When they crossed the bridge of Asnières, they were amused at the sight of the river covered with boats, fishermen, and oarsmen.

Duroy murmured: "I adore the suburbs of Paris. I have memories of dinners which I reckon among the pleasantest in my life."

"And the boats," she replied. "How nice it is to glide along at sunset."

Then they became silent, as though afraid to continue these outpourings as to their past life, and remained so, already enjoying, perhaps, the poetry of regret.

Duroy, seated face to face with his wife, took her hand and slowly kissed it, and kept pressing it gently, without her making any response to this appeal. At length he said: "It seems to me very funny that you should be my wife."

She seemed surprised as she said: "Why so?"

"I do not know. It seems strange to me. I want to kiss

you, and I feel astonished at having the right to do so."

She calmly held out her cheek to him, which he kissed as he would have kissed that of a sister.

He continued: "The first time I saw you—you remember the dinner Forestier invited me to—I thought: 'Hang it all, if I could only find a wife like that.' Well, it's done. I have one."

She said in a low tone: "That is very nice," and looked him straight in the face shrewdly, and with smiling eyes.

He reflected: "I am too cold. I am too stupid. I ought to get along faster than this," and clasping her to him, kissed her with eager and quivering lips. She freed herself, and, quickly rising to her feet, said: "Come, George; do leave off. We are not children; we can very well wait till we get to Rouen."

He remained seated, very red and chilled by this sensible remark; then, having recovered more self-possession, he said, with some liveliness: "Very well, I will wait; but I shan't be able to say a dozen words till we get there. And remember that we are only passing through Poissy."

"I will do the talking then," she said, and sat down quietly beside him.

She spoke with precision of what they would do on their return. They must keep on the suite of apartments that she had resided in with her first husband, and Duroy would also inherit the duties and salaries of Forestier at the *Vie Française*. Before their marriage, besides, she had planned with the assurance of a man of business all the financial details of their household. They had married under a contract preserving to each of them their respective estates, and every incident that might arise— death, divorce, and the birth of one or more children— was duly provided for. The young fellow contributed a capital of four thousand francs, he said, but of this sum he had borrowed fifteen hundred. The rest was what he had saved during the year, in view of the event. Her contribution was forty thousand francs, which she said had been left her by Forestier.

She turned to him as a subject of conversation. "He was a very steady, economical, hard-working fellow. He would have made a fortune in a very short time."

Duroy no longer listened, wholly absorbed by other thoughts. She stopped from time to time, to follow out some inward train of ideas, and then went on: "In three or four years you can be easily earning thirty to forty thousand francs a year. That is what Charles would have had if he had lived."

George, who had begun to find the lecture rather a long one replied: "I thought we were not going to Rouen to talk about him," referring to a remark she had made.

She gave him a slight tap on the cheek, saying, with a laugh: "That is so. I am in the wrong."

He placed his hands on his knees, pretending to be a very good boy.

"You look like a simpleton like that," said she.

He replied, in the tone of a schoolboy stumbling through his lesson: "Yes, I do. I expect you to give me thorough instruction—in twenty lessons. Ten for the elements, reading, and grammar; ten for accomplishments and rhetoric. I don't know anything myself."

She exclaimed, highly amused:

"My dear little pupil, trust my experience, my great experience. Kisses in a railway train are not worth anything. They only upset one." Then she blushed still more as she murmured: "One should never eat cut wheat while it is green."

He chuckled, kindling at the double meanings from her pretty mouth, and made the sign of the cross, with a movement of the lips as though murmuring a prayer, adding aloud: "I have placed myself under the protection of St. Anthony, patron saint of temptations. Now I am adamant."

Night was stealing gently on, folding in its transparent shadow, like fine gauze, the broad landscape stretching away to the right. This evening gloom, entering the open window, penetrated the souls of the now silent pair.

The whistle of the train announced that they were nearing a station. She remarked, flattening the ruffled locks about her forehead with the tips of her fingers: "It was very silly. We are quite childish."

But he was kissing her hands in turn with feverish rapidity, and replied: "I adore you, my little Madeleine."

Until they reached Rouen they remained almost motionless, cheek against cheek, their eyes turned to the window, through which, from time to time, the lights of houses could be seen in the darkness, satisfied with feeling themselves so close to each other.

They put up at a hotel overlooking the quay.

Next morning, as it was striking eight, Duroy looked at his wife, then suddenly, with the joyful impulse of the fortunate man who has just found a treasure, he clasped her in his arms, exclaiming: "My little Madeleine, I am sure that I love you ever so much, ever so much."

She smiled with her confident and satisfied smile, and murmured, as she returned his kisses: "And I, too—perhaps."

But he felt uneasy about the visit to his parents. He had already forewarned his wife, had prepared and lectured her, but he thought fit to do so again.

"You know," he said, "they are only rustics—country rustics, not theatrical ones."

She laughed. "I know that; you have told me so often enough. Come, get up and let me get up."

He jumped out of bed, and said, as he drew on his socks: "We shall be very uncomfortable there, very uncomfortable. There is only an old bed with a straw in my room. Spring mattresses are unknown at Canteleu."

She had put on her dressing gown—a white flannel dressing gown—which Duroy at once recognized. The sight of it was unpleasant to him. Why? His wife had, he was aware, a round dozen of these morning garments. She could not destroy them in order to buy a new one. No matter, he would have preferred that they were not the same she had worn with the other. It seemed to him that the soft, warm material must have retained something from its contact with Forestier.

They started an hour later, for they were to lunch with the old people, who had been notified some days previous. A rusty, open carriage bore them along with a noise of jolting hardware through a long and rather ugly boulevard, passed between some fields through which flowed a stream, and began to ascend the slope. Madeleine, somewhat fatigued, had dozed off beneath the penetrating caress of the sun, which warmed her delightfully as she lay stretched back in the old carriage, as though in a bath of light and country air.

Her husband awoke her, saying: "Look!"

They had halted two-thirds of the way up the slope, at a spot famous for its view, to which all tourists drive. They overlooked the long and broad valley through which the bright river flowed in sweeping curves.

The driver waited until the travelers' ecstasies were over. He knew from experience the duration of the admiration of all the breeds of tourists. But when he started again, Duroy suddenly caught sight of two old people advancing toward them some hundreds of yards farther on, and jumped out, exclaiming: "There they are. I recognize them."

They were walking quickly and in silence to meet their long-looked-for boy, without noticing these city folk, followed by their carriage. They passed by, when George, who was laughing, cried out: "Good day, Daddy Duroy!"

They both stopped short, amazed at first, then stupefied with surprise. The old woman recovered herself first, and stammered, without advancing a step: "Is't thou, boy?"

The young fellow answered: "Yes, it is I, mother," and stepping up to her, kissed her on both cheeks with a son's hearty kiss. Then he rubbed his face against his father's, by way of greeting. Old Duroy had taken off his cap, a very high black silk cap, made Rouen-fashion, like those worn by cattle dealers.

Then George said: "This is my wife," and the two country people looked at Madeleine. They looked at her as one looks at a phenomenon, with an uneasy fear, blended with a species of approving satisfaction in the father, and in the mother with a kind of jealous enmity.

The man, who was of a joyous nature and inspired by a liveliness born of sweet cider and alcohol, grew bolder, and asked, with a twinkle in the corner of his eyes: "May I kiss her, all the same?"

"Certainly," replied his son; and Madeleine, ill at ease, held out both cheeks to the sounding smacks of the rustic, who then wiped his lips with the back of his hand. The old woman, in her turn, kissed her daughter-in-law with a hostile reserve. No, this was not the daughter-in-law of her dreams; the plump, fresh housewife, rosy-cheeked as an apple and round as a brood mare; but not this fine lady, with her furbelows and her musk. For to the old girl all perfumes were musk.

They set out again, walking behind the carriage which bore the trunk of the newly wedded pair. The old fellow took his son by the arm, and keeping him a little in the rear of the others, asked with interest:

"Well, how goes business, lad?"

"Pretty fair."

"So much the better. Has thy wife any money?"

"Forty thousand francs," answered George.

His father gave vent to an admiring whistle, and could only murmur: "Dang it!" so overcome was he by the mention of the sum. Then he added in a tone of serious conviction: "Dang it all, she's a fine woman!" For he found her to his taste, and he had passed for a good judge in his day.

Madeleine and her mother-in-law were walking side by side, without exchanging a word. The two men rejoined them. They reached Father Duroy's tavern, "The Bellevue," a bit of a house consisting of a ground floor and a garret, which stood at the beginning of the village to the left. A pine branch above the door indicated, in ancient fashion, that thirsty folk could enter.

The things were laid for lunch, in the common room of the tavern, on two tables placed together and covered with two napkins. A neighbor, come in to help serve lunch, bowed on seeing a fine lady appear; and then, recognizing George, exclaimed: "Good Lord! is that you, youngster?"

He replied gayly: "Yes, it is I, Mother Brulin," and kissed her as he had kissed his father and mother. Then turning to his wife, he said: "Come into our room and take your hat off."

They were ushered through a door to the right, into an unheated room with tiled floor, whitewashed walls, and a bed with white cotton curtains. A crucifix above a cup of holy water and two colored pictures, one representing Paul and Virginia under a blue palm tree, and the other Napoleon the First on a yellow horse, were the only ornaments of this clean and dispiriting apartment.

As soon as they were alone, he kissed Madeleine, saying: "I am glad to see the old folks again. When one is in Paris one does not think about it; but when one meets again, it gives one pleasure, all the same."

But his father, thumping the partition with his fist, cried out: "Come along, come along; the soup is ready," and they had to sit down to table.

It was a long country repast, with a succession of ill-assorted dishes, a sausage after a leg of mutton, and an omelette after the sausage. Father Duroy, excited by cider and some glasses of wine, turned on the tap of his choicest jokes—those he reserved for great occasions of festivity—smutty adventures that had happened, as he maintained, to friends of his.

Mother Duroy did not speak, but remained sad and glum, watching her daugher-in-law out of the corner of her eye, with hatred awakened in her heart—the hatred of an old toiler, an old rustic with fingers worn and limbs bent by hard work—for this lady, who inspired her with the repulsion of an accursed creature, an impure being, created for idleness and sin.

Madeleine scarcely ate or spoke, but looked sad, though she had the usual mournful, resigned smile. She was downcast. Why? She had wanted to come. She had not been unaware that she was going among country folk—poor country folk. What had she dreamed they would be like, she who did not usually dream? Did she know herself? Do not women always hope for something that is not? Had she fancied them more poetical? No; but perhaps better informed, more noble, more affectionate, more ornamental. She recalled her own mother, of whom she never spoke to any one—a governess, brought up at Saint Denis, and dead from poverty and grief when she, Madeleine, was twelve years old. An unknown hand had had her brought up. Her father, no doubt. Who was he? She did not exactly know, although she had vague suspicions.

The lunch still dragged on. Customers were now coming in and shaking hands with old Duroy, uttering exclamations of wonder on seeing his son, and slyly winking as they scanned the young wife out of the corner of their eye, which was as much as to say: "Hang it, she's no fool, George Duroy's wife." Others, less intimate, sat down at the wooden tables, calling for "A pot," "A jugful," "Two brandies," "A camphor julep," and began to play at dominoes, noisily rattling the little bits of black and white bone.

Mother Duroy kept passing to and fro, serving the customers with her melancholy air, taking money and wiping the tables with the corner of her blue apron.

As soon as dinner was over, Madeleine drew her husband out of the house, in order not to stay in this gloomy room, always reeking with the rank smell of old pipes and spilt liquor. As soon as they were outside, he said: "You are tired of it already."

She began to protest, but he stopped her, saying: "No, I saw it very plainly. If you like, we will leave to-morrow."

"Very well," she murmured.

They strolled gently onward. They had entered a narrow path, overshadowed by tall trees and running between two lines of shrubbery of impenetrable blackness.

"Where are we?" asked she.

"In the forest," he replied.

"It is a large one?"

"Very large; one of the largest in France."

An odor of earth, trees, and moss—that fresh yet old scent of the woods, made up of the sap of bursting buds and the dead and mouldering foliage of the thickets—seemed to linger in the path. Raising her head, Madeleine could see the stars through the tree tops; and although no breeze stirred the boughs, she could yet feel around her the vague quivering of this ocean of leaves. A strange thrill shot through her soul and fleeted across her skin—a strange pain gripped her at the heart. Why? She did not understand. But it seemed to her that she was lost, engulfed, surrounded by perils, abandoned by every one, alone; alone in the world, beneath this living vault quivering there above her.

She murmured: "I am rather frightened. I should like to go back."

"Well, let us do so."

"And—we will leave for Paris to-morrow?"

"Yes, to-morrow."

She slept badly, continually aroused by all the country sounds so new to her—the cry of the screech owl, the grunting of a pig in a sty adjoining the house, and the noise of a cock who kept on crowing from midnight. She was up and ready to start at daybreak.

When George announced to his parents that he was going back, they were both astonished; then they understood the origin of the wish.

The father merely said: "Shall I see you again soon?"

"Yes; in course of the summer."

The old woman growled: "I hope you won't regret what you have done."

He left them two hundred francs as a present to soothe their feelings, and the carriage, which a boy had been sent in quest of, having made its appearance at about ten o'clock, the newly married couple embraced the old country folk and started off once more.

"Well, that's good."

As they were descending the hill, Duroy began to laugh.

"There," he said, "I had warned you. I ought not to have introduced you to Monsieur and Madame Du Roy de Cantel, Senior."

She began to laugh, too, and replied: "I am delighted

now. They are good folk, whom I am beginning to like very well. I will send them some presents from Paris." Then she murmured: "Du Roy de Cantel, you will see that no one will be astonished at the terms of the notification of our marriage. We will say that we have been staying for a week with your parents on their estate." And bending toward him, she kissed the tip of his mustache, saying: "Good morning, Georgey."

He replied: "Good morning, Maisie," as he passed an arm round her waist.

In the valley below they could see the broad river like a ribbon of silver unrolled beneath the morning sun, the factory chimneys belching forth their clouds of smoke into the sky, and the pointed spires rising above the old town.

X. Suspicion

The Duroys had been back in Paris a couple of days, and the journalist had taken up his old work, pending the moment when he should definitely assume Forestier's duties, and give himself wholly up to politics. He was going home that evening to his predecessor's abode to dinner, with a light heart and a desire to embrace his wife. Passing by a florist's at the end of the Rue Notre Dame de Lorette, he was struck with the notion of buying a bouquet for Madeleine, and chose a large bunch of half-opened roses, a very mass of perfumed buds.

At each story of his new staircase he eyed himself complacently in the mirrors, the sight of which continually recalled to him his first visit to the house.

He rang the bell, having forgotten his key, and the same manservant, whom he had also kept on by his wife's advice, opened the door.

"Has your mistress come home?" asked George.

"Yes, sir."

But on passing through the dining-room he was greatly surprised to find the table laid for three, and the hangings of the drawing-room door being looped up, saw Madeleine arranging in a vase on the mantel a bunch of roses exactly similar to his own. He was annoyed, displeased; it was as though he had been robbed of his idea, his little attention, and all the pleasure he anticipated from it.

"You have invited some one to dinner, then?" he inquired, as he entered the room.

She answered without turning around, and continuing to arrange the flowers: "Yes and no. It is my old friend, Comte de Vaudrec, who has been accustomed to dine here every Monday, and who has come as usual."

George murmured: "Ah! very good."

He remained standing behind her, bouquet in hand, with a longing to hide it or throw it away. He said, however, "I have brought you some roses."

She turned round suddenly, smiling, and exclaiming:

"Ah! how nice of you to have thought of that."

And she held out her arms and lips to him with an outburst of joy so real that he felt consoled. She took the flowers, smelled them, and with the vivacity of a delighted child placed them in the empty vase opposite the other. Then she murmured, as she looked at the effect: "How glad I am! My mantelpiece is furnished now." She added almost immediately, in a tone of conviction: "You know Vaudrec is awfully nice; you will be friends with him at once."

A ring at the door announced the Count. He entered quietly, quite at his ease, as though he were at home. After having gallantly kissed the young wife's fingers, he turned to the husband and cordially held out his hand, saying:

"How goes it, my dear Duroy?"

It was no longer his former stiff and starched bearing, but an affable one, showing that the situation was no longer the same. The journalist, surprised, strove to make himself agreeable in response to these advances. Within five minutes one might have supposed they had known and loved one another for ten years.

Then Madeleine, whose face was radiant, said: "I will leave you together. I must go and see about dinner." And she went out, followed by a glance from both men. When she returned, she found them talking theatricals apropos of a new play, and so thoroughly of the same opinion that a species of rapid friendship awoke in their eyes at the discovery of this absolute identity of ideas.

The dinner was delightful, so intimate and cordial, and the Count stayed on quite late, so comfortable did he feel in this pretty new household.

As soon as he had left, Madeleine said to her husband: "Is he not perfect? He improves in every way on acquaintance. He is a true friend—safe, devoted, faithful. Ah, without him——"

She did not finish the sentence, and George replied: "Yes, I find him very agreeable. I think that we shall get on very well together."

She resumed: "You do not know, but we have some work to do together before going to bed. I had not time to speak to you about it before dinner, because Vaudrec came in at once. I have had some important news, news from Morocco. It was Laroche-Mathieu, the deputy, the future minister, who brought it me. We must work up an important article, a sensational one. I have the facts and figures. We will set to work at once. Bring the lamp."

He took it, and they passed into the study. The same books were ranged on the bookshelves, on top of which were the three vases bought at the Golfe Juan by Forestier on the eve of his death. Under the table the dead man's rug awaited the feet of Duroy, who, on sitting down, took up an ivory penholder slightly chewed at the end by the other's teeth. Madeleine leaned against the mantelpiece, and having lit a cigarette, related her news, and then explained her ideas and the plan of the article she wished written. He listened attentively, scribbling notes as he did so, and when she had finished, raised objections, took up the subject again, enlarging it, and developing in his turn not the plan of an article, but of a campaign against the existing Ministry. This attack would be the commencement. His wife had left off smoking, so strongly was her interest aroused, so vast was the vision that opened before her as she followed out George's train of thought.

She murmured from time to time: "Yes; yes. That is very good. That is capital. That is very clever."

And when he had finished speaking in turn, she said: "Now let us write."

But he always found it hard to begin and had difficulty in finding words. Then she approached softly, and, leaning over his shoulder, began to whisper sentences in his ear. From time to time she would hesitate and ask: "Is that what you want to say?"

He answered: "Yes; exactly."

Duroy, from time to time, added a few original lines which gave force and depth to the line of attack. When their article was finished, George read it aloud.

They both thought it excellent, and smiled, delighted and surprised, as if each had become a revelation to the other.

The article appeared with the signature of George du Roy de Cantel, and caused a great sensation. There was an excitement about it in the Chamber. Daddy Walter congratulated the author, and intrusted him with the political editorship of the *Vie Française*. The "Echoes" were taken up again by Boisrenard.

Then there began in the paper a violent and cleverly conducted campaign against the Ministry. The attack, now ironical, now serious, now jesting, and now virulent, but always skillful and based on facts, was delivered with a certitude and continuity which astonished every one. Other papers continually cited the *Vie Française*, taking whole passages from it, and those in office asked themselves whether they could not gag this unknown and inveterate foe with the gift of a prefecture.

Duroy became a political celebrity. He felt his influence increasing by the pressure of hands and the lifting of hats. His wife, too, filled him with astonishment and admiration by the ingenuity of her mind, the accuracy of her information, and the number of her acquaintances. Continually he would find in his drawing-room, on returning home, a senator, a deputy, a magistrate, a general, who treated Madeleine as an old friend, with sober familiarity. Where had she met all these people? In society, so she said. But how had she been able to gain their confidence and their affection? He could not understand it.

"She would make a formidable diplomatist," he thought.

She often came in late at meal times, out of breath, flushed, quivering, and before even taking off her veil would say: "I have something good to-day. Fancy, the Minister of Justice has just appointed two magistrates who belonged to the fusion committees. We will give him a dose he will not forget in a hurry."

And they would give the minister a dose, and another the next day, and a third the day after. The deputy Laroche-Mathieu, who dined at the Rue Fontaine every Tuesday, after the Comte de Vaudrec, who began the week, would shake hands with husband and wife with an appearance of extreme delight. He never ceased repeating: "By Jove, what a campaign! If we don't succeed after that!"

He hoped, indeed, to succeed in getting hold of the portfolio of foreign affairs, which he had had in view for a long time.

It was said everywhere of him: "Laroche will be a minister"; and he believed more firmly than any one else that he would be. He was one of the chief stockholders in Daddy Walter's paper, and his colleague and partner in many financial schemes.

Duroy backed him up with confidence and with vague hopes as to the future. He was, besides, only continuing the work begun by Forestier, to whom Laroche-Mathieu had promised the Cross of the Legion of Honor when the day of triumph should come. The decoration would adorn the breast of Madeleine's second husband, that was all. Nothing was changed in the main.

It was seen about this time that Duroy's comrades organized a joke against him, at which he was beginning to grow angry. They no longer called him anything but Forestier. As soon as he entered the office, some one would call out: "I say, Forestier!"

He would pretend not to hear, and would look for the letters in his pigeonhole. The voice would resume in louder tones: "Hi, Forestier."

Daddy Walter himself had declared, when astonishment was expressed at the flagrant similarity in style and inspiration between the leaders of the new political editor and his predecessor: "Yes, it is Forestier, but a fuller, stronger, more manly Forestier."

This wounded his pride, wounded his vanity, that touchy pride and vanity of the writer which produce the nervous susceptibility, ever on the alert, equally in the reporter and the genial poet. The word "Forestier" made his ears tingle. He dreaded to hear it, and felt himself redden when he did so. This name was to him a biting jest, more than a pest, almost an insult. It said to him: "It is your wife who does your work as she did that of the other. You would be nothing without her."

His rancor was daily increased by a thousand insignificant details, which stung him like pin pricks, by the incessant reminders of the other arising out of a word from Madeline, from the manservant, from the waiting maid.

One evening toward the end of June, as he was smoking a cigarette at the window, the fineness of the evening inspired him with a wish for a drive, and he said: "Madeleine, shall we go as far as the Bois de Boulogne?"

"Why, yes."

They took an open carriage and drove up the Champs Elyseés, and then along the main avenue of the Bois de Boulogne.

"Do you remember the forest close to your home, how gloomy it was?" said she. "It seemed to me that it was full of horrible creatures, and that there was no end to it, while here it is delightful. One feels caresses in the very breeze, and I know that Sèvres lies on the other side of the wood."

He replied: "Oh, in the forest at home there was nothing but deer, foxes, and wild boars, and here and there the hut of a forester."

This word, akin to the dead man's name, issuing from his mouth, surprised him just as if some one had shouted it out to him from the depths of a thicket, and he became suddenly silent, assailed anew by the strange and persistent uneasiness, the gnawing, invincible, jealous irritation that had been spoiling his existence for some time past. After a minute or so he asked: "Did you ever come here like this of an evening with Charles?"

"Yes, often," she answered.

And all of a sudden he was seized with a wish to return home, a nervous desire that gripped him at the heart. But the image of Forestier had returned to his mind and possessed and laid hold of him. He could no longer speak or think of anything else, and said in a spiteful tone: "I say, Maisie!"

"Yes, dear."

"Did you ever deceive poor Charles?"

He had put his lips close to his wife's ear and whispered: "Come, come, confess."

She jerked herself away, and said abruptly: "You are crazy. As if one answered such questions."

She said this in so singular a tone that a cold shiver ran through her husband's veins, and he remained dumfounded, astonished, almost breathless, as though from some mental shock.

The carriage was now passing along the lake, on which the sky seemed to have scattered its stars. Two swans, vaguely outlined, were swimming slowly, scarcely visible in the shadow. George called out to the driver: "Turn back!" and the carriage returned, meeting the others going at a walk, with their lanterns gleaming like eyes in the night.

In what a strange manner she had said it!

"Was it a confession?" Duroy kept asking himself.

And this almost certainty that she had deceived her first husband now drove him wild with rage. He longed to beat her, to strangle her, to tear her hair out. Oh, if she had only replied: "But, darling, if I had deceived him it would have been with yourself," how he would have kissed, clasped, worshiped her.

The carriage was going faster. It passed the fortifications. Duroy saw before him a reddish light in the sky like the glow of an immense forge, and heard a vast, confused, continuous rumor, made up of countless different sounds, the breath of Paris panting this summer night like an exhausted giant.

George reflected: "I should be very stupid to fret about it. Every one for himself. Fortune favors the bold. Everything is only egotism. Egotism as regards ambition and fortune is better than egotism as regards woman and love."

Madeleine, to whom this silence was irksome, said: "Suppose we have an ice at Tortoni's café before going in."

He glanced at her sideways. Her delicate profile was lit up by the bright light from the row of gas jets of a café. He thought: "She is pretty. Well, so much the better. Jack is as good as his master, my dear. But if ever they catch me worrying again about you, it will be warm at the North Pole." Then he replied aloud: "Certainly, dear," and in order that she should not guess anything, he kissed her.

It seemed to the young wife that her husband's lips were frozen. He smiled, however, with his wonted smile, as he gave her his hand to alight in front of the café.

XI. Enter Madame Walter

On reaching the office next day, Duroy sought out Boisrenard.

"My dear fellow," said he, "I have a service to ask of you. It has been considered a joke for some time past to call me Forestier. I begin to find it very stupid. Will you have the kindness to quietly let our friends know that I will slap the face of the first that starts this joke again? It will be for them to reflect whether it is worth risking a sword thrust for. I address myself to you because you are a calm-minded fellow, who can hinder matters from coming to a painful crisis, and also because you were my second."

Boisrenard undertook the commission. Duroy went out on business, and returned an hour later. No one called him Forestier.

When he reached home he heard ladies' voices in the drawing-room, and asked: "Who is there?"

"Madame Walter and Madame de Marelle," replied the servant.

His heart beat fast for a moment, and then he said to himself: "Well, let's see," and opened the door.

Clotilde was beside the fireplace, standing in a ray of light from the window. It seemed to George that she grew slightly paler on perceiving him. Having first bowed to Madame Walter and her two daughters, seated like two sentinels on each side of their mother, he turned toward Madame de Marelle. She held out her hand, and he took it and pressed it meaningly, as though to say: "I still love you." She responded to this pressure.

He inquired: "How have you been during the century that has elapsed since our last meeting?"

She replied with perfect ease: "Quite well; and you, Bel-Ami?" and, turning to Madeleine, added: "You will allow me to call him Bel-Ami still?"

"Certainly, dear; I will allow whatever you please."

A shade of irony seemed hidden in these words.

Madame Walter spoke of an entertainment that was going to be given by Jacques Rival at his residence, a grand fencing match, at which ladies of fashion were to be present, saying: "It will· be very interesting. But I am so vexed we have no one to take us there, my husband being obliged to be away at that time."

Duroy at once offered his services. She accepted, saying: "My daughters and I will be very much obliged to you."

He looked at the younger daughter and thought: "She is not at all bad-looking, this little Susan; not at all."

The elder sister, Rose, was ugly, dull-looking, and insignificant; one of those girls whom you do not notice, do not speak to, and do not talk about.

The mother rose, and, turning to George, said: "Then I may count upon you for next Thursday, two o'clock?"

"You may count upon me, Madame," he replied.

As soon as she had taken her departure, Madame de Marelle rose in turn, saying: "Good-afternoon, Bel-Ami."

As soon as he was alone with his wife, Madeleine broke out into a laugh, a frank, gay laugh, and, looking him fair in the face, said: "You know that Madame Walter is smitten with you."

"Nonsense," he answered incredulously.

"It is so, I tell you; she spoke to me about you with wild enthusiasm. It is strange on her part. She would like to find two husbands such as you for her daughters.

Fortunately, as regards her, such things are of no moment."

He did not understand what she meant, and inquired: "How of no moment?"

She replied, with the conviction of a woman certain of the soundness of her judgment: "Oh, Madame Walter is one of those who have never even had a whisper about them, never, you know, never. She is unassailable in every respect. Her husband you know as well as I do. But with her it is quite another thing. She has suffered enough through marrying a Jew, but she has remained faithful to him. She is an honest woman."

Duroy was surprised. "I thought her a Jewess, too," said he.

"She, not at all. She is a lady patroness of all the good works of the Church of the Madeleine. Her marriage, even, was celebrated religiously. I do not know whether there was a dummy baptism as regards Monsieur Walter, or whether the church winked at it."

George murmured: "Ah! so she like me."

"Positively and thoroughly. If you were single, I should advise you to ask for the hand of—Susan, eh? rather than that of Rose."

He replied, twisting his mustache: "Hum! their mother is not yet out of date."

Madeleine, somewhat out of patience, answered: "Their mother! I wish you may get her, dear. But I am not alarmed on that score. It is not at her age that a woman is guilty of a first fault. One must set about it earlier."

George was reflecting: "If it were true, though, that I could have married Susan." Then he shrugged his shoulders: "Bah! it is absurd. As if her father would ever had accepted me as a suitor."

He promised himself, though, to keep a more careful watch in the future over Madame Walter's bearing toward him, without asking whether he might ever derive any advantage from this.

On the Thursday he said to Madeleine: "Are not you coming to the fencing match at Rival's?"

"No. It would not interest me. I shall go to the Chamber of Deputies."

He went to call for Madame Walter in an open landau, for the weather was delightful. He was surprised at seeing her so handsome and young-looking. She had the calm, lady-like manner, a certain matronly bearing that caused her to pass almost unnoticed before the eyes of gallants. She scarcely spoke, besides, except to make ordinary, conventional and commonplace remarks, her ideas being proper, methodical, well-ordered, and void of all extravagance.

Her daughter, Susan, in pink, looked like a newly varnished Watteau, while her elder sister seemed the governess intrusted with the care of this pretty doll of a girl.

Before Rival's door a line of carriages were drawn up. Duroy offered Madame Walter his arm, and they went in.

The fencing match was to take place under the patronage of the wives of all the senators and deputies connected with the *Vie Française,* for the benefit of the orphans of the Sixth Arrondissement of Paris. Madame Walter had promised to come with her daughters, while refusing the position of lady patroness, for she only aided with her name works undertaken by the clergy. Not that she was very devout, but her marriage with a Jew obliged her, in her own opinion, to observe a certain religious attitude, and the gathering organized by the journalist had a species of Republican import that might be construed as anti-clerical.

Jacques Rival received the guests in the hall of his dwelling, where a refreshment buffet had been fitted up, the cost of which was to be deducted from the receipts. He indicated with an amiable gesture the little staircase leading to the cellar, saying: "Downstairs, ladies, downstairs; the match will take place in the basement."

He darted forward to meet the wife of the manager, and then shaking Duroy by the hand, said: "How are you, Bel-Ami?"

His friend was surprised, and exclaimed: "Who told you that——"

Rival interrupted with: "Madame Walter, here, who thinks the nickname a very nice one."

Madame Walter blushed, saying: "Yes, I will admit that, if I knew you better, I would do like little Laurine and call you Bel-Ami, too; the name suits you very well."

Duroy laughed, as he replied: "But I beg of you, madame, to do so."

She had lowered her eyes and remarked: "No. We are not sufficiently intimate."

He murmured: "Will you allow me to hope that we shall become more so?"

"Well, we will see," said she.

He moved aside to let her precede him at the beginning of the narrow stairs lit by a gas jet.

Madame Walter and her daughters reached the seats reserved for them in the front row. Duroy, having installed them there, was about to quit them, saying: "I am obliged to leave you; we men must not monopolize the seats."

But Madame Walter remarked, in a hesitating tone: "I should very much like to have you with us all the same. You can tell me the names of the fencers. Come, if you stand close to the end of the seat you will not be in any one's way." She looked at him with her large, mild eyes, and persisted, saying: "Come, stay with us, Monsieur Bel-Ami. We have need of you."

He replied: "I will obey with pleasure, madame."

On all sides could be heard the remark: "It is very funny, this cellar; very pretty, too."

George knew it well, this vault. He recalled the morning he had passed there on the eve of his duel, alone in front of the little white cardboard target that had glared at him from the depths of the inner cellar like a huge and terrible eye.

The voice of Jacques Rival sounded from the staircase: "Just about to begin, ladies."

They were two good professional fencers of second-class merit. They made their appearance, both sparely built, with a military air, and somewhat stiff gestures. Having gone through the salute like automatons, they began to attack one another, resembling in their costumes of white leather and duck two comedy clowns fighting for fun, and the six judges nodded with their air of connoisseurs.

The first couple of fencers were succeeded by Monsieur Planton and Monsieur Carapin, a civilian professional and a military professional. Monsieur Planton was very little, and Monsieur Carapin immensely stout. One would have thought that the first thrust would have reduced his volume like that of a balloon. People laughed. Monsieur Planton skipped about like a monkey; Monsieur Carapin only moved his arm, the rest of his frame being paralyzed by fat.

Then came Monsieur Porion and Monsieur Lapalme, a professional and an amateur, who gave way to exaggerated gymnastics; charging furiously at one another, obliging the judges to scuttle away with their chairs; crossing and re-crossing from one end of the platform to the other, one advancing and the other retreating, with vigorous and comic leaps and bounds. They indulged in little backward springs that made the ladies laugh, and long bounds forward that caused them some emotion. This galloping assault was aptly criticised by some young rascal, who sang out: "Don't kill yourselves over it; it is a time job!" The spectators, shocked at this want of taste, cried "Sh!" The judgment of the experts was passed round.

The first half of the entertainment was concluded by a very fine bout between Jacques Rival and the celebrated Belgian professor, Lebegue. Rival greatly pleased the ladies.

The heat down below was getting terrible. Cries of "More air," "Something to drink," were heard.

A loud voice shouted: "We are suffocating down here. Finish quickly, and let us be off." Another cried out: "The collection." And the whole of the public, gasping, but good-humored all the same, repeated: "The collection, the collection."

Six ladies began to pass along between the seats, and the sound of money falling into the collection pouches could be heard.

Duroy pointed out the celebrities to Madame Walter. There were men of fashion and journalists, those attached to the great newspapers, the old established newspapers, which looked down upon the *Vie Française* with certain reserve, the fruit of their experience. They had witnessed the death of so many of these politico-financial sheets, offspring of a suspicious partnership and crushed by the fall of a ministry. There were also painters and sculptors, who are generally men with a taste for sport; a poet who was also a member of the Academy, and who was pointed out generally, and a number of distinguished foreigners.

Some one called out: "Good-day, my dear fellow." It was the Comte de Vaudrec. Making his excuses to the ladies, Duroy hastened to shake hands with him. On returning he remarked: "What a charming fellow Vaudrec is! How thoroughly blood tells in him!"

Madame Walter did not reply. She was somewhat fatigued, and her bosom rose with an effort every time she drew breath, which caught the eye of Duroy. From time to time he caught a glance, a troubled, hesitating glance which lighted upon him, and was at once averted; and he said to himself: "Eh! What! Have I caught her, too?"

But by degrees the crowd worked their way up the little staircase. At last they would be able to get something to drink. There was an outburst of indignation when they found that those who could not get into the crowded cellar had stripped the refreshment buffet, and had then gone away, declaring that it was very impolite to bring together two hundred people and not give them anything to look at. There was not a cake, not a drop of champagne, syrup, or beer left; not a sweetmeat, not a fruit—nothing. They had sacked, pillaged, swept away everything. These details were related by the servants, who pulled long faces to hide their impulse to laugh right out. "The ladies were worse than the gentlemen," they asserted, "and ate and drank enough to make themselves ill." It was like the story of the survivors after the sack of a captured town.

There was nothing to do but to leave. Gentlemen openly regretted the twenty francs given at the collection; they were indignant that those upstairs should have feasted without paying anything. The lady patronesses had collected upward of three thousand francs. All expenses paid, there remained two hundred and twenty francs for the orphans of the Sixth Arrondissement.

Duroy, escorting the Walter family, waited for his landau. As he drove back with them, seated opposite Madame Walter, he again caught her caressing and fugitive glance, which seemed disturbed.

He returned home joyously. Madeleine was waiting for him in the drawing-room.

"I have some news," said she. "The Morocco affair is becoming complicated. France may very likely send out an expeditionary force within a few months. At all events it will be made a pretext to upset the Ministry, and Laroche-Mathieu will profit by this to get hold of the portfolio of foreign affairs."

Duroy, to tease his wife, pretended not to believe anything of the kind. They would never be mad enough to begin the Tunisian bungle over again. But she shrugged her shoulders impatiently, saying: "But I tell you it is so, it is so! You don't understand that it is a matter of money. Now-a-days in political complications we must not ask: 'Who is the woman?' but 'What is the deal?' "

He murmured "Bah" in a contemptuous tone in order to excite her.

Madeleine turned her back on him, disdaining to pursue the subject; and then, after a moment's silence, resumed: "We shall have visitors on Tuesday. Madame Laroche-Mathieu is coming to dinner with the Vicomtesse de Percemur. Will you invite Rival and Norbert de Varenne? I will call tomorrow and ask Madame Walter and Madame de Marelle. Perhaps we shall have Madame Rissolin, too."

For some time past she had been strengthening her connections, making use of her husband's political influence to attract to her house, willy-nilly, the wives of the senators and deputies who had need of the support of the *Vie Française*.

George replied: "Very well. I will see about Rival and Norbert."

The next day, as she was to go and invite Madame Walter, he resolved to forestall her in order to catch the latter alone and see if she really cared for him. It amused and flattered him. And then—why not?—if it were possible.

He arrived at the Boulevard Malesherbes about two, and was shown into the drawing-room, where he waited till Madame Walter made her appearance, her hand outstretched with pleased eagerness, saying: "What good wind brings you hither?"

"No good wind, but the wish to see you. Some power has brought me here, I do not know why, for I have nothing to say to you. I came, here I am; will you forgive me this early visit and the frankness of this explanation?"

He uttered this in a gallant and jesting tone, with a smile on his lips. She was astonished, and colored somewhat, stammering: "But really—I do not understand—you surprise me."

He observed: "It is a declaration made jestingly, in order not to alarm you."

They had sat down in front of one another. She took the matter pleasantly, saying: "A serious declaration?"

"Yes. For a long time I have been wanting to utter it—for a very long time. But I dared not. They say you are so strict, so rigid."

She had recovered her assurance, and observed: "Why to-day, then?"

"I do not know." Then, lowering his voice, he added: "Or, rather, because I have been thinking of nothing but you since yesterday."

She stammered, growing suddenly pale: "Come, enough of nonsense; let us speak of something else."

But he had fallen at her feet so suddenly that she was frightened. She tried to rise, but he kept her seated by the strength of his two arms passed round her waist, and repeated in a voice of passion: "Yes, it is true that I have loved you madly for a long time past. Do not answer me. What would you have? I am mad. I love you. Oh, if you knew how I love you!"

She was suffocating, gasping, and strove to speak, without being able to utter a word. She pushed him away with her two hands, having seized him by the hair to hinder the approach of the mouth that she felt coming toward her own. She kept turning her head from right to left and from left to right with a rapid motion, closing her eyes in order no longer to see him. He touched her through her dress, handled her, pressed her, and she almost fainted under this strong and rude caress. Then he got up, exclaimed "Farewell, farewell," and rushed away.

He quietly took his stick in the hall and gained the street, saying to himself: "By Jove, I believe I have not made a mistake!"

On returning home at his usual time, he said to his wife: "Well, have you secured all the people for your dinner?"

She answered: "Yes, there is only Madame Walter, who is not quite sure whether she will be free to come."

He shrugged his shoulders, saying: "Oh, yes, she'll come."

He was not certain, however, and remained anxious until the day of the dinner. That very morning Madeleine received a note from her: "I have managed to get free from my engagements with great difficulty, and shall be with you this evening. But my husband cannot accompany me."

He awaited her appearance with some slight uneasiness. She came, very calm, rather cool, and slightly haughty. He became humble, discreet, and submissive. Madame Laroche-Mathieu and Madame Rissolin accompanied their husbands. The Vicomtesse de Percemur talked society. Madame de Marelle looked charming in a strangely fanciful toilet, a species of Spanish costume in black and yellow, which set off her neat figure, her bosom, her rounded arms, and her birdlike head.

Duroy had Madame Walter on his right hand, and during dinner only spoke to her on serious topics, and with an exaggerated respect. From time to time he glanced at Clotilde. "She is really prettier and fresher looking than ever," he thought. Then his eyes returned to his wife, whom he found not bad-looking either, although he retained toward her a hidden, tenacious, and evil anger.

But Madame Walter excited him by the difficulty of victory, and by that novelty always desired by man. She wanted to return home early. "I will escort you," said he.

She refused, but he persisted, saying: "Why will not you permit me? You will wound me keenly. Do not let me think you have not forgiven me. You see how quiet I am."

She answered: "But you cannot desert your guests like that."

He smiled. "But I shall only be away twenty minutes. They will not even notice it. If you refuse, you will cut me to the heart."

She murmured: "Well, then, I agree, if you will be discreet."

But as soon as they were in the carriage he seized her hand, and kissing it passionately, exclaimed: "I love you, I love you. Let me tell you that much. I will not touch you. I only want to repeat to you that I love you."

She stammered: "Oh, after what you promised me! This is wrong, very wrong."

He whispered in her ear, understanding that he must capture her by degrees, this simple woman, that he must get her to make appointments with him, where she would at first, where he wished afterward. "Listen, I must see you; I shall wait for you at your door like a beggar; but I will see you, I will see you to-morrow."

She repeated: "No, do not come. I shall not receive you. Think of my daughters."

"Then tell me where I can meet you—in the street, no matter where, at whatever hour you like, provided I see you. I will bow to you; I will say: 'I love you,' and I will go away."

She hesitated, bewildered. And as the brougham entered the gateway of her residence she murmured hurriedly: "Well, then, I shall be at the Church of the Trinity to-morrow at half-past three." Then, having alighted, she said to her coachman: "Drive Monsieur Duroy back to his house."

As he re-entered his home, his wife asked: "Where did you go?"

He replied, in a low tone: "I went to the telegraph office to send off a message."

Madame de Marelle approached them. "You will see me home, Bel-Ami," said she. "You know I only came such a distance to dinner on that condition." And, turning to Madeleine, she added: "You are not jealous?"

Madame Duroy answered, slowly: "Not over-much."

Clotilde, wrapped in lace, said to Madeleine as she went out: "Your dinner was perfection. In a little while you will have the leading political drawing-room in Paris."

As soon as she was alone with George she clasped him in her arms, exclaiming: "Oh, Bel-Ami, I love you more and more every day."

The cab conveying them rocked like a ship.

"It is not so pleasant," said she.

He answered! "Oh, no." But he was thinking of Madame Walter.

XII. A Fresh Conquest

The Place de la Trinité lay, almost deserted, under a dazzling July sun. An oppressive heat was crushing Paris. It was as though the upper air, scorched and deadened, had fallen upon the city—a thick, burning air that pained the chests inhaling it. The fountains in front of the church fell lazily.

Duroy pulled out his watch. It was only three o'clock. He was half an hour too soon. He laughed as he thought of this appointment. "Churches serve for everything, as far as she is concerned," said he to himself. "They console her for having married a Jew and enable her to assume an attitude of protestation in the world of politics. So much for the habit of making use of religion as an umbrella. If it is fine, it is a walking-stick; if sunny, a parasol; if it rains, a shelter; and if one does not go out, why one leaves it in the hall. And there are hundreds like that, who care for God about as much as a cherry-stone, but who will not hear Him spoken against."

He walked slowly along the edge of the fountain, and then again looked at the church clock, which was two minutes faster than his watch.

He returned toward the door and again looked at his watch. It was still only a quarter past three. He sat down at the entrance to the main aisle, regretting that one could not smoke a cigarette.

Some one came in, and George turned sharply round. It was a poor woman in a woolen skirt, who fell on her knees close to the first chair, and remained motionless, with clasped hands, her eyes turned to heaven, her soul absorbed in prayer. Duroy watched her with interest, asking himself what grief, what pain, what despair could have crushed her heart? She was worn out by poverty, it was plain. She had perhaps, too, a husband who was beating her to death, or a dying child. He murmured, mentally: "Poor creatures. How some of them do suffer." Anger rose up in him against pitiless Nature. Then he reflected that these poor wretches believed, at any rate, that they were taken into consideration up above, and that they were duly entered in the registers of heaven with a debtor and creditor balance.

The rustle of a dress made him start. It was she.

He rose and advanced quickly. She did not hold out her hand, but murmured in a low voice: "I have only a few moments. I must get back home. Kneel down near me, so that we may not be noticed." And she advanced up the aisle, seeking a safe and suitable spot. Her face was hidden by a thick veil, and she walked with careful footsteps that could scarcely be heard.

When she reached the choir, she turned and muttered, in that mysterious tone of voice we always assume in church: "The side aisles will be better. We are too much in view here."

She bowed low to the high altar, turned to the right, and returned a little way toward the entrance; then making up her mind, she took a chair and knelt down. George took possession of the one next to her, and as soon as they were in an attitude of prayer, began: "Thanks, oh, thanks. I adore you. I should like to be always telling you so, to tell you how I began to love you, how I was captivated the first time I saw you. Will you allow me some day to open my heart to tell you all this?"

She listened to him in an attitude of deep meditation, as if she heard nothing.

He felt her shoulder trembling against him and her bosom throbbing, and she stammered abruptly: "I love you, too."

He started as though he had received a blow, and sighed, "Good God!"

She replied, in faltering tones: "Ought I to have told you that? I feel I am contemptible. I, who have two daughters; but I cannot help it, I cannot help it. I could not have believed, I should never have thought—but it is stronger than I. Listen, listen; I have never loved any one but you; I swear it. And I have loved you for a year past in secret, in my secret heart. Oh, I have suffered and struggled till I can do so no more. I love you."

She was weeping, with her hands crossed in front of her face, and her whole frame was quivering, shaken by the violence of her emotion.

He placed the hand he held upon his heart, saying: "Do you feel it beat?" For he had come to the end of his passionate phrases.

But for some moments past the regular footsteps of a promenader had been coming nearer. He had gone the round of the altars, and was now, for the second time at least, coming down the little aisle on the right.

When Madame Walter heard him close to the pillar which hid her, she snatched her fingers from George's grasp and again hid her face. And both remained motionless, kneeling as though they had been addressing fervent supplications to Heaven together.

Duroy, who was thinking of making an appointment elsewhere than at the Church of the Trinity, murmured: "Where shall I see you to-morrow?"

She did not answer. She seemed lifeless—turned into

a statue of prayer. He went on: "Tomorrow, will you let me meet you in the Parc Monceau?"

She turned toward him her uncovered face, a livid face, contracted by fearful suffering, and in a jerky voice ejaculated: "Leave me, leave me now; go away, go away, only for five minutes. I suffer too much beside you. I want to pray, and I cannot. Go away; let me pray alone for five minutes. I cannot. Let me implore God to pardon me—to save me. Leave me for five minutes."

Her face was so upset, so full of pain, that he rose without saying a word, and then, after a little hesitation, asked: "Shall I come back presently?"

She gave a nod, which meant "Yes, presently," and he walked away toward the choir.

She understood that it was all over, that the struggle was a useless one. She would not yield, however; and she was seized by one of those nervous crises that hurl women quivering, yelling, and writhing on the ground. She trembled in every limb, feeling that she was going to fall and roll between the chairs, screaming. Some one approached with rapid steps. It was a priest. She rose, and rushed toward him, holding out her clasped hands, and stammering: "Oh, save me, save me!"

He halted in surprise, saying: "What is it you wish, Madame?"

"I want you to save me. Have pity on me. If you do not come to my assistance I am lost."

He looked at her, asking himself whether she was not mad, and then said: "What can I do for you?"

He was a tall and somewhat stout young man, with full pendulous cheeks, dark, with a carefully shaven face, a good-looking city curate belonging to a wealthy district, and accustomed to rich penitents.

"Hear my confession and advise me, sustain me, tell me what I am to do."

He replied: "I hear confessions every Saturday from three to six o'clock."

Having seized his arm, she gripped it tightly as she repeated: "No, no, no, at once, at once. You must. He is here, in the church. He is waiting for me."

"Who is waiting for you?" asked the priest.

"A man who will ruin me, who will carry me off if you do not save me. I cannot flee from him. I am too weak—too weak. Oh, so weak—so weak!" She fell at his feet sobbing: "Oh, have pity on me, father! Save me, in God's name, save me!"

And, fumbling in his pocket, he drew out a ring full of keys, selected one, and walked rapidly toward the little wooden cabinet. He entered the centre door, which he closed behind him, and Madame Walter, throwing herself into the narrow recess at the side, stammered fervently, with a passionate burst of hope: "Bless me, father, for I have sinned!"

Duroy, having taken a turn round the chair, passed down the left aisle.

Approaching the main entrance, he saw the poor woman still on her knees, and still praying. He thought: "By Jove! she keeps hard at it." He was no longer moved, and no longer pitied her. He passed on, began quietly to walk up the right-hand aisle to find Madame Walter again. He marked the place where he had left her from a distance, astonished at not seeing her. He thought he had made a mistake in the pillar; went on as far as the end one, and then returned. She had gone, then. He was surprised and enraged. Then he thought she might be looking for him, and made the circuit of the church again. Not finding her, he returned, and sat down on the chair she had occupied, hoping that she would rejoin him there, and waited. Soon a low murmur of voices aroused his attention. He had not seen any one in that part of the church. Whence came this whispering? He rose to see, and perceived in the adjacent chapel the doors of the confessional. The skirt of a dress issuing from one of these trailed on the pavement. He approached to examine the woman. He recognized her. She was confessing. He felt a violent inclination to take her by the shoulders and to pull her out of the box. Then he thought: "Bah! it is the priest's turn now; it will be mine to-morrow." And he sat down quietly in front of the confessional, biding his time, and chuckling now over the adventure. He waited a long time. At length, Madame Walter rose, turned round, saw him, and came up to him. Her expression was cold and severe. "Sir," said she, "I beg of you not to accompany me, not to follow me, and not to come to my house alone. You will not be received. Farewell!"

And she walked away with a dignified bearing. He let her depart, for one of his principles was never to force matters. Then, as the priest, somewhat upset, issued in turn from his box, he walked up to him and, looking him right in the eyes, growled to his face: "If you did not wear a petticoat, what a slap you would get across your ugly chops." After which he turned on his heels and went out of the church, whistling between his teeth.

The journalist, finding himself at liberty, went to the office of the *Vie Française*. As soon as he entered he saw by the busy air of the messengers that something out of the common was happening, and at once went into the manager's room. Daddy Walter, in a state of nervous excitement, was standing up dictating an article in broken sentences; issuing orders to the reporters, who surrounded him, between two paragraphs; giving instructions to Boisrenard, and opening letters.

As Duroy came in, the governor uttered a cry of joy: "Ah! how lucky; here is Bel-Ami." He stopped short, somewhat confused, and excused himself. "I beg your pardon for speaking like that, but I am very much disturbed by certain events. And then I hear my wife and daughter speaking of you as Bel-Ami from morning till night, and have ended by falling into the habit myself. You are not offended?"

"Not at all!" said George, laughingly; "there is nothing in that nickname to displease me."

Daddy Walter went on: "Very well, then I christen you Bel-Ami, like everyone else. Well, the fact is, great things are taking place. The Ministry has been overthrown by a vote of three hundred and ten to a hundred and two. Our prorogation is again postponed, postponed to the Greek calends, and here we are at the twenty-eighth of July. Spain is angry about the Morocco business, and it is that which has overthrown Durand de l'Aine and his following. We are right in the swim. Marrot is intrusted with the formation of a new Cabinet. He takes General Boutin d'Acre as Minister of War, and our friend Larouche-Mathieu for foreign affairs. We are going to become an official organ. I am writing a leader, a simple declaration of our principles, pointing out the line to be followed by the Ministry." The old boy smiled, and continued: "The line they intend following, be it understood. But I want something interesting about Morocco; something up-to-date; a sensational article; something or other. Get up one for me."

Duroy reflected for a moment, and then replied: "I have the very thing for you. I will give you a study of the political situation of the whole of our African colony, with Tunis on the left, Algeria in the middle, and Morocco on the right; the history of the races inhabiting this vast extent of territory; and the narrative of an excursion on the frontier of Morocco to the great oasis of Figuig, where no European has penetrated, and which is the cause of the present conflict. Will that suit you?"

"Admirably!" exclaimed Daddy Walter. "And the title?"

" 'From Tunis to Tangiers.' "

"Splendid!"

Duroy went off to search the files of the *Vie Française* for his first article, "Souvenirs d'un Chasseur d'Afrique," which, rebaptized, touched up, and modified, would do admirably, since it dealt with colonial policy, the Algerian population, and an excursion in the province of Oran. In three-quarters of an hour it was re-written, touched up, and brought to date, with a flavor of realism, and praises of the new Cabinet. The manager, having read the article, said: "It is capital, capital, capital. You are an invaluable fellow. I congratulate you."

And Duroy went home to dinner delighted with his day's work, despite the check at the Church of the Trinity, for he felt the battle won. His wife was anxiously waiting for him. She exclaimed as soon as she saw him: "Do you know that Laroche-Mathieu is Minister for Foreign Affairs?"

"Yes; I have just written an article on Algeria in connection with it."

"What?"

"You know, the first we wrote together, 'Souvenirs d'un Chasseur d'Afrique,' revised and corrected for the occasion."

She smiled, saying: "Ah! that is very good." Then, after a few moments' reflection, she continued: "I was thinking—that continuation you were to have written then, and that you—put off. We might set to work on it now. It would make a nice series, and very appropriate to the situation."

He replied, sitting down to table: "Exactly, and there is nothing in the way of it now that sucker of a Forestier is dead."

She said quietly, in a dry and hurt tone: "That joke is more than out of place, and I beg of you to put an end to it. It has lasted too long already."

He was about to make an ironical answer, when a telegram was brought him containing these words: "I had lost my senses. Forgive me, and come at four o'clock to-morrow to the Parc Monceau."

He understood, and with heart suddenly filled with joy he said to his wife, as he slipped the message into his pocket: "I will not do so any more, darling; it was stupid, I admit."

And he began his dinner. While eating, he kept repeating to himself the words: "I had lost my senses. Forgive me, and come at four o'clock tomorrow to the Parc Monceau." He began to laugh, and Madeleine asked: "What is it?"

"Nothing," he answered: "I was thinking of a priest I met just now, who had a very comical face."

Duroy arrived exactly on time at the appointed place next day. On the benches of the park were seated citizens overcome by heat, and careless nurses who seemed to be dreaming while their children were rolling on the gravel of the paths. He found Madame Walter in the little antique ruin in which there is a flowing spring. She was walking round the little circle of columns with an uneasy and unhappy air. As soon as he had greeted her she exclaimed: "What a number of people there are in this garden!"

He seized the opportunity: "It is true; will you come somewhere else?"

"But where?"

"No matter where, in a cab, for instance. You can draw down the blind on your side and you will be quite invisible."

"Yes, I prefer that; here I am dying with fear."

"Well, come and meet me in five minutes at the gate opening on to the outer boulevard. I will have a cab."

And he darted off.

As soon as she had rejoined him, and had carefully drawn down the blind on her side, she asked: "Where have you told the driver to take us."

George replied: "Do not trouble yourself; he knows what to do."

He had given the man his address in the Rue de Constantinople.

She resumed: "You cannot imagine what I suffer on account of you, how I am tortured and tormented. Yesterday in the church I was cruel, but I wanted to flee from you at any cost. I was so afraid to find myself alone with you. Have you forgiven me?"

He squeezed her hands: "Yes, yes. What would I not forgive you, loving you as I do?"

She looked at him with a supplicating air: "Listen, you must promise to respect me—not to—not to—otherwise I cannot see you again."

He did not reply at once; he wore under his mustache that subtle smile that disturbed women. He ended by murmuring: "I am your slave."

Then she began to tell him how she had discovered that she was in love with him on learning that he was going to marry Madeleine Forestier. She gave details, little details of dates, etc. Suddenly she paused. The cab had stopped. Duroy opened the door.

"Where are we?" she asked.

"Get out and come into this house," he replied. "We shall be more at ease there."

XIII. A Secret of Diplomacy

Autumn had come. The Duroys had passed the whole of the summer in Paris carrying on a vigorous campaign in the *Vie Française* during the short vacation of the deputies.

The journal had gained considerably in importance through its known connection with the party in office. It published political intelligence in advance of the most important papers, and hinted discreetly the intentions of its friends the Ministry, so that all the papers of Paris and the provinces took their views from it. It was quoted and feared, and people began to respect it.

Madeleine's drawing-room had been an influential centre, in which several members of the Cabinet met every week. The President of the Council had even dined twice at her house, and the wives of statesmen who had formerly hesitated to cross her threshold now boasted of being her friends, and paid her more visits than were returned by her. The Minister for Foreign Affairs reigned almost as a master in the household. He called at all hours, bringing despatches, news, items of information, which he dictated either to the husband or the wife, as if they had been his secretaries.

When Duroy, after the minister's departure, found himself alone with Madeleine, he would break out in a menacing tone and with bitter insinuations against the goings-on of this commonplace parvenu.

But she would shrug her shoulders contemptuously, repeating: "Do as much as he has done yourself. Become a minister, and you can have your own way. Till then, hold your tongue."

He growled: "He worries me to death, that minister of yours. He is a nincompoop."

She remarked, quietly. "He is no more my minister than he is yours. He is more useful to you than to me."

He turned half round toward her, saying sneeringly: "I beg your pardon, but he does not pay court to me."

She observed, slowly: "Nor to me either; but he is making our fortune."

He was silent for a few moments, and then resumed: "If I had to make a choice among your admirers, I should still prefer that old fossil De Vaudrec. What has become of him? I have not seen him for a week."

"He is indisposed," replied she, unmovedly. "He wrote to me that he was even obliged to keep his bed from an attack of gout. You ought to call and ask how he is. You know he likes you very well, and it would please him."

George said: "Yes, certainly, I will go some time to-day."

And he went out. Monsieur Laroche-Mathieu was awaiting him, for he was lunching at ten o'clock that morning, the Council having to meet at noon, before the opening of Parliament. As soon as they were seated at table alone with the minister's private secretary, for Madame Laroche-Mathieu had been unwilling to change her own meal times, Duroy spoke of his article, sketched out the line he proposed to take, consulting notes scribbled on visiting cards, and when he had finished said: "Is there anything you think should be modified, my dear minister?"

"Very little, my dear fellow. You are, perhaps, a trifle too strongly affirmative as regards the Morocco business. Speak of the expedition as if it were going to take place; but, at the same time, letting it be understood that it will not take place, and that you do not believe in it the least in the world. Write in such a way that the public can easily read between the lines that we are not going to poke our noses into that adventure."

"Quite so. I understand, and I will make myself thoroughly understood. My wife commissioned me to ask you, on this point, whether General Belloncle will be sent to Oran. After what you have said, I conclude he will not."

The statesman answered: "No."

Then they spoke of the coming session. Laroche-Mathieu began to spout, rehearsing the phrases that he was about to pour forth on his colleagues a few hours later. A tiny, twisted mustache curled up its two ends above his lip, like scorpions' tails, and his hair, anointed with brilliantine and parted in the middle, was puffed out over his temples, after the fashion of a provincial lady-killer.

The private secretary ate and drank quietly, no doubt accustomed to these floods of loquacity; but Duroy, whom jealousy of achieved success cut to the quick, thought: "Go on, you proser. What idiots these political jokers are!" And comparing his own worth to the frothy importance of the minister, he said to himself: "By Jove! if I had only a clear hundred thousand francs to offer myself as a candidate at home, near Rouen, and dish my cunning dullards of Normandy folk in their own sauce, what a statesman I should make beside these short-sighted rascals!"

Presently Laroche-Mathieu rang for his brougham, and holding out his hand to the journalist, said: "You quite understand, my dear fellow?"

"Perfectly, my dear minister; you may rely upon me."

And Duroy strolled leisurely to the office to begin his article, for he had nothing to do till four o'clock. But, on reaching the office, a telegram was handed to him. It was from Madame Walter, and ran as follows:

"I must see you to-day. Most important. Expect me two o'clock, Rue de Constantinople. Can render you great service. Till death.   VIRGINIE."

He began to swear: "Hang it all, what an infernal bore!" And seized with a fit of ill-temper, he went out again at once, too irritated to work.

From the first he had been trying to break off with her, without being able to wear out her eager attachment. He had found that he did not relish this mature and melodramatic conquest, and had simply kept away, hoping to put an end to the adventure in that way. She insisted on seeing him, however, summoning him at all hours to a hasty meeting at a street corner, at a shop, or in a public garden. She would then repeat to him in a few words, always the same, that she worshiped and idolized him, and leave him, vowing that she felt so happy to have seen him. He had to call at the Walters' home, but found more pleasure in playing with Susan, who amused him by her whimsicalities. In her doll-like frame was lodged an active, arch, sly, and startling wit, always ready to show itself off. She joked at everything and everybody with biting readiness. George stimulated her imagination, excited it to irony, and they understood one another marvelously. She kept appealing to him every moment: "I say, Bel-Ami. Come here, Bel-Ami."

He would at once leave the mother and go to the daughter, who would whisper some bit of spitefulness, at which they would laugh heartily.

Although disgusted with Madame Walter, he observed some circumspection on account of the *Vie Française*, and strove by dint of coolness, harshness, tempered by attention, and even rude words at times, to make her understand that there must be an end to it.

His affection for Madame de Marelle had, on the contrary, augmented during the summer. He called her his "little rascal," and she certainly charmed him. Their two natures had kindred links; they were both members of the adventurous race of vagabonds, those vagabonds in society who so strongly resemble, without being aware of it, the vagabonds of the highways.

He had fancied himself at length pretty well rid of Madame Walter, when he received at the office of the paper the telegram summoning him to meet her at two o'clock.

He thought: "What does this old screech-owl want with me now? I wager she has nothing to tell me. She will only repeat that she adores me. Yet I must see what it means. She speaks of an important affair, and a great service; perhaps it is so."

He walked slowly, dreading the meeting with Madame Walter. "Ah! I will just receive her nicely if she has nothing to tell me! Cambronne's language will be academic compared to mine. I will tell her that I will never set foot in her house again, to begin with."

He went in, and as soon as she caught sight of him she exclaimed: "Ah! you got my telegram. How fortunate!"

He put on a grumpy expression, saying: "By Jove, yes; I found it at the office just as I was going to start off to the Chamber. What is it you want now?"

She had raised her veil, and drew near with the timid and submissive air of an oft-beaten dog.

"How cruel you are to me! How harshly you speak to me! What have I done to you? You cannot imagine how I suffer through you. Do you remember what you said to me in the church? And now, how do you speak to me? How do you receive me? Oh, God, oh, God, what pain you give me!"

He stamped his foot, and exclaimed violently: "Ah, bosh! That's enough of it. I can't see you a moment without hearing all that foolery."

She had taken a step forward in order to bar the way, and quickly pulling out a handkerchief from her pocket, wiped her eyes with an abrupt movement. Her voice grew firmer by the effect of her will as she said, in tones tremulous with pain: "No—I came to—to tell you some news—political news—to put you in the way of gaining fifty thousand francs—or even more—if you like."

He inquired, suddenly softened: "How so? What do you mean?"

"They are going to take possession of Morocco, but do not wish to let you know of it."

"Sit down," said George, and sat down himself in an armchair. Then she drew toward him a low stool, and sitting down on it between his knees, went on in a coaxing tone: "As I am always thinking about you, I pay attention now to everything that is whispered around me."

And she began quietly to explain to him how she had guessed for some time past that something was being hatched unknown to him; that they were making use of him, while dreading his coöperation.

At length, the day before, she had understood it all. It was a business transaction, a tremendous affair, hatched on the quiet. She smiled now, happy in her dexterity, and grew excited, speaking like a financier's wife accustomed to see the market manipulated, to see stocks rise and fall, ruining within two hours thousands of small investors who had placed their savings in undertakings guaranteed by the names of men honored and respected in the world of politics or finance.

She repeated: "Oh, it is a big thing that they have

done. Very big. It was Walter who did it all, though, and he knows all about such things. Really it is a first-class job."

He grew impatient at these preliminaries, and exclaimed: "Come, tell me what it is at once."

"Well, then, this is what it is. The Tangiers expedition was decided upon between them on the day that Laroche-Mathieu took the Ministry of Foreign Affairs and, little by little, they have bought up the whole of the Morocco loan, which had fallen to sixty-four or sixty-five francs. They bought it up very cleverly by means of shady brokers, who did not awaken any mistrust. They have even hoodwinked the Rothschilds, who were astonished to find Morocco stock always in demand, and who were answered by having agents pointed out to them —all stool pigeons. That quieted the big financiers. And now the expedition is to take place, and as soon as we are there, the French Government will guarantee the debt. Our friends will gain fifty or sixty millions. You understand the matter? You understand, too, how afraid they have been of every one, of the slightest indiscretion?"

She had leaned her head against the young fellow's waistcoat, and with her arms resting on his legs, pressed up against him, feeling that she was interesting him now, and ready to do anything for a caress, for a smile.

"You are quite certain?" he asked.

"I should think so," she replied with confidence.

"It is very smart, indeed. As to that swine of a Laroche-Mathieu, just see if I don't pay him out one of these days. Oh, the scoundrel! Just let him look out for himself. He shall go through my hands."

Then he began to reflect, and went on: "We ought, though, to profit by all this."

"You can still buy some of the loan," said she; "it is only at seventy-two francs."

He said: "Yes, but I have no money under my hand."

She raised her eyes toward him, eyes full of entreaty, saying: "I have thought of that, and if you were very nice, you would let me lend you some."

He answered abruptly and almost harshly: "As to that, no, indeed."

She murmured in an imploring voice: "Listen, there is something that you can do without borrowing money. I wanted to buy ten thousand francs' worth of the stock to make a little nest-egg. Well, I will take twenty thousand, and you shall stand in for half. You understand that I am not going to hand the money over to Walter. So there is nothing to pay for the present. If it suceeds, you gain seventy thousand francs. If not, you will owe me ten thousand, which you can pay when you please."

He remarked: "No, I do not like such partnerships."

Then she argued, in order to get him to make up his mind. She proved to him that he was really pledging his word for ten thousand francs, that he was running risks, and that she was not advancing him anything, since the actual outlay was made by Walter's bank. She pointed out to him, besides, that it was he who had carried on in the *Vie Française* the whole of the political campaign that had rendered the scheme possible. He would be very foolish not to profit by it. He still hesitated, and she added: "But you reflect that in reality it is Walter who is advancing you these ten thousand francs, and that you have rendered him services worth a great deal more than that."

"Very well, then," said he, "I will go halves with you. If we lose, I will repay you the ten thousand francs."

She was so pleased that she took both his hands, and began to kiss them eagerly. He repulsed her gently, saying, "Come, be good now."

She looked at him disconsolately, saying: "Oh, George, can't I even kiss your hands?"

He replied: "No, not to-day. I have a headache, and it upsets me."

She sat down again and asked: "Will you come and dine with us to-morrow? It would give me such pleasure."

He hesitated, but dared not refuse, so said: "Certainly."

As he was leaving she stood very close to him, and one of her long black hairs caught in his waistcoat. She noticed it, and a wild idea crossed her mind, one of those superstitious notions which are often the whole of a woman's reason. She began to twist this hair gently round a button. Then she fastened another hair to the next button, and a third to the next. One to every button. He would tear them out of her head presently when he turned to go, and hurt her. What happiness! And he would carry away something of her without knowing it, he would carry away a tiny lock of her hair which he had never yet asked for. It was a tie by which she attached him to her, a secret, invisible bond, a talisman she left with him.

He said, all at once: "I must leave you, because I am expected at the Chamber at the close of the sitting. I cannot miss attending to-day."

She sighed, "Already," and then added, resignedly: "Go, dear, but you will come to dinner to-morrow." And suddenly, she drew aside. There was a short and sharp pain in her head, as though needles had been stuck into the skin. Her heart throbbed, she was pleased to have suffered a little by him. "Good-by," said she.

After considerable reflection, Duroy called a messenger and sent the following note to Madame de Marelle: "I am going to intrust you with a commission for your husband. Tell him from me to buy to-morrow ten thousand francs' worth of the Morocco loan, which is quoted at seventy-two, and I promise him that he will gain from sixty to eighty thousand francs before three months are over. Charge him to observe the most absolute secrecy. Tell him from me that the expedition to Tangiers is decided on, and that the French Government will guarantee the Morocco loan. But do not mention it to a soul. It is a State secret that I am intrusting to you."

*   *   *

He walked down as far as the boulevard, and sauntering along stopped in front of a jeweler's shop to look at a chronometer which he had fancied for a long time back, and which was ticketed eighteen hundred francs. He thought all at once, with a thrill of joy at his heart: "If I gain my seventy thousand francs, I can afford it." And he began to think of all the things he would do with these seventy thousand francs. In the first place, he would get elected deputy. Then he would buy his chronometer, and would speculate on the Bourse, and would——

He did not want to go to the office, preferring to consult Madeleine before seeing Walter and writing his article, and started for home. He had reached the Rue Drouot, when he stopped short. He had forgotten to ask after the Comte de Vaudrec, who lived in the Chaussée d'Antin. He therefore turned back, still sauntering; thinking of a thousand things, mainly pleasant, of his coming fortune.

He asked the concierge of the house in which the Comte de Vaudrec resided: "How is Monsieur de Vaudrec? I hear that he has been indisposed the last few days."

The man replied: "The Count is very bad indeed, sir. They are afraid he will not live through the night; the gout has gone to his heart."

Duroy was so startled that he no longer knew what he ought to do. Vaudrec dying! Confused and disquieting ideas shot through his mind that he dared not even admit to himself. He stammered: "Thank you; I will call again," without knowing what he was saying. Then he jumped into a cab and was driven home. His wife had come in. He went into her room, breathless, and said at once: "Have you heard? Vaudrec is dying."

She was sitting down reading a letter. She raised her eyes and repeated thrice: "Oh, what do you say, what do you say, what do you say?"

"I say that Vaudrec is dying from an attack of gout that has gone to the heart." Then he added: "What do you think of doing?"

She had risen, her face livid and her cheeks shaken by a nervous quivering, then she began to cry terribly, hiding her face in her hands. She stood shaken by sobs and torn with grief. But suddenly she mastered her sorrow, and wiping her eyes, said: "I—I am going there—don't bother about me—I don't know when I shall be back—don't wait for me."

He replied: "Very well, dear." They shook hands, and she went off so hurriedly that she forgot her gloves.

George, having dined alone, began to write his article. He did so exactly in accordance with the minister's instructions, giving his readers to understand that the expedition to Morocco would not take place. Then he took it to the office, chatted for a few minutes with the governor, and went out smoking, light-hearted, though he knew not why. His wife had not come home, and he went to bed and fell asleep.

Madeleine came in toward midnight. George, suddenly aroused, sat up in bed. "Well?" he asked.

He had never seen her so pale and so deeply moved. She murmured: "He is dead."

"Ah—and he did not say anything?"

"Nothing. He had lost consciousness when I arrived."

George was thinking. Questions rose to his lips that he did not dare to put. "Come to bed," said he.

She undressed rapidly and slipped into bed beside him, when he resumed: "Were there any relations present at his death-bed?"

"Only a nephew."

"Ah! Did he see this nephew often?"

"Never. They had not met for ten years."

"Had he any other relatives?"

"No, I do not think so."

"Then it is this nephew who will inherit?"

"I do not know."

"He was very well off, Vaudrec?"

"Yes, very well off."

"Do you know what his fortune was?"

"No, not exactly. One or two millions, perhaps."

He said no more. She blew out the light, and they remained, side by side, in the darkness—silent, wakeful, and reflecting. He no longer felt inclined for sleep. He now thought the seventy thousand francs promised by Madame Walter insignificant. Suddenly he fancied that Madeleine was crying. He inquired, in order to make certain: "Are you asleep?"

"No."

Her voice was tearful and quavering, and he said: "I forgot to tell you when I came in that your minister has played us a nice trick."

"How so?"

He told her at length, with all details, the scheme hatched between Laroche-Mathieu and Walter. When he had finished she asked: "How do you know this?"

He replied: "You will excuse me not telling you. You have your means of information, which I do not seek to penetrate. I have mine, which I wish to keep to myself. I can, in any case, answer for the correctness of my information."

Then she murmured: "Yes, it is quite possible. I fancied they were up to something without us."

But George, who no longer felt sleepy, had drawn closer to his wife, and gently kissed her ear. She repulsed him sharply: "I beg of you to leave me alone. I am not in a mood for fooling." He turned resignedly toward the wall, and, having closed his eyes, ended by falling asleep.

XIV. A Testimony of Regard

The church was draped with black, and over the main entrance a huge coat-of-arms, surmounted by a coronet, announced to the passers-by that a nobleman was being buried. The ceremony was just over, and those present at it were slowly dispersing, defiling past the coffin and the nephew of the Comte de Vaudrec, who was now shaking hands and returning bows. When George Duroy and his wife came out of the church they began to walk homeward side by side, silent and preoccupied. At length George said, as though speaking to himself: "Really, it is very strange."

"What, dear?" asked Madeleine.

"That Vaudrec should not have left us anything."

She blushed suddenly, as though a rosy veil had been cast over her white skin, and said: "Why should he leave us anything? There was no reason why he should do so." Then, after a few moments' silence, she went on: "There is, perhaps, a will in the hands of some notary. We know nothing as yet."

He reflected for a short time, and then murmured:

"Yes, it is probable, for, after all, he was the most intimate friend of both of us. He dined with us twice a week, called at all hours, and was at home at our place, quite at home in every respect. He loved you like a father, and had no children, no brothers and sisters, nothing but a nephew, and a nephew he never used to see. Yes, there must be a will. I do not care for much, only a remembrance to show that he thought of us, that he loved us, that he recognized the affection that we felt for him. He certainly owed us some such mark of friendship."

She said in a pensive and indifferent manner: "It is possible, indeed, that there may be a will."

As they entered their rooms, the man-servant handed a letter to Madeleine. She opened it, and then held it out to her husband. It ran as follows:

"Office of Maître Lamaneur, Notary,
"17 Rue des Vosges.

"MADAME: I have the honor to beg you to call at my office on Tuesday, Wednesday, or Thursday, between the hours of two and four, on business that concerns you. I am, etc., LAMANEUR."

George had reddened in turn. "That is what it must be," said he. "It is strange, though, that it is you who are summoned, and not myself, who am legally the head of the family."

She did not answer at once, but after a brief period of reflection said: "Shall we go round there by and by?"

"Yes, certainly."

They set out as soon as they had lunched. When they entered Maître Lamaneur's office, the head clerk rose with marked attention and ushered them into the lawyer's private office. The notary was a round little man, round all over. His head looked like a ball almost nailed on to another ball, resting on short little legs that almost resembled balls, too. He bowed, pointed to two chairs, and, turning toward Madeleine, said:

"Madame, I have sent for you in order to acquaint you with the will of the Comte de Vaudrec, in which you are interested."

George could not help muttering: "I thought so."

The notary went on: "I will read to you the document, which is very brief."

He took a paper from a box in front of him, and read as follows:

"I, the undersigned, Paul Emile Cyprien Gontran, Comte de Vaudrec, being sound in body and mind, hereby express my last wishes. As death may overtake us at any moment, I wish in provision of his attacks to take the precaution of making my will, which will be placed in the hands of Maître Lamaneur. Having no direct heirs, I leave the whole of my fortune, consisting of stocks to the amount of six hundred thousand francs and landed property worth about five hundred thousand francs, to Madame Claire Madeleine Duroy, without any charge or condition. I beg her to accept this gift of a departed friend as the proof of a deep, devoted, and respectful affection."

The notary added: "That is all. This document is dated last August, and replaces one of the same nature, written two years back, with the name of Madame Claire Madeleine Forestier. I have this first will, too, which would prove, in the case of opposition on the part of the family, that the Comte de Vaudrec did not change his mind."

Madeleine, very pale, looked at her feet. George nervously twisted the end of his mustache between his fingers. The notary continued, after a moment of silence: "It is of course understood, sir, that your wife cannot accept the legacy without your consent."

Duroy rose and said dryly: "I must ask time to reflect."

The notary, who was smiling, bowed, and said in an amiable tone: "I understand the scruples that cause you to hesitate, sir. I should say that the nephew of Monsieur de Vaudrec, who became acquainted this very morning with his uncle's last wishes, stated that he was prepared to respect them, provided the sum of a hundred thousand francs was allowed him. In my opinion the will is un-assailable, but a law suit would cause a stir which it may perhaps suit you to avoid. The world often judges things ill-naturedly. In any case, can you give me your answer on all these points before Saturday?"

George bowed, saying: "Yes, sir."

Then he bowed again ceremoniously, ushered out his wife, who had remained silent, and went out himself with so stiff an air that the notary no longer smiled.

As soon as they got home, Duroy abruptly closed the door, and, throwing his hat on the bed, said:

"You were more than a mere friend to Vaudrec."

Madeleine, who was taking off her veil, turned round with a start, exclaiming: "I? Oh!"

"Yes, you. A man does not leave the whole of his for-tune to a woman, unless——"

She was trembling, and was unable to remove the pins fastening the transparent tissue. After a moment's reflec-tion she stammered, in an agitated tone: "Come, come—you are mad—you are—you are. Did not you yourself, just now, have hopes that he would leave us something?"

George remained standing beside her, following all her emotions like a magistrate seeking to note the least hesi-tation on the part of an accused. He said, laying stress on every word: "Yes, he might have left something to me, your husband—to me, his friend—you understand, but not to you—my wife. The distinction is capital, essential from the point of propriety and of public opinion."

Madeleine in turn looked at him fixedly in the eyes,

in a penetrating and singular fashion, as though seeking to read something there, as though trying to discover that unknown part of a human being which we never fathom, and of which we can scarcely even catch rapid glimpses at moments which are like doors left half open, revealing the mysterious depths of the mind. She said slowly: "It seems to me, however, that a legacy of this importance would have been looked on as at least equally strange left to you."

He asked abruptly: "Why so?"

She said: "Because——" hesitated, and then continued. "Because you are my husband, and have only known him for a short time, after all—because I have been his friend for a very long while—and because his first will, made during Forestier's lifetime, was already in my favor."

George began to stride up and down. He said: "You cannot accept."

She replied in a tone of indifference: "Precisely so. Then it is not worth while waiting till Saturday; we can let Maître Lamaneur know at once."

He stopped short in front of her, and they again stood for some moments with their eyes riveted on each other, striving to fathom the impenetrable secret of their hearts, to cut down to the quick of their thoughts.

They tried to see one another's conscience unveiled in an ardent and mute interrogation; the struggle of two beings who, living side by side, were always ignorant of one another, suspecting, sniffing round, watching, but never understanding one another to the muddy depths of their souls. And suddenly he muttered to her face, in a low voice: "Come, tell me the whole story of your friendship with De Vaudrec."

She shrugged her shoulders, saying: "Vaudrec was very fond of me, very—but there was nothing more—never."

He stamped his foot. "You lie. It is not possible."

She replied quietly: "It is so, though."

He began to walk up and down again, and then, halting once more, said: "Explain, then, how he came to leave the whole of his fortune to you."

She did so in a careless and disinterested tone, saying: "It is quite simple. As you said just now, he had only ourselves for friends, or rather myself, for he has known me from a child. My mother was a companion at the house of some relatives of his. He was always coming here, and as he had no natural heirs, he thought of me. That there was a little love for me in the matter is possible. But where is the woman who has not been loved thus? Why should not such secret, hidden affection have placed my name at the tip of his pen when he thought of expressing his last wishes? He brought me flowers every Monday. You were not at all astonished at that, and yet he did not bring you any, did he? Now he has given me his fortune for the same reason, and because he had no one to offer it to. It would have been, on the contrary, very surprising for him to have left it to you. Why should he have done so? What were you to him?"

She spoke so naturally and quietly that George hesitated. He said, however: "All the same, we cannot accept this inheritance under such conditions. The effect would be deplorable. All the world would believe it, all the world would gossip about it and laugh at me. My fellow journalists are already only too disposed to feel jealous of me and to attack me. I should have, before any one, a care for my honor and my reputation. It is impossible for me to allow my wife to accept a legacy of this kind. Forestier might perhaps have tolerated it, but not I."

She murmured mildly: "Well, dear, do not let us accept. It will be a million the less in our pockets, that is all."

He was still walking up and down, and began to think aloud, speaking for his wife's benefit, without addressing himself directly to her: "Yes, a million; so much the worse. He did not understand, in making his will, what a fault in tact, what a breach of propriety he was committing. He did not see in what a false, a ridiculous position he would place me. Everything is a matter of detail in this life. He should have left me half, that would have settled everything."

He sat down, crossed his legs, and began to twist the end of his mustache, as he did in moments of boredom, uneasiness, and difficult reflection. Madeleine took up some embroidery at which she worked from time to time, and said, while selecting her wools: "I have only to hold my tongue. It is for you to reflect."

He was a long time without replying, and then said hesitatingly: "The world will never understand that Vaudrec made you his sole heiress, and that I allowed it. Do you understand now how our acceptance of it would be interpreted? It would be necessary to find a side issue, some clever way of palliating matters. To let it go abroad, for instance, that he had divided the money between us, leaving half to the husband and half to the wife."

She observed: "I do not see how that can be done, since the will is plain."

"Oh! it is very simple. You could leave me half the inheritance by a deed of gift. We have no children, so it is feasible. In that way the mouth of public malevolence would be closed."

She replied somewhat impatiently: "I do not see any the more how the mouth of public malevolence is to be closed, since the will is there, signed by Vaudrec."

He said angrily: "Have we any need to show it and to paste it up on the walls? You are really stupid. We will say that the Comte de Vaudrec left his fortune between us. That is all. But you cannot accept this legacy without my authorization. I will only give it on condition of a division, which will hinder me from becoming a laughing-stock."

She looked at him again with a penetrating glance, and said: "As you like. I am willing."

Then he rose and began to walk up and down again. He seemed to be hesitating anew, and now avoided his wife's penetrating glance. He was saying: "No; certainly not. Perhaps it would be better to give it up altogether. That is more worthy, more correct, more honorable. And yet by this plan nothing could be imagined against us—absolutely nothing. The most scrupulous people could have nothing to say." He paused in front of Madeleine. "Well, then, if you like, darling, I will go back alone to Maître Lamaneur to explain matters to him and consult him. I will tell him of my scruples, and add that we have decided on dividing the fortune to prevent gossip. From the moment that I accept half this inheritance, it is plain that no one has the right to smile. It is equal to saying aloud: 'My wife accepts because I accept, I, her husband, the best judge of what she may do without compromising herself.' Otherwise a scandal would have arisen."

Madeleine merely murmured: "Just as you like."

He went on with a flow of words: "Yes, it is all as clear as daylight with this arrangement of dividing it in halves. We inherit from a friend who did not want to make any difference between us—any distinction; who did not wish to appear to say: 'I preferred one or the other after death, as I did during life.' He liked the wife best, be it understood, but in leaving the fortune to both, he wished plainly to express that his preference was purely platonic. And you may be sure that, if he had thought of it, that is what he would have done. He did not reflect. He did not foresee the consequences. As you said very appropriately just now, it was you to whom he offered flowers every week; it is to you that he wished to leave his last remembrance, without taking into consideration that——"

She checked him with a shade of irritation: "All right;

I understand. You have no need to make so many explanations. Go to the notary's at once."

He stammered, reddening: "You are right. I am off."

He took his hat, and then, at the moment of going out, said: "I will try to settle the difficulty with the nephew for fifty thousand francs, eh?"

She replied, with dignity: "No. Give him the hundred thousand francs he asks. Take them from my share if you like."

He muttered, shamefacedly: "Oh, no; we will share that. Giving up fifty thousand francs apiece, there still remains to us a clear million." He added: "Good-by, then, for the present, Maisie." And he went off to explain to the notary the partnership, which he asserted had been thought out by his wife.

They signed the next day a deed of gift of five hundred thousand francs, which Madeleine Duroy abandoned to her husband. On leaving the notary's office, as the day was fine, George suggested that they should walk as far as the boulevards. He showed himself pleasant, and full of attention and affection. He laughed, pleased at everything, while she remained thoughtful and somewhat severe.

It was a somewhat cool autumn day. The people in the streets seemed in a hurry, and walked rapidly. Duroy led his wife to the front of the shop in which he had so often gazed at the longed-for chronometer. "Shall I buy you some jewelry?" said he.

She replied indifferently: "Just as you like."

They went in, and he asked: "What would you prefer—a necklace, a bracelet, or a pair of earrings?"

The sight of the trinkets in gold and precious stones overcame her studied coolness, and she scanned with kindling and inquisitive eyes the glass cases filled with jewelry. And, suddenly moved by desire, she said: "That is a very pretty bracelet."

It was a chain of quaint pattern, every link of which had a different stone set in it.

George inquired: "How much is this bracelet?"

"Three thousand francs, sir," replied the jeweler.

"If you will let me have it for two thousand five hundred it is a bargain."

The man hesitated, and then replied: "No, sir, that is impossible."

Duroy went on: "Come, you can throw in that chronometer for fifteen hundred; that will make four thousand, which I will pay at once. Is it agreed? If not, I will go somewhere else."

The jeweler, in a state of perplexity, ended by agreement, saying: "Very good, sir."

And the journalist, after giving his address, added:

"You will have the monogram, G. R. C., engraved on the chronometer under a baron's coronet."

Madeleine, surprised, began to smile, and when they went out took his arm with a certain affection. She found him really clever and capable. Now that he had an income, he needed a title. It was quite right.

The jeweler bowed them out, saying: "You can depend upon me; it will be ready on Thursday, Baron."

They paused before the Vaudeville, at which a new piece was being played.

"If you like," said he, "we will go to the theatre this evening. Let us see if we can get a box."

They took a box, and he continued: "Suppose we dine at a restaurant."

"Oh! yes, I should like that."

He was happy as a king, and sought what else they could do. "Suppose we go and ask Madame de Marelle to spend the evening with us. Her husband is at home, I hear, and I shall be delighted to see him."

They went there. George, who slightly dreaded the meeting, was not ill pleased that his wife was present to prevent anything like an explanation. But Clotilde did not seem to remember anything against him, and even obliged her husband to accept the invitation.

The dinner was good and the evening pleasant. George and Madeleine got home late. The gas was out, and to light them upstairs the journalist struck a wax match from time to time. On reaching the first floor landing, the flame, suddenly starting forth as he struck, caused their two lit-up faces to show in the glass standing out against the darkness of the staircase. They resembled phantoms, appearing suddenly and ready to vanish into the night.

Duroy raised his hand to light up their reflections, and said, with a laugh of triumph: "Behold the millionaires!"

XV. Little Susan Comes Forward

The conquest of Morocco had been accomplished two months back. France, mistress of Tangiers, held the whole of the African shore of the Mediterranean as far as Tripoli, and had guaranteed the debt of the newly annexed territory. It was said that two ministers had gained a score of millions over the business, and Laroche-Mathieu was almost openly named. As to Walter, no one in Paris was ignorant of the fact that he had brought down two birds with one stone, and made thirty or forty millions out of the loan and eight to ten millions out of the copper and iron mines, as well as out of a large stretch of territory bought for almost nothing prior to the conquest, and sold after the French occupation to companies formed to promote colonization. He had become in a few days one of the lords of creation, one of those omnipotent financiers more powerful than monarchs, who cause heads to bow, mouths to stammer, and all that is base, cowardly, and envious to well up from the depths of the human heart. He was no longer the Jew Walter. He was Monsieur Walter, the wealthy Israelite.

He wished to let it be known. Aware of the monetary embarrassments of the Prince de Carlsbourg, who owned one of the finest mansions in the Rue de Faubourg Saint Honoré, with a garden opening on the Champs Elysées, he proposed to him to buy his house and furniture, just as it stood, within twenty-four hours. He offered three millions, and the Prince, tempted by the amount, accepted. The following day, Walter installed himself in his new domicile. Then he had another idea, the idea of a conqueror who wishes to conquer Paris, the idea of a Bonaparte. The whole city was flocking at that moment to see a great painting by the Hungarian artist, Karl Marcowitch, exhibited at a dealer's named Jacques Lenoble, and representing Christ walking on the water. The art critics, filled with enthusiasm, declared this picture the most superb masterpiece of the century. Walter bought it for four hundred thousand francs, and took it away, thus cutting suddenly short the flow of public curiosity, and forcing the whole of Paris to speak of him in terms of envy, blame, or approbation. Then he had it announced in the newspapers that he would invite every one known in Parisian society to view at his house some evening this triumph of the foreign master, in order that it might not be said that he had hidden away a work of art. His house would be open, let those who would come. It would be enough to show at the door the letter of invitation.

This ran as follows: "Monsieur and Madame Walter beg of you to honor them with your company on December 30, between nine and twelve P. M., to view the picture by Karl Marcowitch, 'Jesus Walking on the Waters,' illuminated by electric light." Then, as a postcript, in small letters: "Dancing after midnight." So those who wished to stay might do so, and out of these the Walters would recruit their future acquaintances. The others would view the picture, the mansion, and their owners with worldly curiosity, insolent and indifferent, and would then go away as they came. But Daddy Walter knew very well that they would return later on, as they had done in the case of his Israelite brethren, grown rich like himself. The main thing was that they should enter his house, all these titled paupers who were mentioned in the papers, and they would enter it to see the face of a man who had gained fifty millions in six weeks; they would enter it to see and note who else came there; they would also enter it because he had had the good taste and dexterity to summon them to admire a Christian picture at the home of a child of Israel.

Duroy was furious at his chief's triumph. He had thought himself rich with the half million francs extorted from his wife, and now he considered himself to be poor, fearfully poor, when comparing his modest fortune with the shower of millions that had fallen around him, without his being able to pick any of it up. He was angry with every one; with his wife, who, deceived by Laroche-Mathieu, had persuaded him not to invest in the Morocco loan; and, above all, with the minister who had tricked him, who had made use of him, and who dined at his table twice a week. Laroche-Mathieu now reigned in the Duroy household, having taken the place and the days of the Comte de Vaudrec, and spoke to the servants like a second master. George tolerated him with a quiver running through him like a dog who wants to bite and dares not.

He had declared at first that he would not go to his chief's entertainment, and that he would never more set foot in his house. For two months Madame Walter had been writing letters, begging him to come, whenever he liked, in order, she said, that she might hand over the seventy thousand francs she had gained for him. He did not reply, and threw these into the fire. Not that he had renounced receiving his share of their profits, but he wanted to madden her, to treat her with contempt. She was too rich. He wanted to show his pride. The very day of the exhibition of the picture, as Madeleine pointed out to him that he was very wrong not to go, he replied: "Leave me in peace. I shall stay at home."

Then, after dinner, he suddenly said: "It will be better, after all, to undergo this infliction. Get dressed at once."

She was expecting this, and said: "I will be ready in a quarter of an hour."

He dressed growling, and even in the cab he continued to vent his anger.

The courtyard of the Carlsbourg mansion was illuminated by four electric lights, looking like four small bluish moons, one at each corner. A splendid carpet was laid down the high flight of steps, on each of which a footman in livery stood motionless as a statue.

Duroy muttered: "Here is a fine splurge for you," and shrugged his shoulders, his heart filled with jealousy.

His wife said: "Keep still, and do as much yourself!"

They went in and handed their wraps to the footmen, who advanced to meet them.

The reception rooms were already crowded. Most of the ladies were in outdoor dress to show that they came there as to any other exhibition. Those who intended re-

maining for the ball were armed and bare-necked.
Madame Walter, surrounded by her friends, was in the
second room, acknowledging the greetings of the visitors.
Many of these did not know her, and walked about as
though in a museum, without troubling themselves about
the masters of the house. When she perceived Duroy she
remained motionless awaiting Duroy. He greeted her ceremoniously, while Madeleine overwhelmed her with affection and compliments. Then George left his wife with
her and lost himself in the crowd, to listen to the spiteful
things that assuredly must be said.

George recognized some well-known people—the Duchess de Ferracine, the Count and Countess de Ravenel,
General Prince d'Andremont, the beautiful Marchioness
des Dunes, and all those folk who are seen at first per-
formances. He was suddenly seized by the arm, and a
young and pleased voice murmured in his ear: "Ah! here
you are at last, you naughty Bel-Ami. How is it one no
longer sees you?"

It was Susan Walter, scanning him with her enamel-
like eyes from beneath the curly cloud of her fair hair.
He was delighted to see her again, and frankly pressed
her hand. Then, excusing himself, he said: "I have not
been able to come. I have had so much to do during the
past two months that I have not been out at all."

She said, with a serious air: "That is wrong, very
wrong. You have caused us a great deal of sorrow, for we
adore you, mamma and I. As to myself, I cannot get on
without you. When you are not here I am bored to death.
You see I tell you so plainly, so that you may no longer
have the right to disappear like that. Give me your arm,
I will show you 'Jesus Walking on the Waters' myself;
it is right at the end, beyond the conservatory. Papa had
it put there so that they should be obliged to see everything before they could get to it. It is astonishing how
proud papa is of this place."

They went on quietly among the crowd. People turned round to look at this good-looking fellow and this charming little doll. A well-known painter said:

"What a pretty pair! They go capitally together."

George was thinking: "If I had been really clever, this is the girl I should have married. I could have done it. How is it I did not think of it? How did I come to take that other one? What a piece of stupidity! We always act too impetuously, and never reflect sufficiently."

Susan was saying: "Oh! do come often, Bel-Ami; we will go in for all sorts of extravagances, now papa is so rich. We will amuse ourselves like madcaps."

He answered, still following up his idea: "Oh! you will marry now. I will not give you six months before you are caught with that same bait. You will be a marchioness, a duchess, or a princess, and will look down on me from a very great height, miss."

She grew indignant, tapped him on the arm with her fan, and vowed that she would marry according to the dictates of her heart.

He sneered: "We shall see about that; you are too rich."

She remarked, "But you, too, have come in for an inheritance."

He uttered in a tone of contempt: "Oh! not worth speaking about. Scarcely twenty thousand francs a year. Not much in these days."

"But your wife has also inherited."

"Yes. A million between us. Forty thousand francs income. We cannot even keep a carriage on it."

They had reached the last of the reception rooms, and before them lay the conservatory—a huge winter garden full of tall, tropical trees, sheltering clumps of rare flowers. They walked on carpets exactly like moss, between two thick rows of shrubs. All at once Duroy noticed on his left, under a wide dome of palms, a broad basin of white marble, large enough to bathe in, on the edge of which four large Delft swans poured forth water through their open beaks. The bottom of the basin was strewn with golden sand, and swimming about in it were some enormous goldfish, quaint Chinese monsters, with projecting eyes and scales edged with blue, mandarins of the waters who recalled, thus suspended above this gold-colored ground, the quaint embroideries of the Flowery Land. The journalist halted with beating heart. He said to himself: "Here is luxury. These are the houses in which one ought to live. Others have attained it. Why should not I?"

He thought of methods of doing so; did not find them at once, and grew irritated at his powerlessness. His companion, somewhat thoughtful, did not speak. He looked at her sideways, and again thought: "All that was necessary was to have married this little puppet."

But Susan all at once seemed to wake up. "Attention!" said she; and pushing George through a group which barred their way, she made him turn sharply to the right. They were now in front of the painting. It was the powerful and unexpected work of a master; one of those works which stir the mind and give you something to dream of for years. People who look at such things at the outset remain silent, and then go thoughtfully away, and only speak later on of the worth of the painting.

Duroy, having contemplated it for some time, said: "It is nice to be able to afford such trifles."

But as he was pushed against by others coming to see it, he went away, still keeping on his arm Susan's little hand, which he squeezed slightly. She said: "Would you like a glass of champagne? Come to the refreshment buffet. We shall find papa there."

And they slowly passed back through the rooms in which the crowd was increasing, noisy and at home, the fashionable crowd of a public fête. George all at once thought he heard a voice say: "It is Laroche-Mathieu and Madame Duroy." These words flitted past his ear like those distant sounds borne by the wind. Whence came they? He looked about on all sides, and indeed saw his wife passing by on the minister's arm. They were chatting intimately in a low tone, smiling, and with their eyes fixed on one another's.

They reached the dining room—an immense apartment, with marble columns, and walls hung with old tapestry. Walter perceived his descriptive writer, and darted forward to take him by the hands. He was intoxicated with joy. "Have you seen everything? Have you shown him everything, Susan? What a lot of people, eh, Bel-Ami! Did you see the Prince de Guerche? He came and drank a glass of punch here just now," he exclaimed.

Then he darted toward the Senator Rissolin, who was towing along his wife, bewildered and bedecked like a stall at a fair. A gentleman bowed to Susan, a tall, thin fellow, slightly bald, with yellow whiskers, and that air of good breeding which is everywhere recognizable. George heard his name mentioned, the Marquis de Cazolles, and became suddenly jealous of him. How long had she known him? Since her accession to wealth, no doubt. He divined a suitor.

He was taken by the arm. It was Norbert de Varenne. The old poet was airing his long hair and worn dress coat with a weary and indifferent air.

He had a glass filled for himself, and, bowing to Duroy, who had taken another, said: "I drink to the triumph of wit over wealth." Then he added softly:

"Not that wealth on the part of others hurts me, or that I am angry at it. But I protest on principle."

George no longer listened to him. He was looking for Susan, who had just disappeared with the Marquis de

Cazolles, and, abruptly quitting Norbert de Varenne, set out in pursuit of the young girl. A dense crowd in quest of refreshments checked him. When he at length made his way through it, he found himself face to face with the De Marelles. He had not for some time past met the husband, who seized both his hands, saying:

"How can I thank you, my dear fellow, for the advice you gave me through Clotilde? I have gained close on a hundred thousand francs over the Morocco loan. It is to you I owe them. You are a valuable friend."

Several men turned round to look at the pretty and elegant brunette. Duroy replied: "In exchange for that service, my dear fellow, I am going to take your wife, or rather to offer her my arm. Husband and wife are best apart, you know."

Monsieur de Marelle bowed, saying: "You are quite right. If I lose you, we will meet here in an hour."

"Exactly."

The pair plunged into the crowd, followed by the husband. Clotilde kept saying: "How lucky these Walters are! That is what it is to have business intelligence."

George replied: "Bah! Clever men always make a position one way or another."

She said: "There are two girls who will have from twenty to thirty millions apiece. Without reckoning that Susan is pretty."

He said nothing. His own idea coming from another's mouth irritated him. She had not yet seen the picture of "Jesus Walking on the Waters," and he proposed to take her to it. They amused themselves by talking scandal of the people they recognized, and making fun of those they did not. Saint-Potin passed by, bearing on the lapel of his coat a number of decorations, which greatly amused them. An ex-ambassador following him showed far fewer.

Duroy remarked: "What a mixed salad of society."

Boisrenard, who shook hands with him, had also

adorned his buttonhole with the green and yellow ribbon worn on the day of the duel.

But, on passing through the greenhouse, he noticed his wife seated beside Laroche-Mathieu, both almost hidden behind a clump of plants. It appeared as if they were saying: "We have appointed a meeting here, a meeting in public. For we do not care a rap what people think."

Madame de Marelle agreed that the Jesus of Karl Marcowitch was astounding, and they retraced their steps.

Susan seized on them as they passed through a doorway, exclaiming: "Ah! here you are. Well, pretty boy, you must remain alone. I am going to take away Clotilde to show her my room."

The two moved rapidly away, gliding through the throng with that undulating, snakelike motion women know how to adopt in a crowd. Almost immediately a voice murmured: "George."

It was Madame Walter, who went on in a low tone:

"Oh! how you do make me suffer without reason. I told Susan to get your companion away in order to be able to say a word to you. Listen, I must speak to you this evening, I must, or you don't know what I will do. Go into the conservatory. You will find a door on the left leading out into the garden. Follow the path in front of it. At the end of it you will find an arbor. Wait for me there in ten minutes' time. If you won't, I declare to you that I will create a scene here at once."

He replied loftily: "Very well. I will be at the spot you mention within ten minutes."

And they separated. But Jacques Rival almost made him late. He had taken him by the arm and was telling him a lot of things in a very excited manner. He slowly went along the walk, seeing his way with difficulty after coming out of the bright light of the reception rooms. He could distinguish to the right and left leafless shrubs, the little branches of which were quivering. Light filtered through their branches, coming from the windows of the mansion.

He saw something white in the middle of the path in front of him, and Madame Walter, with bare arms and neck, said in a quivering voice: "Ah! here you are; you want to kill me, then?"

He answered quietly: "No melodramatics, I beg of you, or I shall bolt at once."

She had seized his arm, and with her lips close to his, said: "But what have I done to you? You are behaving toward me like a wretch. What have I done to you?"

He tried to repulse her. "You wound your hair round every one of my buttons last time I saw you, and it almost brought about a rupture between my wife and myself."

She was surprised for a moment, and then, shaking her head, said: "Oh! your wife would not mind. It was one some one else who made a scene over it."

He looked at her with astonishment. She was no longer the big, frolicsome tomboy he had known, but a bewildered, desperate woman, capable of anything. A vague project, however, arose in his mind. He replied: "My dear, love is not eternal. We meet and leave one another. But when it drags on it becomes a terrible bore. I will have no more of it. That is the truth. However, if you can be reasonable, and receive and treat me as a friend, I will come as I used to. Do you feel capable of that?"

She murmured: "I am capable of anything in order to see you."

"Then it is agreed on," said he; "we are friends, and nothing more."

She stammered: "It is agreed on;" and then, holding out her lips to him: "One more kiss; the last."

He refused gently, saying: "No, we must keep to our agreement."

She turned aside, wiping away a couple of tears, and

then, drawing from her bosom a bundle of papers, offered it to Duroy, saying: "Here; it is your share of the profit in the Morocco affair. I was so pleased to have gained it for you. Here, take it."

He wanted to refuse, observing: "No, I will not take that money."

Then she grew indignant. "Ah! so you won't take it now. It is yours, yours only. If you do not take it, I will throw it into the gutter. You won't act like that, George?"

He received the little bundle, and slipped it into his pocket.

"We must go in," said he; "you will catch cold."

She murmured: "So much the better, if I could die."

She took one of his hands, kissed it passionately, with rage and despair, and fled toward the house. He returned, quietly reflecting. Then he reëntered the conservatory with haughty forehead and smiling lip. His wife and Laroche-Mathieu were no longer there. The crowd was thinning. It was becoming evident that they would not stay for the dance. He perceived Susan arm in arm with her sister. They both came toward him to ask him to dance the first quadrille with the Comte de Latour-Yvelin.

He was astonished, and asked: "Who is he?"

Susan answered maliciously: "A new friend of my sister's."

Rose blushed, and murmured: "You are very spiteful, Susan; he is no more my friend than yours."

Duroy familiarly took Susan by the elbow, and said in his caressing voice: "Listen, my dear, you believe me to be your friend?"

"Yes, Bel-Ami."

"You have confidence in me?"

"Perfect confidence."

"Well, then, will you promise me one thing?"

"Yes; but what is it?"

"To consult me every time that your hand is asked for, and not to accept any one without taking my advice."

"Very well."

"And to keep this a secret between us two. Not a word of it to your father or your mother."

"Not a word."

"It is a promise, then?"

"It is a promise."

Rival came up with a bustling air. "Mademoiselle, your papa wants you for the dance."

She said: "Come along, Bel-Ami."

But he refused, having made up his mind to leave at once, wishing to be alone in order to think. Too many new ideas had entered his mind, and he began to look for his wife. In a short time he saw her drinking chocolate at the buffet with two gentlemen unknown to him. She introduced her husband without mentioning their names to him. After a few moments, he said:

"Shall we go?"

"Whenever you please."

She took his arm, and they walked back through the reception rooms, in which the public were growing few. She said: "Where is Madame Walter? I should like to wish her good-by."

"It is better not. She would try to keep us for the ball, and I have had enough of this."

"That is so; you are quite right."

All the way home they were silent. But as soon as they were in their room, Madeleine said smilingly, before even taking off her veil: "I have a surprise for you."

He growled ill-temperedly: "What is it?"

"Guess."

"I will make no such effort."

"Well, the day after to-morrow is the first of January."

"Yes."

"The time for New Year's gifts."

"Yes."

"Here's one for you that Laroche-Mathieu gave me just now."

She gave him a little black box resembling a jewel case. He opened it indifferently, and saw the cross of the Legion of Honor. He grew somewhat pale, and then smiled, and said: "I should have preferred ten millions. That did not cost him much." She had expected an outburst of joy, and was irritated at this coolness. "You are really incredible. Nothing satisfies you now," said she.

He replied tranquilly: "That man is only paying his debt, and he still owes me a great deal."

She was astonished at his tone, and resumed: "It is, though, a big thing at your age."

He remarked: "All things are relative. I could have something bigger now."

He had taken the case, and, placing it on the mantel-shelf, looked for some moments at the glittering star it contained. Then he closed it and went to bed, shrugging his shoulders.

The *Journal Officiel* of the first of January announced the nomination of Monsieur Prosper-George du Roy, journalist, to the dignity of chevalier of the Legion of Honor, for special services. The name was written in two words, which gave George more pleasure than the derivation itself.

An hour after having read this piece of news, he received a note from Madame Walter, begging him to come and dine with her that evening with his wife, to celebrate his new honors. He hesitated for a few moments, and then, throwing this note, written in ambiguous terms, into the fire, said to Madeleine: "We are going to dinner at the Walters' this evening."

She was astonished. "Why, I thought you never wanted to set foot in the house again."

He only remarked: "I have changed my mind."

When they arrived, Madame Walter was alone in the little Louis XVI boudoir she had appropriated to the reception of personal friends. Dressed in black, with her hair powdered, she looked charming.

She had the air at a distance of an old woman, and close at hand of a young one, and when one looked at her well, of a pretty snare for the eyes.

"You are in mourning?" inquired Madeleine.

She replied sadly: "Yes, and no. I have not lost any relatives. But I have reached the age when one wears the mourning of one's life. I wear it today to inaugurate it. In future I shall wear it in my heart."

Duroy thought: "Will this resolution last?"

The dinner was somewhat dull. Susan alone chattered incessantly. Rose seemed preoccupied. The journalist was warmly congratulated. During the evening they strolled chatting through the reception rooms and the conservatory. As Duroy was walking behind the rest with Madame Walter, she held him back by the arm.

"Listen," said she, in a low voice: "I will never speak to you of anything again, never. But come and see me, George. It is impossible for me to live without you, impossible."

He answered quietly: "I understand. It is useless to speak of all that again. You see, I came here to-day, at once, on receiving your letter."

Walter, who had walked on in advance with his two daughters and Madeleine, was waiting for Duroy beside the picture of "Jesus Walking on the Waters."

"Just imagine," said he, laughing, "I found my wife yesterday on her knees before this picture, as if in a chapel. She was paying her devotions."

Madame Walter replied in a firm voice—a voice thrilling with secret exultation: "It is that Christ who will save my soul. He gives me strength and courage every time I look at Him." And, pausing in front of the Divinity standing amidst the waters, she murmured: "How handsome He is. How afraid of Him those men are, and yet how they love Him. Look at His head, His eyes, how simple, and yet how supernatural at the same time."

Susan exclaimed: "But He resembles you, Bel-Ami. I am sure. He resembles you. If you had a beard, or if He were clean shaven, you would be both alike. Oh! but it is striking!"

She insisted on his standing beside the picture, and they all, indeed, recognized that the two faces resembled one another. Every one was astonished. Walter thought it very singular. Madeleine, smiling, declared that Jesus had a more manly air. Madame Walter stood motionless, gazing fixedly at the face of Duroy beside the face of Christ.

XVI. *In Flagrante Delictu*

During the remainder of the winter the Duroys often visited the Walters. George even dined there by himself continually, Madeleine saying that she was tired, and preferred to remain at home. He had adopted Friday as a regular day, and Madame Walter never invited any one that evening; it belonged to Bel-Ami, to him alone. After dinner they played cards, and fed the goldfish, amusing themselves like a family circle.

Toward the end of March the marriage of the two sisters was all at once alluded to. Rose, it was said, was to marry the Comte de Latour-Yvelin, and Susan the Marquis de Cazolles. These two gentlemen had become familiars of the household, those familiars to whom special favors and marked privileges are granted. George and Susan continued to live in a species of free and fraternal intimacy, romping for hours, making fun of every one, and seeming greatly to enjoy one another's company. They had never spoken again of the possible marriage of the young girl nor of the suitors who offered themselves.

Mr. Walter had brought George home to luncheon one morning. Immediately after the repast Madame Walter was called to see one of the tradesmen, and the young fellow said to Susan: "Let us go and feed the goldfish."

They each took a piece of bread from the table and went into the conservatory. As they leaned over the edge of the marble basin, George and Susan saw their own faces looking up from the water, and smiled at them. All at once he said in a low voice: "It is not kind to hide things from me, Susan."

"What do you mean, Bel-Ami?" asked she.

"Don't you remember what you promised me here on the evening of the fête?"

"No."

"To consult me every time your hand was asked for."

"Well?"

"Well, it has been asked for."

"By whom?"

"You know very well."

"No. I swear to you."

"Yes, you do. That great fop, the Marquis de Cazolles."

"He is not a fop, in the first place."

"It may be so, but he is stupid, ruined by play, and worn out by dissipation. It is really a bad match for you, so pretty, so fresh, and so intelligent."

She inquired, smiling: "What have you against him?"

"I? Nothing."

"Yes, you have. He is not all that you say."

"Nonsense. He is a fool and an intriguer."

She turned round somewhat, leaving off looking into the water, and said: "Come, what is the matter with you?"

He said, as though a secret were being wrenched from the bottom of his heart: "I—I—am jealous of him."

She was slightly astonished, saying: "You?"

"Yes, I."

"Why so?"

"Because I am in love with you, and you know it very well, you naughty girl."

She said in a severe tone: "You are mad, Bel-Ami."

He replied: "I know very well that I am mad. Ought I to have admitted that—I, a married man, to you, a young girl? I am more than mad, I am guilty. I have no possible hope, and the thought of that drives me out of my senses. And when I hear it said that you are going to be married, I have fits of rage, so that I could kill some one. You must forgive me this, Susan."

He was silent. The young girl murmured half sadly, half gayly: "It is a pity that you are married. What is to be done? It cannot be helped. It is done."

He turned suddenly toward her and said, speaking close to her face: "If I were free, would you marry me?"

She replied in a tone of sincerity: "Yes, Bel-Ami, I would marry you, for you please me far better than any of the others."

He rose and stammered: "Thanks, thanks; do not say 'yes' to any one yet, I beg of you; wait a little longer, I entreat you. Will you promise me this much?"

She murmured, somewhat uneasy, and without understanding what he wanted: "Yes, I promise you."

Duroy threw the lump of bread he still held in his

hand into the water, and fled as though he had lost his head, without wishing her good-by.

Susan, surprised and uneasy, got up and returned slowly to the dining room. The journalist had left.

He came home very calm, and as Madeleine was writing letters, said to her: "Are you going to dine at the Walters' on Friday? I am going."

She hesitated and replied: "No. I do not feel very well. I would rather stay at home."

He remarked: "Just as you like."

Then he took his hat and went out again at once. For some time past he had been keeping watch over her, following her about, knowing all her movements. The hour he had been awaiting was at length at hand. He had not been deceived by the tone in which she had said: "I would rather stay at home."

He was very amiable toward her during the next few days. He even appeared lively, which was not usual, and she said: "You are growing quite nice again."

He dressed early on the Friday, in order to make some calls before going to the Walters', he said. He started just before six, after having kissed his wife, and went and took a cab at the Place Notre Dame de Lorette. He said to the driver: "Stop in front of Number 17 Rue Fontaine, and stay there till I tell you to go on again. Then drive to the Cock Pheasant restaurant in the Rue Lafayette."

The cab started at a slow trot, and Duroy drew down the blinds. As soon as he was opposite his door, he did not take his eyes off it. After waiting ten minutes he saw Madeleine come out and go in the direction of the outer boulevards. As soon as she had gone far enough he put his head through the window, and said to the driver: "Go on." The cab started again, and landed him in front of the Cock Pheasant, a well-known middle-class restaurant. George went into the main dining-room and ate slowly, looking at his watch from time to time. At half-past seven, when he had finished his coffee, drunk two *petits verres* of the best brandy, and slowly smoked a good cigar, he went out, hailed another cab that was going by empty, and was driven to the Rue La Rouche-foucauld. Without making any inquiry of the concierge, he went upstairs, to the third story of the house he had told the man to drive to, and when a servant opened the door to him, said: "Monsieur Guibert de Lorme is at home, is he not?"

"Yes, sir."

He was ushered into the drawing-room, where he waited for a few moments. Then a gentleman came in, tall, and with a military bearing, gray-haired, though still young, and wearing the ribbon of the Legion of Honor. Duroy bowed and said: "As I foresaw, commissary, my wife is now dining under suspicious circumstances in furnished rooms in the Rue des Martyrs."

The commissary of police bowed, saying: "I am at your service, sir."

George continued: "You have until nine o'clock, have you not? That limit of time passed, you can no longer enter a private dwelling to prove a crime."

"No, sir; seven o'clock in winter, nine o'clock from the thirty-first of March. It is the fifth of April, so we have till nine o'clock."

"Very well, commissary, I have a cab downstairs."

"As you like, sir." The commissary left the room, and then returned with an overcoat, hiding his tri-colored sash.

They went first to the police office to pick up three officers in plain clothes, who were awaiting them, for George had given notice during the day that the surprise would take place that evening. One of the men got on the box beside the driver. The other two entered the cab, which reached the Rue des Martyrs. Duroy said:

"I have a plan of the rooms. They are on the second floor. We shall first find a little anteroom, then a dining room, then the bedroom. The three rooms open into one another. There is no way out to facilitate flight."

When they arrived opposite the house it was only a quarter past eight, and they waited in silence for more than twenty minutes. But when he saw the three-quarters about to strike, George said: "Let us start now."

They went up the stairs without troubling themselves about the doorkeeper, who, indeed, did not notice them.

At the end of two or three minutes George again pulled the bell several times in succession. They noted a noise from the further end of the rooms, and then a light step approached. Some one was coming to spy who was there. The journalist then rapped smartly on the panel of the door. A voice, a woman's voice, with an attempt to disguise it, asked: "Who is there?"

The commissary replied: "Open, in the name of the law."

The voice repeated: "Who are you?"

"I am the commissary of police. Open the door, or I will have it broken in."

The voice went on: "What do you want?"

Duroy said: "It is I. It is useless to try to escape."

The light step, the tread of bare feet, was heard to withdraw, and then in a few seconds to return.

George said: "If you won't open, we will break in the door." He grasped the handle, and pushed slowly with his shoulder. As there was no longer any reply, he suddenly gave such a violent and vigorous shock that the old lock gave way. The screws were torn out of the wood, and he almost fell over Madeleine, who was standing in the anteroom.

An hour later, George Duroy entered the offices of the *Vie Française*. Monsieur Walter was already there, for he continued to manage and supervise his paper with great care. It had enormously increased in circulation, and greatly helped the schemes of his bank. The manager raised his head and said: "Ah! here you are. You look very strange. Why did you not come to dinner with us? What have you been up to?"

The young fellow, sure of his effect, said, emphasizing every word: "I have just overthrown the Minister of Foreign Affairs."

The other thought he was joking, and said: "Overthrown what?"

"I am going to turn out the cabinet. That is all. It is quite time to get rid of that carrion."

The old man thought that his editor must be drunk. He murmured: "Come, you are talking nonsense."

"Not at all. I have just caught Monsieur Laroche-Mathieu *in flagrante delictu* with my wife. The commissary of police has verified the fact. The minister is done for." Walter, amazed, pushed his spectacles right back on his forehead, and said: "You are not hoaxing me?"

"Not at all. I am even going to write an article on it."

"But what do you want to do?"

"To upset that scoundrel, that wretch, that barefaced criminal." George placed his hat on an armchair, and added: "Woe to those who cross my path. I never forgive."

The manager still failed to understand. He murmured: "But—your wife?"

"My application for a divorce will be lodged to-morrow morning. I shall return her to the departed Forestier."

"You mean to get a divorce?"

"Yes. I made myself ridiculous. But I had to do it in order to catch them. That's done. I am master of the situation."

Monsieur Walter could not get over it, and watched

Duroy with startled eyes, thinking: "Hang it, here is a fellow to beware of."

George went on: "I am now free. I have some money. I shall offer myself as a candidate at the October elections for my native place, where I am well known. I could not take a position or make myself respected with that woman who was suspected by every one. She had caught me like a fool, humbugged and ensnared me. But since I became alive to her little game I kept watch on her." He began to laugh, and added: "It was poor Forestier who was the fool without imagining it, confiding and tranquil. Now I am free. Now I shall get on."

And Daddy Walter, still looking at him with unveiled eyes, his spectacles remaining pushed up on his forehead, said to himself: "Yes, he will get on, the rascal."

George rose: "I am going to write the article. It must be done discreetly. But you know it will be terrible for the minister. He has gone under. He cannot be fished up again. The *Vie Française* no longer needs to stand in awe of him."

The older man hesitated a few moments, and then made up his mind. "Do so," said he; "so much the worse for those who get into such scrapes."

XVII. The Last Plot

Three months had elapsed, and Duroy's divorce had just been granted. His wife had resumed the name of Forestier, and, as the Walters were to leave on the 15th of

July for Trouville, it was decided that he and they should spend a day in the country together before they started. Bel-Ami had asked to be the only man of the party, for he could not endure the presence of the Marquis de Cazolles. But at the last moment it was decided that the Comte de Latour-Yvelin should be called for on the way. He had been invited the day before. The carriage passed along the Avenue des Champs Elysées at a swinging trot, and then traversed the Bois de Boulogne. It was splendid summer weather, not too warm. They crossed the Seine, skirted Mount Valerien, and gained Bougival in order to follow the river as far as Le Pecq.

The Comte de Latour-Yvelin, a man advancing toward middle age, with long, light whiskers, gazed tenderly at Rose. They had been engaged for a month. George, who was very pale, often looked at Susan, who was pale, too. Their glances constantly met and seemed to blend, to understand one another, to secretly exchange a thought, and then to avoid one another. Madame Walter was quiet and happy.

The luncheon was long. Before starting back to Paris, George suggested a turn on the terrace. They stopped at first to admire the view. All ranged themselves in a line along the parapet, and went into ecstasies over the far-stretching horizon.

Walter said: "Such a panorama is not to be found anywhere in the world. There is not one to match it in Switzerland."

Then they all began to walk on slowly, to take a stroll and enjoy the view. George and Susan remained behind. As soon as they were a few paces distant from the others, he said to her in a low and restrained voice: "Susan, I adore you. I love you to madness."

She murmured: "So do I love you, Bel-Ami."

He went on: "If I do not have you for my wife, I shall leave Paris, and this country."

She replied: "Ask papa for my hand. Perhaps he will consent."

He made a gesture of impatience. "No, I tell you for the twentieth time that is useless. The door of your house would be closed to me. I would be dismissed from the paper, and we should not be able even to see one another. Those would be the consequences if I should propose for you in the conventional manner. They have promised you to the Marquis de Cazolles. They hope that you will end by saying 'yes,' and they are waiting for that."

She asked: "What is to be done?"

He hesitated, glancing at her sideways. "Do you love me enough to run a risk?"

She answered resolutely: "Yes."

"Very well, there is one way and only one. The thing must come from you and not from me. You are a spoiled child; they let you say whatever you like, and they will not be too much astonished at one act of daring the more on your part. Listen, then: This evening, on reaching home, you must go to your mamma first, your mamma alone, and tell her you want to marry me. She will be greatly moved and very angry——"

Susan interrupted him with: "Oh! mamma will agree."

He went on quickly: "No, you do not know her. She will be more vexed and angrier than your father. You will see how she will refuse. But you must be firm, you must not give way, you must repeat that you want to marry me and no one else. Will you do this?"

"I will."

"On leaving your mother, you must tell your father the same thing in a very serious and decided manner."

"Yes, yes; and then?"

"And then it is that matters become serious. If you are determined, very determined—very, very determined to be my wife, my dear, dear little Susan—I will—run away with you."

She gave a great start of joy, and almost clapped her hands. "Oh! how delightful. You will run away with me. When will you run away with me?"

All the old poetry of nocturnal elopements, postchaises, country inns; all the charming adventures told in books flashed through her mind, like an enchanting dream about to be realized. She repeated: "When will you run away with me?"

He replied, in low tones: "This evening—to-night."

She asked, quivering: "And where shall we go?"

"That is my secret. Reflect on what you are doing. Remember that after such a flight you can only be my wife. It is the only way, but it is—it is very dangerous—for you."

She declared: "I have made up my mind; where shall I meet you?"

"Can you get out of the hotel alone?"

"Yes. I know how to undo the little door."

"Well, when the doorkeeper has gone to bed, toward midnight, come and meet me on the Place de la Concorde. You will find me in a cab drawn up in front of the Ministry of Marine."

"I will come."

"Really?"

"Really."

He took her hand and pressed it. "Oh! how I love you. How good and brave you are! So you don't want to marry Monsieur de Cazolles?"

"Oh, no!"

"Your father was very angry when you said no?"

"I should think so. He wanted to send me back to the convent."

"You see that it is necessary to be energetic."

"I will be so."

She looked at the vast horizon, her head full of the idea of being run off with. She would go further than that—with him. She would be run away with. She was proud of it. She scarcely thought of her reputation—of what shame might befall her.

Was she aware of it? Did she even suspect it?

Madame Walter, turning around, exclaimed: "Come along, little one. What are you doing with Bel-Ami?"

They rejoined the others and spoke of the seaside, where they would soon be. Then they returned home by way of Chatou, in order not to go over the same road twice. George no longer spoke. He reflected. If this little girl had a little courage, he was going to succeed at last. For three months he had been enveloping her in his net. He had made himself loved by her, as he knew how to make himself loved. He had captured her childish soul without difficulty. He had at first made her promise that she would refuse Monsieur de Cazolles. He had just made her promise that she would fly with him. For there was no other way. Madame Walter, he well understood, would never agree to give him her daughter. Thinking of all this, he replied in broken phrases to the remarks addressed to him, and which he did not hear. He only seemed to come to himself when they reëntered Paris.

Susan, too, was thinking, and the bells of the four horses rang in her ears, making her see endless miles of highway under eternal moonlight, gloomy forests traversed, wayside inns, and the hurry of the hostlers to change horses, for every one guesses that they are being pursued.

When the landau entered the courtyard of the town house, they wanted to keep George to dinner. He refused, and went home. After having eaten a little, he went through his papers, as if about to start on a long journey. He burned some compromising letters, hid others, and wrote to some friends. From time to time he looked at the clock, thinking: "Things must be getting warm there." And a sense of uneasiness gnawed at his heart. Supposing he should fail? But what had he to fear? He could always get out of it. Yet it was a big game he was playing that evening.

He went out toward eleven o'clock, wandered about some time, took a cab, and had it drawn up in the Place de la Concorde, in front of the Ministry of Marine. From time to time he struck a match to see the time by his watch. As he saw midnight approaching, his impatience became feverish. Every moment he thrust his head out of the window to look. A distant clock struck twelve, then another, nearer, then two together, then a last one, very far away. When the latter had ceased to sound, he thought: "It is all over. It is a failure. She won't come." He had made up his mind, however, to wait till daylight. In these matters one must be a patient.

He heard the quarter strike, then the half hour, then three-quarters, and all the clocks struck "one," as they had struck midnight. He no longer expected her; he was merely remaining, racking his brain to divine what could have happened. All at once a woman's head was put through the carriage window, and a voice said: "Are you there, Bel-Ami?"

He started, almost choked with emotion: "Is that you, Susan?"

"Yes, it is I."

He could not manage to turn the handle quickly enough, and repeated: "Ah! it is you, it is you; come inside."

She came in and fell against him. He said: "Go on," to the driver, and the cab started.

She gasped, without saying a word.

He asked: "Well, how did it go off?"

She murmured, almost fainting: "Oh! it was terrible, especially with mamma."

The cab rolled along the street. George took one of the young girl's hands and began to kiss it slowly and with respect. He scarcely knew what to say to her, being scarcely accustomed to platonic lovemaking. But all at once he thought he noticed that she was crying. He inquired, with alarm: "What is the matter with you, darling?"

She replied, in tearful tones: "Poor mamma, she will not be able to sleep if she has found out that I have gone."

Her mother, indeed, was not asleep.

As soon as Susan had left the room, Madame Walter remained face to face with her husband. She asked, bewildered and stunned: "Good God! What is the meaning of this?"

Walter exclaimed furiously: "It means that that schemer has bewitched her. It is he who made her refuse Cazolles. He thinks her dowry worth trying for." He began to walk angrily up and down the room, and went on: "You were always luring him here, too, yourself; you flattered him, you cajoled him, you could not coddle him enough. It was Bel-Ami here, Bel-Ami there, from morning till night. This is your reward."

She murmured with livid face: "I—I lured him?"

He shouted in her face: "Yes, you. You are all mad over him—Madame de Marelle, Susan, and the rest. Do you think I did not see that you could not pass a couple of days without having him here?"

She drew herself up tragically: "I will not allow you to speak to me like that. You forget that I was not brought up like you, behind a counter."

He stood for a moment, stupefied, and then uttered a furious "Damn it all," and rushed out, slamming the door after him. As soon as she was alone she thought for a long time over the possible innocence or perfidy of this man. What a scoundrel if he had prepared the blow! And what would happen? What dangers and what tortures she foresaw! If he knew nothing all could yet be arranged. They would travel about with Susan for six months, and it would be all over. But how could she meet him herself afterward? She looked at the clock, it was past one. She said to herself: "I cannot remain like this, I shall go mad. I must know. I will wake up Susan and question her."

She went, barefooted, in order not to make a noise, with a candle in her hand, toward her daughter's room. She opened the door softly, went in, and looked at the bed. It had not been lain in. She did not comprehend matters at first, and thought that the girl might still be arguing with her father. But all at once a horrible suspicion crossed her mind, and she rushed to her husband's room. She reached it in a bound, blanched and gasping for breath. He was in bed reading.

He asked, startled: "Well, what is it? What is the matter with you?"

She stammered: "Have you seen Susan?"

"I? No; why?"

"She has—she has—gone! She is not in her room."

He sprang to the floor, thrust his feet into his slippers, and, with his shirt tails floating in the air, rushed in turn to his daughter's room. As soon as he saw it, he no longer retained any doubt. She had fled. He dropped into a chair and placed his lamp on the ground in front of him.

His wife had rejoined him, and stammered: "Well?"

He had no longer the strength to reply; he was no longer enraged, he only groaned: "It is done, he has got her. We are done for."

She did not understand, and said: "What do you mean, done for?"

"Yes, by Jove. He will certainly marry her now."

She gave a cry like that of a wild beast: "He, never! You must be mad."

He replied sadly: "It is no use screaming. He has run

away with her. The best thing is to give her to him. By setting to work in the right way no one will know anything of this escapade."

She repeated, shaken by terrible emotion: "Never, never; he shall never have Susan. I will never consent."

Walter murmured dejectedly: "But he has got her. It is done. And he will keep her and hide her as long as we do not yield. So, to avoid scandal, we must give in at once."

He ended by getting angry, and taking up, as a practical man, the cudgels on behalf of Bel-Ami: "Hold your tongue," said he. "I tell you again that it must be so; it absolutely must. And who knows? Perhaps we shall not regret it. With men of that stamp one never knows what may happen. You saw how he overthrew in three articles that fool of a Laroche-Mathieu, and how he did it with dignity, which was infernally difficult in his position as the husband. At all events, we shall see. It just comes to this, that we are trapped. We cannot get out of it."

She felt a longing to scream, to roll on the ground, to tear her hair out. She said at length, in exasperated tones: "He shall not have her. I won't have it."

Walter rose, picked up his lamp, and remarked:

"There you are, stupid just like all women. You never do anything except from passion. You do not know how to bend yourself to circumstances. You are all stupid. I tell you that he shall marry her. He must."

He went out, shuffling along in his slippers. He was a comical figure in his night-shirt as he traversed the broad corridor of the huge, silent house, and noiselessly reëntered his room.

Madame Walter remained standing, torn by intolerable grief. She did not yet quite understand it. She was only conscious of suffering. Then it seemed to her that she could not remain there motionless till daylight. She felt within her an urgent need of fleeing, of running away, of seeking help, of obtaining succor. She took her candle, left the room, and went downstairs to the conservatory. The picture of Jesus was right at the end of it in a small drawing-room, shut off by a glass door, in order that the humidity from the soil should not damage the canvas. It formed a kind of chapel in a forest of strange trees. The poor woman walked slowly, oppressed by the shadows, amid which appeared, by the flickering light of her candle, immense plants, recalling monsters, living creatures, hideous deformities. All at once she caught sight of the picture of Christ. She opened the door separating her from it, and fell on her knees. She prayed to Him, wildly at first, stammering forth words of true, passionate, and despairing invocations. Then, the ardor of her appeal slackening, she raised her eyes toward Him, and was struck with anguish. He resembled Bel-Ami so strongly, in the trembling light of this solitary candle lighting the picture from below, that it was no longer Christ—it was Bel-Ami who was looking at her. They were his eyes, his forehead, the expression of his face, his cold and haughty air.

She stammered: "Jesus, Jesus, Jesus!" and the name "George" rose to her lips. All at once she uttered a loud cry and fell on her back. Her candle, overturned, went out.

The next morning, Madame Walter was found stretched out senseless, almost asphyxiated, before "Jesus Walking on the Waters." She was so ill that they feared for her life. She only fully recovered the use of her senses the following day. Then she began to weep. The disappearance of Susan was explained to the servants as due to her being suddenly sent back to the convent. And Monsieur Walter replied to a long letter of Duroy by granting him his daughter's hand. Bel-Ami had posted this letter at the moment of leaving Paris, for he had prepared it in advance the evening of his departure. He said in it, in respectful terms, that he had long loved the young girl; that there had never been any agreement between them; but that finding her come freely to him to say: "I wish to be your wife," he considered himself authorized in keeping her, even in hiding her, until he had obtained an answer from her parents, whose legal power had for him less weight than the wish of his betrothed. He begged Monsieur Walter to address his reply "Post-restante," a friend being charged to forward the letter to him.

When he had obtained what he wished, he brought back Susan to Paris, and sent her on to her parents, abstaining from appearing himself for some little time.

They had spent six days on the banks of the Seine at La Roche Guyon.

The young girl had never enjoyed herself so much. She had played at pastoral life. As he passed her off as his sister, they lived in a free and chaste intimacy—a kind of loving friendship. He thought it a clever stroke to respect her. On the day after their arrival, she had bought some underwear and some peasant's clothes, and set to work fishing, with a huge straw hat, ornamented with wild flowers, on her head. She thought the country delightful. There was an old tower and an old château, in which beautiful tapestries were exhibited.

George, dressed in a fisherman's jersey, bought from a local tradesman, escorted Susan now on foot along the banks of the river, now in a boat. They kissed at every moment, she in all innocence, and he ready to succumb to temptation. But he was able to restrain himself; and when he said to her: "We will go back to Paris to-morrow, your father has granted me your hand," she murmured simply: "Already? It was so nice being with you, Bel-Ami."

XVIII. He Laughs Who Wins

It was dark in the little suite of rooms in the Rue de Constantinople; for George Duroy and Clotilde de Marelle, having met at the door, had gone in at once, and she had said to him, without giving him time to open the Venetian blinds: "So you are going to marry Susan Walter?" He admitted it quietly, and added: "Did not you know it?"

She exclaimed, standing before him, furious and indignant: "So you are going to marry Susan Walter? That is a little too much of a good thing. For three months you have been pretending to me in order to hide it from me. Every one knew it but I. It was my husband who told me of it."

Duroy began to laugh, though somewhat confused all the same; and having placed his hat on a corner of the mantelshelf, sat down in an armchair. She looked him straight in the face, and said, in a low and irritated tone: "Ever since you left your wife you have been preparing for this move, and you only amused yourself with me to fill up the interim. What a rascal you are!"

He asked: "Why so? I had a wife who deceived me. I caught her, I obtained a divorce, and I am going to marry another. What could be simpler?"

She murmured, quivering: "Oh! how cunning and dangerous you are!"

He began to smile again.

"By Jove! Simpletons and fools are always some one's dupes."

But she continued to follow out her idea: "I ought to have guessed your character from the beginning. But, no; I could not believe that you could be such a blackguard as that."

He assumed an air of dignity, saying: "I beg of you to be careful about the words you are making use of."

His indignation revolted her: "What? You want me to put on gloves in dealing with you now. You have behaved toward me like a vagabond ever since I have known you, and you want to make out that I am not to tell you so. You deceive every one; you take advantage of every one; you filch money and enjoyment wherever you can, and you want me to treat you as an honest man!"

He rose, and, with quivering lip, said: "Be quiet, or I will turn you out of here."

"Do you think I don't know how you robbed Madeleine of half Vaudrec's money? Do you think I don't know how you obliged Susan to marry you?"

He seized her by the shoulders, and, shaking her with both hands, exclaimed: "Don't speak of her, at any rate. I won't have it."

She screamed out: "You deceived her; I know you did."

He would have accepted no matter what, but this falsehood exasperated him. The truths she had told him to his face had caused thrills of anger to run through him, but this lie respecting the young girl who was going to be his wife aroused in the palm of his hand a furious longing to strike her.

He repeated: "Be quiet—have a care—be quiet," and shook her as one shakes a branch to make the fruit fall.

She screamed, with her hair coming down, her mouth wide open, her eyes aglow: "You deceived her!"

He let her go, and gave her such a smack on the face that she fell down beside the wall. But she turned toward him, and, raising herself on her hands, once more shouted: "You deceived her!"

He rushed at her, and, holding her down, struck her as though striking a man. She left off shouting, and began to moan beneath his blows. She no longer stirred, but hid her face against the wall and uttered plaintive cries. He left off beating her and rose up. Then he walked about the room a little to recover his coolness, and, an idea occurring to him, he went and filled a basin with cold water, and dipped his head into it. Then he washed his hands and came back to see what she was doing, carefully wiping his fingers. She had not budged, was still, quietly weeping.

"Are you going to stop blubbering?" he said.

She did not answer. He stood in the middle of the room, feeling somewhat awkward and ashamed in presence of this form stretched out before him. All at once he formed a resolution, and took his hat from the mantelshelf, saying: "Good-night. Give the key to the doorkeeper when you leave. I shan't wait for your convenience." He went out, closed the door, went to the concierge, and said: "Madame is still there. She will be leaving in a few minutes. Tell the landlord that I give notice to leave at the end of September. It is the sixteenth of August, so I am within the limit."

And he walked hastily away, for he had some pressing calls to make touching the purchase of the last wedding gifts.

The wedding was fixed for the 20th of October, after the meeting of the Chambers. It was to take place at the Church of the Madeleine. There had been a great deal of gossip about it, without any one knowing the exact truth. Different tales were in circulation. It was whispered that an elopement had taken place, but no one was certain about anything. According to the servants, Madame Walter, who would no longer speak to her future son-in-law, had poisoned herself out of rage the very evening the match was decided on, after having taken her daughter off to a convent at midnight. She had been brought back almost dead. Certainly, she would never get over it. She had now the appearance of an old woman; her hair had become quite gray, and she had gone in for religion, taking the sacrament every Sunday.

At the beginning of September, the *Vie Française* announced that the Baron du Roy de Cantel had become editor-in-chief, Monsieur Walter retaining the title of manager. A battalion of well-known writers, reporters, political editors, art and threatrical critics, detached from old important papers by dint of monetary influence, were taken on. The old journalists, the serious and respectable ones, no longer shrugged their shoulders when speaking of the *Vie Française*. Rapid and complete success had wiped out the contempt of serious writers for the beginnings of this paper.

The marriage of its chief editor was what is styled a Parisian event, George Duroy and the Walters having excited a great deal of curiosity for some time past. All the people who are written about in the papers promised themselves to be there.

The event took place on a bright autumn day.

At eight in the morning, the sight of the staff of the Madeleine stretching a broad red carpet down the lofty flight of steps overlooking the Rue Royale caused passers-by to pause, and announced to the people of Paris that an important ceremony was about to take place. The clerks on the way to their offices, the work girls, the shopmen, paused, looked, and vaguely speculated about the rich folk who spent so much money over getting spliced. Toward ten o'clock idlers began to halt.

They would remain for a few minutes, hoping that it would perhaps begin at once, and then move away. At eleven, squads of police arrived and set to work almost immediately to make the crowd move on, as fresh groups formed every moment. The first guests soon made their appearance—those who wanted a good seat so as to see everything. They took the chairs bordering the main aisle. By degrees came others, ladies rustling silks, and serious-looking gentlemen, almost all bald, walking with well-bred air, and graver than usual in this locality.

The church slowly filled. A flood of sunlight entering the huge doorway lit up the front rows of guests.

In the chancel, which looked somewhat gloomy, the altar, laden with tapers, shed a yellow light, pale and insignificant beside the main entrance. People recognized one another, beckoned to one another, and gathered in groups. The literary men, less respectful than the society men, chatted in low tones and looked at the ladies.

Norbert de Varenne, who was looking out for an acquaintance, perceived Jacques Rival near the centre of the rows of chairs, and joined him. "Well," said he, "the race is to the crafty."

The other, who was not envious, replied: "So much the better for him. His career is made." And they began to point out the people they recognized.

"Do you know what has become of his wife?" asked Rival.

The poet smiled. "Yes, and no. She is living in a very retired style, I am told, in the Montmartre district. But —there is a but—I have noticed for some time past in the *Plume* some political articles terribly like those of Forestier and Duroy. They are by Jean Le Dal, a handsome, intelligent young fellow, of the same breed as our friend George, and who has made the acquaintance of his late wife. From whence I conclude that she had, and always will have, a fancy for beginners. Besides, she is quite well off and continues to wield considerable silent force on the body politic."

Rival observed: "She is not bad-looking. Madeleine is very clever and very sharp. But, tell me, how is it that Duroy comes to be married in church after a divorce?"

Norbert replied: "He is married in church because, in the eyes of the Church, he was not married before."

"How so?"

"Our friend, Bel-Ami, from indifference or economy, thought the registrar sufficient when marrying Madeleine Forestier. He therefore dispensed with the ecclesiastical benediction of the Holy Mother Church. Consequently, he comes before her to-day as a bachelor, and she lends him all her pomp and ceremony, which will cost Daddy Walter a pretty penny."

Rival resumed: "Tell me, my dear fellow, you who go so often to the Walters', is it true that Duroy and Madame Walter never speak to one another now?"

"Never. She did not want to give him the girl. But he had a hold, it seems, on the father through skeletons in the house—skeletons connected with the Morocco business. He threatened the old man with frightful revelations. Walter recollected the example he made of Laroche-Mathieu, and gave in at once. But the mother, obstinate like all women, swore that she would never again speak a word to her son-in-law. She looks like a statue, a statue of Vengeance, and he is very uneasy at it, although he puts a good face on the matter, for he knows how to control himself, that fellow does."

Fellow journalists came up and shook hands with them. Bits of political conversation could be caught.

All at once the beadle struck the pavement trice with the butt of his halberd. Every one turned round with a prolonged rustling of skirts and a moving of chairs. The bride appeared on her father's arm in the bright light of the doorway.

She had still the air of a doll, a charming white doll crowned with orange flowers. She stood for a few moments on the threshold; then, when she made her first step up the isle, the organ gave forth a powerful note, announcing the entrance of the bride in loud, metallic tones. She advanced with bent head, but not timidly; vaguely moved, pretty, charming, a miniature bride. Madame Walter followed them, giving her arm to the father of her other son-in-law, the Marquis de Latour-Yvelin, aged seventy-two. She did not walk, but dragged herself along, ready to faint at each forward movement.

Then George Duroy appeared with an old lady unknown. He, too, kept his head up without turning aside his eyes, fixed and stern under his slightly bent brows. His moustache seemed to bristle on his lip. He was set down as a very good-looking fellow. He had a proud bearing, a good figure and a straight leg. He wore his clothes well, the little red ribbon of the Legion of Honor showing like a drop of blood on his dress coat.

The organ was playing, pouring forth through the immense building the sonorous and rhythmic accents of its glittering throats, which cry aloud unto Heaven the joy or grief of mankind. The great doors were closed, and all at once it became as gloomy as if the sun had just been turned out.

Now, George was kneeling beside his wife in the choir, before the lighted altar. The new Bishop of Tangiers, crozier in hand and mitre on head, made his appearance from the vestry to join them together in the Eternal name. He put the customary questions, exchanged the rings, uttered the words that bind like chains, and addressed to the newly wedded couple a Christian allocution.

He was declaiming: "You are among the fortunate ones of this world, among the wealthiest and most respected. You, sir, whom your talent raises above others;

you who write, who teach, who advise, who guide the people, you have a noble mission to fulfill, a noble example to set."

Duroy listened, intoxicated with pride. A prelate of the Roman Catholic Church was speaking thus to him. And he felt behind him a crowd, an illustrious crowd, gathered on his account. It seemed to him that some power impelled and lifted him up. He was becoming one of the masters of the world—he, the son of two poor peasants of Canteleu. He saw them all at once in their humble wayside inn, at the summit of the slope, overlooking the broad valley of Rouen, his father and mother, serving the country-folk of the district with drink. He had sent them five thousand francs on inheriting from the Comte de Vaudrec. He would now send them fifty thousand, and they would buy a little estate. They would be satisfied and happy.

The Bishop had finished his harangue.

Bel-Ami, on his knees beside Susan, had bowed his head. He felt at that moment almost a believer, almost religious; full of gratitude toward the Divinity who had thus favored him, who treated him with such consideration. And, without exactly knowing to whom he was addressing himself, he thanked Him for his success.

When the ceremony was concluded he rose up, and, giving his wife his arm, passed into the vestry. Then began the interminable defiling past of the visitors. George, wild with joy, believed himself a king whom a nation had come to acclaim. He shook hands, stammered unmeaning remarks, bowed, and replied: "You are very good to say so."

All at once he caught sight of Madame de Marelle. She drew near, somewhat timid, somewhat uneasy, and held out her hand. He took it in his and retained it. Then he felt the discreet appeal of a woman's fingers, the soft pressure that forgives. And for his own part he squeezed it, that little hand, as though to say: "I still love you."

Their eyes met, smiling, bright. She murmured in her pleasant voice: "I hope to have the pleasure of seeing you again soon, Monsieur."

He replied, gayly: "Soon, Madame."

She passed on. Other people were pushing forward.

The crowd flowed by like a stream. At length it grew thinner. The last guests took leave.

George took Susan's arm in his to pass through the church again. It was full of people, for every one had regained their seats in order to see them pass together. They went by slowly, with calm steps and uplifted heads, their eyes fixed on the wide sun-lit space of the open door. He felt little quiverings run all over his skin, those cold shivers caused by overpowering happiness. He saw no one. His thoughts were solely for himself. When he gained the threshold he saw the crowd collected—a dense, agitated crowd gathered there on his account—on account of George Duroy. The people of Paris were gazing at, and envying, him. Then, raising his eyes, he could see afar off, beyond the Place de la Concorde, the Chambers of Deputies, and it seemed to him that he was going to make one jump from the portico of the Madeleine to that of the Palais Bourbon.

He slowly descended the long flight of steps between two ranks of spectators. But he did not see them; his thoughts had now turned backward, and before his eyes, dazzled by the brilliant sun, there floated the image of Madame de Marelle, re-adjusting before the mirror the little curls on her temples, always disarranged.